Marrition

H ..cGENCY ROMANCE NOVEL

Dorothy Sheldon

Copyright © 2025 by Dorothy Sheldon
All Rights Reserved.
This book may not be reproduced or transmitted in any form without the written permission of the publisher. In no way is it legal to reproduce, duplicate, or transmit any part of this document in either electronic means or in printed format. Recording of this publication is strictly prohibited and any storage of this document is not allowed unless with written permission from the publisher.

Table of Contents

Chapter 1 3
Chapter 2 8
Chapter 3 17
Chapter 4 22
Chapter 5 28
Chapter 6 35
Chapter 7 42
Chapter 8 47
Chapter 9 54
Chapter 10 62
Chapter 11 69
Chapter 12 73
Chapter 13 80
Chapter 14 84
Chapter 15 86
Chapter 16 89
Chapter 17 93
Chapter 18 97
Chapter 19 100
Chapter 20 104
Chapter 21 112
Chapter 22 115
Chapter 24 125
Chapter 25 132
Chapter 26 138
Chapter 27 145
Chapter 28 152
Epilogue 157
Extended Epilogue 163

Chapter 1

Miss Isabella Drayton gazed out of the window across the park to the hills in the distance. It's going to be fine, she thought, taking a deep breath and turning to smile at her cousin, Miss Penelope Drayton.

"How do I look?" asked Isabella, as she gazed at her reflection in the mirror, before turning to Penelope, anxious for her approval.

Tonight, Isabella needed to look perfect for her betrothed, Lord Lawrence Whitby, Baron Moreton, and yet she didn't feel that glow of happiness which she had always anticipated she would feel on the evening of her betrothal ball.

"You look lovely, Bella," Penelope reassured her as she watched Maisie, Isabella's maid, putting the final touches to Isabella's hair, lifting the strands of deep chestnut and adding a green ribbon. Maisie stood back when she'd finished declaring her mistress was ready for the ball.

"I can't believe this is happening," whispered Isabella, talking to herself, as she walked across the room to the window and impulsively pushed up the sash pane.

"Here let me, Miss," said Maisie, hurrying across and helping to lift the heavy framed window.

"Thank you, Maisie," Isabella said, "I felt a little faint, and in need of some air."

"Maisie, go and fetch the smelling salts," Penelope urged. "Make haste."

Isabella could see the look of concern on Penelope's face as she stared at her friend and cousin. "Bella, what is amiss? You look pale and you're trembling."

Isabella turned back from the window. "I don't know. I thought I was well and that I had accepted this wasn't a love match."

Penelope sought to reassure her. "Lawrence is a good man. You like him and it's obvious he cares about you."

"I know," said Isabella as she pushed the window down firmly again. "You're right. I made the decision to marry Lawrence months ago, and he's kind, considerate, and he'll let me continue my scientific studies into plants."

"This is just nerves. You're the belle of the ball, Bella," Penelope said encouragingly, but still looking concerned. "Everyone must feel nervous on the night of their betrothal ball. It shall pass."

"I always thought I'd be racing down that staircase to meet my future husband, and our guests, and dance with him all night, and he would look at me as if he could never let me go."

"You shall waltz through life," replied Penelope, laughing as the tension on her cousin's face eased. "You suit each other very well. I know you shall be happy together."

"You're quite right. I've thought this through so many times and it's for the best." Isabella smiled and smoothed the light muslin skirt on her ivory dress. "Everyone will be talking about my gown. Madame Dubois has excelled herself this time. They won't notice if I'm a little pale." Taking another slow breath, she tried to ignore the subtle knot of anxiety that had taken root earlier that day.

The door opened and Maisie returned with the bottle of smelling salts. "Here, Miss," she said, handing the glass bottle to Penelope.

"Thank you, Maisie. Miss Isabella feels a little better. It seems all she needed was a blast of fresh air."

"Mr. Fletcher asked me to tell you that the first guests are arriving," Maisie informed them.

Penelope looked at Isabella with a smile on her face. "We'd better take our places then. I wish Aunt Jane could have seen you tonight, Bella. She would have been so proud of you."

"I still miss Mama, and Papa too. I have their memory with me tonight though." Isabella paused as she looked in the direction of the miniature paintings of her parents, placed in a prominent position on the wall of her bedchamber. "Come along Penelope, let us go and dance all night."

"I certainly plan to do that," giggled Penelope. "I fully expect to meet my true love and future husband this evening, and nothing is going to stop me."

They made their way down the wide staircase towards the hallway where Uncle Henry stood waiting. Lord Henry Drayton was uncle to both Isabella and Penelope, and their guardian. He looked up and smiled at his niece, offering her his arm. "My dear girl, you look beautiful," he exclaimed. "And so do you, Penelope," he added, offering her his other arm. "Our guests are arriving. We should go and greet them."

As they walked into the ballroom, Uncle Henry looked around. "Where is Lawrence? He should be here with you. I saw him earlier, so I know he's arrived."

"He's probably with his Mama," suggested Penelope, a disparaging tone in her voice.

Isabella glanced at her friend. The duty and dedication her betrothed showed to his mother had been endearing at first, but as the months went on, she wondered if Lawrence would ever give the same priority to their relationship. She had lost count of the number of times he had cancelled a visit or engagement due to his mother needing his presence to help calm her nerves.

Isabella's biggest fear of her decision to marry Lawrence was the thought of living with his mother at Moreton Hall. Normally it would be expected that his mother would move into the Dower house and leave the running of the household at the hall to Isabella. However, this was not something that Isabella could see Lady Moreton readily agreeing to.

Isabella took a deep breath and felt a stab of irritation towards her betrothed. *This is our special evening to celebrate our betrothal. He should be here with me to greet our guests.*

A question from Uncle Henry brought her back to the present. "Hasn't Lady Moreton brought her companion? I've never seen her without Miss Dymchurch beside her?"

"I've no idea, Uncle, but here are some of the first guests arriving," Isabella replied pointing to the entrance of the ballroom. "It is time to smile and greet people."

As they moved to stand in position Isabella whispered to Penelope. "Don't mention Lawrence's mother again. And indeed, he ought to be here with me, rather than in the ballroom fetching his mother's lemonade, which is, I daresay, where I suspect he shall be."

"Lawrence definitely should be with you," persisted Penelope. "People will notice and are sure to chatter about it."

"Oh, I'm sure Lady Elliott and Lady Somerville will comment on his absence," Isabella agreed. "I have to stay calm and composed though."

"Of course you do," whispered Penelope. "The floral arrangements in the great hall are so exquisite that no one may notice Lawrence's absence. As long as he ensures his presence for the opening dance, everything will be fine."

"I do hope so," replied Isabella as the first guests entered through the heavy oak door and moved towards them.

This is it, Isabella thought, a feeling of resignation mingling with a tremor of fear she couldn't quite name. Her betrothal ball. *In less than a month I'll be Baroness Moreton.*

Isabella felt Penelope nudge her arm gently. "Are you ready, Bella? You look beautiful." Isabella nodded, hoping she exuded the air of a confident, serene, bride-to-be, hiding the faint whisper of vague unease.

Lawrence was kind, undeniably so. He'd promised her freedom for her botanical pursuits after their marriage. Her mind told her this was a fortunate match. Why then, did she feel as though Lawrence only wished to marry her for appearances sake and she could have been anyone. *I guess there is nothing about me which inspires him in any way. I'm not even sure about affection. Why isn't he here with me to at least put on a show of affection?*

This really wasn't how she'd imagined her betrothal ball. She remembered talking with her mother about meeting the man she would fall in love with. Her mother had loved her father with a passionate devotion, they had been almost inseparable and had died together when their carriage had skidded with a broken axle on a dark December night two years ago. She heard a guest speaking with her uncle and raised her head to smile in the way *ton* society expected.

"Isabella, I have the pleasure of introducing you to Lord Jason and Lady Julia, Farthington," said Uncle Henry, briefly resting his hand on her shoulder with a show of paternal affection. "You must join my niece and take tea sometime, Lady Farthington. I believe you both share an interest in music," Uncle Henry added. The fine lady had such pale cheeks she looked almost ethereal as she smiled back.

"How charming, I'd be delighted," Lady Farthington coo-ed in response, before moving on.

After the guests had moved on into the ballroom Isabella realized she had no idea who she had been speaking to. She had been almost in a trance as they had gone past and been introduced. Her Uncle Henry looked at her with an expression of pride on his face. "You are going to make an accomplished society matron," he beamed. "Now where is that betrothed of yours. I've a mind to send Mr. Fletcher to locate him."

Isabella had begun to reply, when a number of guests arrived at the same time. "Keep smiling, my dear," Uncle Henry told her. "You too Penelope."

Isabella placed her hand around the bracelet she wore on her left wrist, twisting it round, feeling the warmth of the pearls against her fingers. Her gift from Lawrence to celebrate their agreement to marry. She needed to adjust to her future in the same way that she twisted and moved the pearls strung on the bracelet. She had a strong sensation of being like the pearls, firmly settled on her bracelet in a position she had to accept, and for a brief moment she wanted to pull the string apart and send the pearls bouncing along the polished wooden floor giving them a new direction.

Isabella forced the thoughts away, as fanciful thinking. She believed she was content with Lawrence and was fully aware that marriage was as much about practicalities and family alliances as romantic love. Her parents were unusual in experiencing true love and Lawrence offered security, appropriate connections, and a promised freedom for her studies.

We shall suit each other very well. What more could anyone reasonably expect from a ton society marriage? Isabella's fingers clasped around the soft pearls again. *Where was Lawrence? This really was too inconsiderate of him.*

As she smiled in welcome at the next guests, half listening to their news of a trip to town, she felt her thoughts floating away to what felt like another life. The shadow of a tall, intelligent man, who had told her he loved her, that memory of warmth, with an undercurrent of something more, a frisson of excited anticipation each time they had met that summer.

Upstairs in her bedchamber, in the pocket of her old woolen hooded cloak which she used to walk through the woods on cold days, she still kept a smooth, shiny pebble which he'd given her on a walk by the lake more than five years ago. She'd kept it over the years, a link with the past, its surface rubbed and smooth by all the times she'd held it in her hand on those long walks she enjoyed, especially in the months after her parents' death. Walking alone, or playing Beethoven on the pianoforte with the crashing deep chords, had kept her functioning in that period of shock and deep mourning.

It must now be time to throw the pebble in the lake and say goodbye to that long ago flirtation with love and romance. She'd turned down his proposal, taken by surprise and unsure how to respond, and never had a second chance to make it right and change her mind.

"Isabella, are you feeling faint again?" Penelope's concerned voice broke into her conscious.

"No, no, I'm well. I think I found myself in a daydream for a few seconds. I'm back now," she assured her cousin.

"Uncle Henry has sent Mr. Fletcher to find Lawrence. Look, there's Everett, he's Viscount Kennington now. You two used to be such close friends growing up. We all jested that you'd marry one day. Oh, and Clarissa, I didn't know Everett's sister was out in society. And …" Penelope paused, and Isabella noticed her friend's voice sounded fainter and a little more breathy. "There's Lord Brownridge. I hoped, I mean I thought he might be visiting Kennington Manor."

"Oh, you did, did you?" laughed Isabella, the feeling of faintness disappearing as quickly as it arrived. "He's spotted you, and I somehow suspect that Lord Brownridge won't be able to take his eyes off you for the rest of the evening."

Penelope blushed furiously. "Bella, hush now," she chided.

Isabella gave a small nod. "Very well, Penelope. But I'll be stunned if he doesn't ask you to dance at least twice."

"Oh Isabella, pray stop!"

This gentle teasing of Penelope helped cover up her discomfiture at the sight of the tall, confident figure entering Drayton Park with his sister on his arm. Everett Kane, Viscount Kennington and his best friend Lord Peter Brownridge.

Chapter 2

Uncle Henry's voice boomed out, delighted to welcome the Viscount and his family. As they approached, Isabella felt her eyes drawn to the man who used to be her best friend. She took another sharp breath and tried to ignore the unexpected fluttering sensation beneath her ribs.

The Viscount's emerald green eyes met hers, as he raised a quizzical eyebrow in that individual style he'd always had. Did he do that as a child? Surely not, but she truly couldn't remember. Lord Kennington, Everett, had always taken life lightly, and made gentle fun of others when they took themselves too seriously.

Memories of their years of close friendship flooded in as she met his eyes across the hall and tried to smile. *I can't deal with this. Not tonight. Just let me greet him and his family pleasantly and hope I don't see him again this evening.*

"Isabella, it's so good to see you," cried Clarissa. "I'm back after staying most of last year with Aunt Mary, and we need to see each other frequently. I am to travel to London in March for the season, but until then I shall remain at home. That affords nearly a whole year to enjoy the pleasures of local society."

"I shall come visit you next week," Isabella assured her young friend. "Maybe one day, when Everett is out on the estate, and you have free time. Penelope shall come as well."

"What a lovely evening for your betrothal ball," exclaimed Clarissa as she looked around the ballroom. "Drayton Park looks so magical with the light from those crystal chandeliers giving it a golden glow. I'm so excited. This is my first ball."

Isabella smiled at Clarissa's obvious excitement. "Then you must have a very special evening. I shall make sure Lawrence asks you to dance."

Clarissa leaned closer as she whispered, "Everett has promised to dance with me if my card is empty. He doesn't like dancing though." Clarissa added, raising her voice a little as she looked for her brother with the intention of pulling him into the conversation.

Everett stood there, so close she could smell the faint scent of the familiar sandalwood cologne he preferred. Lord Kennington easily stood out as the most handsome, distinguished man at the ball. He'd always dressed discretely but elegantly, with a deceptively simply tied cravat, dark frock coat and hessian boots.

With a lull in the stream of guests arriving, the group talked together. Uncle Henry was clearly delighted to see Everett again and asked him how he had settled in after his return to Kennington Manor.

"I've an excellent Estate Manager and team at the manor. My father, and then Charles ran an efficient estate, so it's been easy to take the reins. I wish it were otherwise though."

Uncle Henry became serious. "Charles died far too young. I wish they could find a remedy to successfully treat the morbid sore throat. It took my poor wife, and our infant son. There's been a lot of sadness in our families in recent years. But tonight is a celebration, and I won't dwell on those memories."

Lord Kennington nodded to Henry before turning to Isabella. "I must congratulate you on your betrothal Miss Drayton."

Isabella took a deep breath and met his gaze. "It's still Isabella, please. We grew up together and we are friends. There is no need for formality."

Everett smiled and his eyes never left hers. "Isabella then, it's good to see you again. It's been so long, yet in some ways it seems like just yesterday we were searching for plant specimens in Brindley Woods and down by the lake."

"It is good to know you're safe and home again, your Lordship," Isabella replied.

He broke into laughter. "So, I'm to call you Isabella, but you're still calling me by my title. That's a little unbalanced. I insist on your calling me Everett. We can, of course, be formal if the occasion demands. I can't think when that would be, but I suppose it's possible."

Isabella smiled back. "Very well, Everett." In that brief moment the connection between them returned, and she knew how much she'd missed him all these years.

She sensed a presence at her side, and felt a hand placed on her arm, followed by a familiar voice. Lawrence.

"Everett, good to see you. You're back at the manor I presume? I must ride over this week."

"Indeed. It's good to be home, Lawrence," Everett replied with a nod of his head.

"And Clarissa. You look stunning," continued Lawrence. "If you have a free dance on that card of yours then I insist on stepping out for the first Quadrille with you."

Isabella could see how Clarissa looked slightly flustered under the gaze of her betrothed.

He's so charming to everyone he meets, she thought.

It seemed that Lawrence knew Everett. Isabella had seen a clear shock of recognition between them, before they spoke. She'd known Everett since they were children, and she knew when he was wary. How did he know Lawrence? Had they been at school together?

She felt Lawrence's hold on her arm, and his warm breath close to her cheek. *This is how it should be. He is my betrothed,* she chided herself, but the element of possession and power between the two men was impossible to ignore.

"Still as studious as ever Kane?" laughed Lawrence. "I'm surprised you could drag yourself away from those moldy old books you used to spend all your time with. We all thought you'd enter the priesthood after Cambridge."

"I enjoy reading and intended to obtain a first in my final exams," Everett replied, a fixed smile on his face, but she could tell it didn't reach his eyes. "What was it you got Lawrence? I can't quite recall," he asked, that eyebrow raised quizzically again.

"Degrees are not worth the paper they're written on," laughed Lawrence, as Isabella struggled to work out his mood. "We go to Oxford or Cambridge because our fathers attended those establishments. If we have the right position in society, then we don't even need to sit an exam."

"Truly? I do wish women could study at a university," Isabella added wistfully. "I'd have loved to go to Cambridge."

"You'd have enjoyed every minute, Bella," Everett once again called her the familiar name used only by family and friends.

Lawrence looked shocked. "My dear Isabella, that would be quite inappropriate for a young lady of grace and favour. You will make a superb hostess and mother. My mother is excited at the thought of grandchildren in her life."

Isabella bit her tongue, irritated by Lawrence's condescending attitude. He'd agreed to support her botanical projects, so why would he belittle women studying? She wondered whether to tell him what she thought of his attitude when Everett spoke again.

"And what subject would you have chosen to study, Bella?"

"Oh, such a difficult choice between English Letters and the Natural Sciences," she declared without a moment's hesitation. "I would struggle to choose between immersing myself in Shakespeare or wildflowers of the British countryside. In fact, when you read Shakespeare's plays they are strewn with references to flowers."

Everett laughed. "And we both know a bank where the wild thyme grows. No Helen of Troy or Aphrodite for you? There are many strong women in Greek classical literature."

"Alas no, I never learned Greek." Isabella looked at her betrothed, wondering why he had appeared a little shocked by her words. "Perhaps I should learn Greek, though I doubt I will have the time."

Everett smiled at Isabella. "Call on me for any help with your future classical studies. We will be in residence at the manor for several months."

"Until I go to town for my season," supplied Clarissa, rejoining the conversation. "Though I suggest, Isabella that you visit to join me, and not Everett with his fusty books." She patted her brother's arm, smiling up at him. "Come along Everett, the ballroom looks enchanting, and I am determined to drink lemonade and then dance all night. Who knows I may meet my true love this evening."

Everett offered Clarissa his arm. "Oh very well Clarissa. Miss Drayton, will you do me the pleasure of dancing Grimstock with me?"

"You remember my favorite country dance! Of course." Isabella agreed without a moment's pause.

Isabella thought Everett looked older, noticing fine lines around his eyes. *It suits him. He looks rather distinguished. Can he have grown in height since we last met,* she wondered, knowing it wasn't possible. All the same she found she had to raise her head more than she remembered to meet his eyes as she agreed to dance the fourth set with him.

Isabella knew he'd planned to take a living close to Kennington Manor-as his brother would live in the Manor being the Viscount- spending his days writing sermons and sketching in the Hills; but instead, he'd gone off to oversee his family's estate in war torn Portugal. There he had joined the army, and she had heard stories that he had somehow become involved in Intelligence work. If the stories were true, he'd been in danger in action several times.

She'd learnt of his return after several years abroad when his brother's death had unexpectedly propelled him into becoming Viscount Kennington.

"I'll allow you that dance with my betrothed bride-to-be, Kane. I've already promised mother that I shall dance Grimstock with her."

Isabella was taken aback by Lawrence's intervention. *What does he mean? He'll allow me to dance with a childhood friend. I suspect Lawrence may be jealous of my affection for Everett. Surely not. There's no need as we've always been like older brother and younger sister to each other.*

Except for that one walk five years ago, she thought, hoping her cheeks hadn't suddenly turned flame red with the memory of that tender moment.

"I must dance with you, Lady Clarissa," she heard Lawrence continue, and Isabella saw her young friend blush coral pink with pleasure.

"Oh yes, I'll add you to my card," Clarissa told him, trying to hide her excitement at completing her first dance card at a ball.

"We'd better get you into that ballroom." Everett called to his friend. "Peter, come along. Clarissa is determined to drink her first lemonade at a ball. We have a mission to discover the refreshments."

As Isabella watched them walk into the ballroom, she could almost feel Clarissa's excitement and it was so infectious. Clarissa was right in her excited appraisal of the decorations. Mr. Fletcher and Mrs. Finchley, the housekeeper, had excelled themselves. The floral decorations were down to her though, and she'd enjoyed every minute spent gathering flowers from the hot house and gardens adding foliage from the local hedgerows to create her designs.

Isabella turned to Penelope as Lawrence moved to stand with her Uncle Henry. "Clarissa is so excited and it's a joy to see."

Penelope nodded. "Indeed, and she's only recently out of mourning for Charles and her mother. It is good to see her so happy."

"Poor Everett, he never expected to become Viscount, harnessed into duty and putting all his effort into the estate," Isabella added fingering her pearl bracelet again. "Life hasn't turned out as he expected. So much sadness for the family, but you're right, it's lovely to see Clarissa shining at her first society ball. "

"We should visit her soon, and take some fashion plates with us," suggested Penelope. "I believe all the guests have now arrived. Uncle Henry is just speaking with Mr. Fletcher about the orchestra commencing the first dance."

Isabella leaned closer to Penelope and whispered, a jesting note in her voice. "Lord Brownridge spoke with you intently."

"Bella, stop this now. We're merely friends who enjoy each other's company. We are to dance the second set together."

Lawrence joined them having finished talking to Uncle Henry. "Come along my dear, we don't want to be late for this first dance to mark our betrothal." He was now perfectly amiable, and Isabella could see how handsome he looked, with his elaborate cascading cravat and elegant hessian boots.

He makes it sound almost as though I've been delaying and I am about to be late for my own ball! But Isabella put the thought aside and nodded, "Of course Lawrence, I'm ready to dance."

"Excellent. Let's get this over with, so I can check on Mama. She's feeling a little melancholy this evening. It will be so good for her to have you at Moreton Hall."

Why did her heart sink at those words? It was what she wanted, what she'd committed to when she'd accepted Lawrence's proposal. She decided to accept it but couldn't help herself when she replied. "I hope she feels better soon. She does suffer so from so many illnesses."

He looked at her sharply and she made herself smile sweetly, chastising herself for letting the words slip out.

"She should have remained at the hall, but she didn't want to miss our betrothal ball. I've told her I'll be at her side whenever you don't need me," Lawrence informed Isabella, rather stiffly.

"It's time for you to make your entrance," announced Uncle Henry. "Lawrence, dear boy, I must tell you how delighted I will be to welcome you into the family when you marry next month. Isabella and you make such a charming couple. I look forward to welcoming my great nephews and nieces to Drayton Park." He guffawed and Lawrence joined the older gentleman, grasping him firmly by the hand.

Isabella smiled, knowing her Uncle expressed genuine pleasure at their union.

"Thank you, I am the happiest of men."

Isabella looked at her betrothed, liking the way he respected her uncle. Uncle Henry clearly doted on Lawrence and had encouraged her to take the step forward into marriage when she'd had misgivings.

I remember him telling me that love has many forms and the love we read about and dream about is not the reality of life. "Marry and be happy, knowing you are well suited," he'd urged her, convinced she would not find a better match than Lord Moreton.

Isabella had to admit that Uncle Henry gave wise advice and Lawrence and herself did get on very well indeed. He had always appeared a good man, handsome as well as wealthy. He lived at Moreton Hall, a delightful house, and was well regarded as a local man of stature, about to be appointed local justice of the peace. She knew they would get along very well together, and she could make the marriage work.

"Would your mother like to dance with me as the ball starts?" Uncle Henry asked Lawrence. "I know she felt a little fragile with her nerves this evening, but I don't want her to feel overlooked."

"Thank you, but she is quite comfortable in the ballroom, seated with Miss Dymchurch, observing proceedings. I shall join them as soon as this dance is over."

"Of course," Isabella murmured, while her thoughts raced. *Why oh why does he need to spend the evening with his mother. I know I could go and join them, but she rarely speaks to me when I see her. Surely, we will have more than one dance at our betrothal ball.*

"Let's go through and you can enjoy your first dance on this special evening," Uncle Henry, offered his arm to Penelope as he spoke, and gestured for Lawrence to take Isabella's arm and lead the way into the ballroom.

Isabella glanced at Lawrence as they walked to the dance floor, with friends and family greeting them along the way. *He really is handsome and so at ease in the world of the ton. This may not be a love match but why shouldn't enough of love follow once we are married to give us a happy life. I believe we shall be happy together.*

"You look wonderful this evening," Lawrence whispered, so close to her ear that she could feel his breath on her cheek. "If Mama were in better spirits, I should dance every dance with you this evening."

She smiled with understanding, though wondering why Lady Moreton needed her son beside her at all times when Miss Dymchurch was in attendance. "We will have many more opportunities to dance, Lawrence.".

Isabella was taken a little by surprise at Lawrence's next words. "We have never waltzed yet. Shall we be daring and lead a waltz? I shall hope to find you while Mama is taking refreshments later this evening."

She was able to hide her momentary shock as she replied. "I shall look forward to that. Of course, Lady Moreton's health must come first."

"I've been trying to persuade her to spend the winter in Bath to take the waters. I believe it will do her the world of good."

"The waters have a good reputation and the winter months in Bath have many recitals and exhibitions. That's an excellent idea," Isabella encouraged him.

Lawrence's face had a rather endearing expression of pleasure as he responded. "I hoped you would think that." However, it was then spoilt as he added, "shall we journey to Bath and spend some weeks there after our marriage."

"Of course," she smiled, with a leaden feeling in her stomach. Bath! She'd hoped to get to know her new household, and have a first Christmas at Moreton.

Isabella knew she was going to find Bath tedious, but being so close to Lady Moreton would test her patience. She considered asking Penelope to join the expedition. Having her friend and cousin in Bath would make it close to bearable.

Lawrence led her on to the dance floor. "Ah, here we are, time to put on a show my dear Isabella."

The small orchestra struck up the introductory bars of a minuet and Lawrence bowed formally, then raised her gloved hand to his mouth and gently kissed her fingers. A wave of approved murmurs spread out among their guests, and her betrothed led her into the steps of the dance. What a good choice for a first dance, she thought, so slow and graceful.

Afterwards, as the music moved on to a cotillion, she saw Uncle Henry retreat from the floor and Lord Brownridge bowing before Penelope.

He's smitten in love, she thought. *And Penelope likes him too. Maybe they will make a match of it?*

She looked towards Lawrence and smiled gently, and he responded with a broad beam on his face. "I'll finish this cotillion and then leave you with your family. I'd ask you to join us with Mama, but her nerves really are quite fraught this evening and I promised I'd give her my full attention." He looked at her, his gray eyes meeting hers directly, drawing her into his gaze, and she wished she felt that quiver of desire which she'd experienced on that long ago walk in the woods. She pushed those memories firmly away though, into a locked vault.

'I understand," she told him, still smiling, despite a stab of intense disappointment.

"I shall return often to check how you are faring. Will you join me to greet Mama, and then I must urge you to make your excuses and leave her. I want to avoid her having one of her turns if at all possible."

What on earth was one of her turns? I'm sure I'll discover that when I move to the hall. She shuddered visibly, wondering if she might be having some sort of turn herself.

As the music guided them into the intricate knots of the dance, Isabella concentrated on the steps, amazed at how effortlessly Lawrence took each step and turn with excellent technical precision. He occasionally looked towards his Mama who was seated with a small entourage of ladies around her, and that great lady nodded her head in recognition. Isabella thought she almost beckoned for Lawrence to join her, moving her fan in a way which signaled he had danced long enough. Sure enough, as the music faded and the dancers around them prepared to move into a quadrille, Lawrence lowered his head to hers as he whispered. "I should join Mama, she must be exhausted and so brave to be here tonight."

"Of course, Lawrence. Should we take her some lemonade or a glass of punch?"

Lawrence appeared to consider the suggestions before dismissing it. "Perhaps later. I believe she wishes to watch quietly and enjoy this evening. She'll take her specially prepared cordial when she retires later for refreshments."

They moved to join the group consisting of Lady Moreton, Miss Dymchurch, and two elderly matrons whom she knew from local society. Lady Pembroke and the Countess of Carbury had often called on her own mother, and from experience she knew that both usually had forthright opinions they were happy to share.

As they got closer Isabella heard the topic of conversation and felt a stab of irritation. She bit her tongue as the words drifted across the ballroom.

"How curious, such a modern approach to marriage," she could hear the countess telling everyone.

"I agree absolutely, Anne," came the strident tones of Lady Pembroke. "I don't know what the world is coming to when a bride declares she plans to continue her botanical research and have links with the ... university." She almost whispered the last word with obvious distaste. "A wife should not abandon her household duties and care of her husband for such unladylike pursuits."

Lady Moreton sighed deeply, as she welcomed her son. "Hush, Catherine, times change, and we must change with them. Lawrence my boy, come and join me. Isabella, I hope that dance card of yours is full. I so miss dancing. I don't recall ever having a space on my dance card."

Lawrence was quick to assure his mother as Isabella stood next to the two women who had been discussing her in such disparaging terms. "I'm sure you were the belle of every ball, Mama."

"Rumour has it that you're going to allow your future wife to continue working in a botanical garden," said Catherine, the Countess of Carbury. "Never heard such a thing before." She peered at Isabella as if she were an insect about to be squashed. "I don't believe a word of it."

"It wouldn't have been countenanced in my day," added Lady Pembroke.

"I'm sure it shall all work out very well," came the surprising contribution of Miss Dymchurch, who generally stayed in the shadows of her employer and spoke only when spoken to. "They are young and in love, that's all that is important." Isabella glanced at her with interest.

There may be more to Miss Dymchurch than I realized. Perhaps she may become a friend when I marry and move to the hall.

"Bravo, Miss Dymchurch," exclaimed Lawrence. "Isabella will continue to strengthen her interest in botanical plants which are native to the British countryside and I'm proud of her achievements. I will support her endeavours as her devoted husband."

Isabella heard a disparaging snort from the elderly Lady Pembroke, but the others all seemed to nod in agreement with Lawrence.

She smiled at her husband-to-be, thankful of him supporting her so publicly, but Isabella also knew that he had the ability to charm this particular group of ladies into agreeing with anything he told them. He looked directly and endearingly around the group and when he smiled at Lady Pembroke she nodded. "I know times change, but I still do believe it is best for a wife to make her husband and household her primary concern."

"And I shall make sure that's the case," Isabella said, wanting to defend herself from criticism, which she felt was unwarranted at her betrothal ball. "I'm looking forward to taking over the reins of the household at Moreton."

As she spoke, she realized her fingers had tightened around her fan, and she wriggled them a little to ease the tension in her body. She glanced towards Lady Moreton and saw the surprised expression on her face. Clearly Lady Moreton did not plan to relinquish the management of the household so easily. Isabella was not surprised because it was what she had suspected.

Lawrence seated himself next to his mother, who immediately turned to him and began talking animatedly.

She's actually turned her back on me. Well, she has been ill, and Lawrence told me to greet his mother and then feel able to leave them, so that's what I intend to do.

Isabella bowed and mouthed a farewell to Miss Dymchurch, and the two society ladies. She turned to do the same to her future-mother-in-law but knew there was no point as she had her head bowed close to her son's, deep in conversation.

She decided to go and find Penelope. Isabella valued Lawrence's commitment to maintaining her work compiling a Floriale Botanica of the English countryside. She hoped that with his support she would be able to publish the Floriale in two years' time. Her dream to contribute to botanical science in this way could be realised.

That will be more important in life than searching for love, and those fleeting, inconvenient stirrings of passion. Lawrence is amiable and supportive, and I plan on building a life at Moreton where I find contentment. I don't want or need any more than that.

Isabella looked around the room, noticing everyone either engaged in conversation, or dancing a quadrille. She wished Lawrence had spent a little longer with her this evening. She strongly suspected the evening gave an indication of how things were going to be in their future life. She was going into the marriage with her eyes wide open; and could easily content herself with her studies and writing. Lawrence had even talked of building Isabella a glass house, with an adjoining study and reference library. That would certainly be a dream come true.

Yet, as the orchestra played the first notes of a country dance, and music began to fill the ballroom, she felt a sudden longing for something more than this. Isabella remembered experiencing that wave of desire for a man, and she forced herself to suppress the memory down into that locked vault hidden deep in the depths of her carefully composed heart.

Chapter 3

Everett smiled at his sister and her delight at attending this, her first ball. At eighteen she should have had the pleasure of many balls but the death of their father, closely followed by their brother Charles had propelled her into deep mourning. Clarissa's season in London had to wait. Now she seemed eager to make up for lost time.

I don't need to worry about her as she's with Peter, and he'll make sure her dance card is full. I probably ought to engage some sort of sponsor or companion, but we have several months before such an encumbrance becomes essential. We can manage without chaperonage at local society events, Everett was thinking.

He really had no idea that bringing a young lady out into society would prove to be such a complicated, involved process. He'd blithely assumed that new gowns and arranging to take a residence in town was all that was required. How wrong he'd been!

As he watched the dancers, he noticed the group of ladies surrounding Lawrence's mother. He found Lillian Whitby, Lady Moreton, tiresome in the extreme. She put her own comfort before that of others, and he knew her reputation for fits of the vapors, and a razor-sharp tongue, was well deserved.

She clearly loves her son though, he thought. Every time he looked at her he could see she had her eye on Lawrence. He wondered how Isabella could cope with living in the same house with her. He'd felt a moment of extreme dismay when news of Bella's betrothal to Baron Moreton had been announced.

I wish her well with her choice. I never expected her to marry. I somehow thought Isabella would remain single, living at Drayton Park, tending her plants. Why would I assume that? I had no reason.

Deep down he still felt the pain of her rejection. He'd been impulsive that long-ago day, he knew he'd spoken too soon, but her answer had stunned him. He'd had a lucky escape, they had both been very young for marriage, so why did he still feel uncomfortable about how it had worked out?

I wish we could have stayed friends. I lost her due to misjudging her feelings for me and recklessly proposing that day in the woods.

His eye was drawn to Isabella, walking across the ballroom alone, looking near to tears. He knew her and he detected no sign of the joy and happiness expected in a bride-to-be. And Lawrence was with his mother again. How ridiculous, should he not be dancing with Isabella? It's a ball to celebrate their betrothal.

Bella... His eyes followed her walking alone through her guests, looking so fragile. The small orchestra began to play the introductory bars of another country dance, and Bella clearly had no dance partner. This was the sort of situation which risked setting the tongues of the matrons wagging. A short conversation over a crystal punch bowl about the sad figure of an abandoned bride at her betrothal ball could easily result in an entry in a London scandal sheet appearing a few days later.

This had nothing to do with him. He no longer had an interest in Miss Isabella Drayton, soon to be Lady Moreton. He would never forget her refusing his offer. He'd meant it half in jest and half in hope that she might accept him. After seeing the stunned expression on her face when he suggested they might make a match, he'd made little of it and never mentioned it again. Soon after he'd chosen to go abroad, glad to lose himself in the war. He'd found a role serving in intelligence, relentlessly risking his life by moving ahead of the main column of advancing troops and checking for potential danger. His fluency in French, thanks to his Grandmother Celestine, had made him a valued addition to Arthur Wellesley's covert service.

When he'd been seriously injured in a skirmish, he'd found refuge in the family estate further from the conflict zone in Portugal and enjoyed focusing on improving their fine port wine. He'd happily have made a life there if Arthur hadn't died.

Everett didn't plan it, and he had no idea how he found himself standing in front of Isabella. She looked up at him, confused, and for a second he lost himself in those hazel eyes, shining like mosaics in the candlelight, as their gaze fused. Everett felt as though the ballroom faded into the shadows and the only reality was the woman standing in front of him. He felt his arm move towards her and forced it back down by his side.

Isabella greeted him brightly. "Everett. I'm delighted you could join us this evening. I must catch up with Clarissa soon. It's wonderful my betrothal ball is her first ball."

He listened and kept looking at her, and the words he'd been about to say tumbled out of his mouth. "I saw you were alone. I thought perhaps …" and his voice faded as he realized he needed to be more formal. "I'm sorry," he said quietly. "I saw you were alone and wondered if you might care to dance. I see Lawrence is occupied entertaining his Mama."

And nothing has changed there, he thought. Even at university Lawrence had been so solicitous of his mother's welfare that some terms he'd been at Moreton Hall more than he'd been in Cambridge.

"I do indeed find myself without a partner. I believe people assumed I would be with Lawrence this evening, but he's had to give his Mama support."

"Ah, yes Lady Moreton does suffer with her nerves. I remember Lawrence was often recalled home from his studies when we were at Cambridge."

"I'd forgotten you studied together, although I never knew you were close at that time," she said, with a question in her voice.

"No, we didn't run in the same circles, and have very different interests," he held back from saying more, and hoped his words were sufficiently neutral.

"I can imagine," Isabella said lightly, smiling up at him. "And yes, Everett, I'd be glad to dance with you. However, on one condition, you must ask Penelope to dance later. She is in danger of spending all evening with Lord Brownridge and those tongues will begin tattling."

"Of course, I shall be happy to agree to that request." Everett offered her his arm. "Shall we dance?" he laughed. "I believe I can remember not to trip over your toes."

Isabella looked surprised. "You haven't danced recently?"

"Only the occasional hop in the drawing room with Clarissa, to keep her content about her lack of society. I believe the last ball I attended was before I left England for the Peninsular."

"You were gone a long time," Isabella's voice was so quiet he only just heard her.

They drew closer to the dance floor, and he could see Lawrence looking in their direction, a look of annoyance on his face. Isabella seemed oblivious to her betrothed's angst, and he felt glad about that.

"Almost five years. I served with Wellesley on the Iberian Peninsula, then after I was injured, I spent time recovering at our estate abroad." He saw the look of horror on her face and felt a sudden rush of warmth through his body at her obvious concern.

"Let's wait to dance," Isabella said. "I'd like to talk, it's so long since we last met. I hadn't realised you'd been hurt." She guided him towards a quiet door which led to a side terrace used mainly by the family with Maisie of course accompanying them. "Come, we can talk here and then join the next dance. Unless you're engaged to dance with another?"

"No, no, I only asked you to dance because I saw you were without a partner, and this is your special evening."

"Excellent!" Isabella led him out onto the terrace, lit by sconces and empty of guests. They stood side by side by the terrace wall, looking out at moonlit shadows of trees in the distance. "Now tell me about this wound. I had no idea, and I've been too busy with my research here to visit others socially and find out news. Uncle Henry never mentioned it." She put her arm gently on his, and he knew it was a habit from years earlier when they had been such close friends, almost like brother and sister, yet now it made him catch his breath. He focused his attention on answering her question and suppressing the shivering signals which pulsed though his body.

He spoke slowly, choosing his words carefully. "It wasn't pleasant being stabbed in a skirmish behind enemy lines, but my injuries were not life threatening. I'd have gone back to active service if Arthur hadn't died so suddenly."

"You worked undercover I believe? In espionage?"

"More of a reconnaissance role. We scouted ahead of the main column of the army, mostly making contact with sympathetic local people in villages, checking there were no hidden surprises before the army moved forward."

"That sounds dangerous," she said quietly. "And you were injured on one of those expeditions into enemy territory?"

He nodded. "My language skills made me an obvious choice for the work. I've learnt fluent French from Grandmother, and a pretty decent level of Spanish and Portuguese due to our family business being based there."

"What happened?"

"This really isn't a topic of conversation for a young lady at her betrothal ball," suggested Everett.

"I want to know Everett," she told him, looking directly into his eyes. "We've been friends since we were children and I'm sorry we've lost touch. I know there are reasons, and I regret so many things from the past, but we are where we are today, and I'd like to know what happened to you."

"Very well, but I'll keep it brief. I refuse to tell you about the incident while strains of the country dance play in the background," he said wondering how he could describe the brutal ambush where he'd been left for dead.

"You may thank me for avoiding this country dance." She was jesting with him but he could hear the gentleness in her voice.

"I was with another intelligence agent scouting out a hilltop village near the border between France and Spain. Someone in our ranks proved to be a traitor and gave the enemy warning. We entered a clearing near the village as arranged and were attacked and left for dead. I survived, but the other man didn't. A priest found me and took me to a local convent where they nursed me out of the danger zone and returned me to our camp."

"I can't imagine how that would have been." Isabella took his hand, her gloved fingers covering his. "Are you recovered? Do you still feel pain?" she asked with concern.

"I recovered slowly, but improved with every week that passed. After I travelled to our estate in Porto to convalesce, I found I rather liked living in the valley there, with the vines, the sunshine and the cork trees. I hope to return and spend more time there when Clarissa is settled and happy."

"At least you are well again, and the news from the continent is encouraging. I'm glad you're home and that we met again tonight." Isabella removed her hand from his. He wanted to reach out and hold her close, but he knew that couldn't happen.

I'm glad to have friendship with Bella. Even as the thought entered his head, he realized that it must be time limited, for as soon as she married Lord Moreton, he would be unlikely to see her again, except at an occasional supper gathering across the room.

The music changed to a more sedate country lament, and he bowed, then held out his arm. "We should dance, Bella. Please do me the honour of dancing the next set with me."

"Of course," she curtsied before taking his arm.

Everett glanced up at the moon, noticing more stars appearing high in the midnight blue sky every few seconds. He wished for an impulsive moment that they could dance alone here on the terrace, under that canopy of stars. The music filled the terrace, and he wanted to twirl Bella in his arms, alone without observers, but he knew that would mean she risked ruin if one of the gossip mongers of the *ton* happened to come out to take the air and discovered them dancing even though Maisie was their chaperone. They needed to return to the ballroom, as the bride-to-be would no doubt soon be missed by her guests.

Oh, Heavens! If Isabella had been his betrothed, he'd have spent every minute of this ball with her. What was Lawrence thinking? That man needed to cut the strings and set his mother adrift, so she could acquire some resilience. He didn't feel sorry for Lawrence, as the reality was the man had never made the transition to an independent adult in life.

Well, his loss is my gain this evening, I'm going to lead Isabella into the next two dances and imagine that life is as simple and carefree as the last time we danced all those years ago. At least I was injured in the chest and head, not my leg, so I can still dance well enough.

Chapter 4

Isabella reached out and gave Everett her arm and felt him tuck it neatly under his. She remembered this same firm, reassuring warmth of close connection from the past. She swallowed, a dry swallow, as she felt fluttering somewhere deep inside, a little like a butterfly moving its wings gently on a warm summer's day.

It's a good day. My friendship with Everett has re-kindled. It's as if we were never apart. Yet so much has changed, I have Lawrence, and my course is set to marriage and a new life.

She shuddered thinking of how Everett had nearly died faraway in Spain. She hadn't known, they had grown so far apart that she had no idea that Everett had undergone such trauma. Isabella bit her lip as they walked together across the terrace towards the door. She had listened out for news of Everett after their friendship faded, and the last she heard he was about to become betrothed to Lady Viola Harrington, but she couldn't remember there ever being an announcement of a betrothal. She couldn't ask him about it, but perhaps Clarissa would tell her what had happened.

The butterfly fluttering inside her moved its wings more quickly and she felt a moment of calm connection followed by intense irritation at herself. *Everett is my friend, this reaction is only what anyone would feel after being re-united with a friend after several years apart. I waited. I waited for him to return, and I believe my answer would have been different if he'd ever asked again, but I never got the chance.*

They returned to the bright, stifling atmosphere of the ballroom and she felt glad to have his arm for support as she smiled at her guests. Uncle Henry and Clarissa were dancing, and she spied Penelope and Lord Brownridge talking near the punch bowl. Lawrence's mother and companion had disappeared, probably into the reception room where a light collation was set out for guests.

As they walked to the dance floor Lawrence appeared before them.

Maybe he's about to break in and insist I dance with him, she thought with surprise.

"Isabella, my dear," he began, nodding at Everett briefly before continuing. "I've settled Mama in the reception salon to take refreshment."

"Do you wish to dance Lawrence? I know Viscount Kennington won't mind stepping aside if I promise him another dance later." She glanced at Everett who nodded in agreement.

"Alas, my dear, I must attend to a matter of business with one of the other guests; it is rather awkward, especially as I have just parted from my mother and was about to seek you for a dance. Nonetheless, such matters must sometimes take precedence, even if our inclinations are to pursue other pleasures."

Everett took her hand and squeezed it affectionately.

"Please dance with Lord Kennington," Lawrence added before turning to Everett. "My thanks Kane, my betrothed deserves to dance tonight, and I'm called away again."

Everett, bowed stiffly. "It's my pleasure, Moreton. Go deal with your urgent business."

Lawrence turned back to Isabella. "When you've danced with Kane, I promised Lady Hargrove that you would discuss choosing scented roses for her terrace. You'll find her with her daughter Frederica by the punch."

"Of course, I'd be delighted."

"Enjoy the evening, my dear. I shall try to return to check on you when I can." Everett moved aside while Lawrence kissed her gloved hand, somewhat formally, before nodding and moving away.

He's begun to tell me who and what to talk about. Lady Hargrove has as much interest in roses as I have in cross stitch. Isabella watched as he crossed the ballroom, disappearing into the crowd of guests.

How could business take priority over dancing with her at their betrothal ball? Surely not! Isabella felt a wave of desolation, mixed with anger at this state of affairs.

This was beginning to feel like it would be a marriage in name only. What's more, Lawrence didn't seem to mind others knowing how inattentive he was to her. If they started out like this how could it develop? She'd thought they would at least be friends, share interests, talk on an evening about their days. She began to wonder if she'd been mistaken. Would they lead separate lives? If Lady Moreton stayed in charge of the household keys at Moreton what role would there be for her?

I have my work; I have other interests and family close-by. I can ask Penelope to stay with me while I get settled. She remembered the specter of Bath on the horizon, with a vision of her wading through the pump room mineral waters with Lady Moreton beside her.

She felt a tear welling up in the corner of her eye and took several slow, steady breaths. The cloying scent of a matron's violet perfume overcame her and she felt a little dizzy.

This wouldn't do. She closed her eyes tightly, determined to find a way to control this emotional flood seeping through her mind and body.

She then felt a hand on her arm, a tender re-assuring touch. "I know you're not all right," he whispered. "Can you dance, or shall we find somewhere to sit? If you need smelling salts and a glass of lemonade, I can see Penelope over there, and can call her to your side in an instant."

"No, no," Isabella tried to be strong, although her voice sounded strained and indistinct to her own ears. "I am quite able to dance." She looked up at him, her eyes blazing. "In fact, I want to dance. I need to dance."

I'm going to dance every dance, even if I have to drag partners onto the dance floor, and that will be fine, as none of them will dare to refuse me as this is my ball. I'll start now with Everett, and that should lead us into supper.

"Very well," Everett agreed, although Isabella could sense the concern in his voice. "Let's dance." He smiled a half smile. "I promise to keep hold of you so you don't faint onto the dance floor. To my eye you still look pale and a little unwell."

"I'm perfectly fine," Isabella snapped, becoming conscious that her very tone of voice suggested she was far from all right. "I'm so sorry. I don't know what has come over me."

"Oh, I believe we both know the cause of your distress, but talking about it isn't going to help your composure. However, dancing should help." With those words he led her to join the other dancers.

She noticed Penelope with Lord Brownridge, and Everett made sure they joined that set of dancers. He guided her to stand close to her friend.

I'll be glad to be enclosed by family and friends. I don't like feeling this fragile. Penelope looks so happy with Peter. I'm starting to believe they will make a match. I want Penelope to have a happy ever after marriage.

As they stood waiting for the music to begin again, she listened to Penelope talking animatedly with Lord Brownridge about a performance she hoped to attend when she spent time in town for the season. To Isabella's surprise Lord Brownridge listened attentively, and she heard him asking an astute question. Penelope lived through her music and maybe she had found a kindred spirit.

I'd never have taken Peter for an expert on Purcell. People have such hidden depths. She felt a momentary shiver as Lawrence's face flashed into her mind. *Hidden depths ... Do I really know my betrothed?*

"What do you think about this orchestra tonight?" Lord Brownridge asked Penelope.

Penelope looked thoughtful. "Oh, they are far better than the average small orchestra. In fact, I suspect the violinist is talented enough to play solo at a recital."

"Your knowledge of music is exceptional, Miss Drayton," Lord Brownridge told her, causing a faint blush to color Penelope's cheeks. "Everett, will you host a recital with that lead violinist in the program? Perhaps a small string ensemble with violin solos? I'd hold it at Darton Manor, but the place is covered in dust sheets with a skeleton staff as I'm hardly ever there. I've promised Miss Drayton a recital."

"Oh, there's no need, truly," protested Penelope.

"Of course," agreed Everett without a second thought. "Let us have a recital."

The music began and they split from the others for the first part of the dance. "That's so kind of you about the recital," Isabella told him earnestly.

"It's a good idea. It won't put pressure on the household staff in the same way as a ball, and Clarissa needs to flex her social wings before her season in town." Everett guided her into a twirl and pulled her back towards him. "I hope you'll be there. It will be after your wedding, so I'm aware you can't commit."

"I shall certainly be there if I can. Penelope looks overjoyed at the prospect."

As their hands connected during the complicated patterns of the dance, Isabella became conscious that something had ignited between them during those moments on the terrace. As Everett took her hand, a faint spark of recognition that this contact was agreeable flickered within her, and she anticipated the next touch with a growing sense of anticipation as they proceeded through the steps of the dance.

Between the patterns of the dance, their conversation flowed with ease, as Everett asked about her botanical specimens and if she planned to publish her work. She told him about her hopes to publish a botanical guide, an encyclopedia about the plants of the English countryside.

"Have you seen that rare orchid again?" Everett asked. It was obvious to Isabella that he hoped she would remember. "The one we found one day on the other side of the lake?"

"I have, every year since, and I have a specimen I'm propagating with hopes of planting in another similar area in the wild. You have a suitable place in that woodland copse at the manor if you're interested in being a site where the development of the species can be monitored."

"You sound so knowledgeable and scientific, Isabella. I'm in awe of your knowledge and passion for your studies."

She felt a warm glow at his words. "Thank you, that means a lot, Everett. I mostly face disapproval of my commitment to botany."

They parted, danced briefly with others in the pattern, before returning to each other again. "How about your art. Are you sketching still?" Isabella asked him. "You had such talent at capturing the essence of a person or place."

"I sketch every day, it's the way I break off from estate business and gather my thoughts. I hardly ever finish a sketch or move on to watercolors, though I still have my pigments ready if I ever have time. I did paint quite a lot of the time while convalescing in Portugal. I have quite a series of sketches and watercolors depicting the vineyard and woodlands on our family property there. I can show you if you're interested."

"I'd like that very much."

I'm enjoying our conversation. I'd forgotten how much we know about each other and always supported each other's strengths. I remember Everett used to sketch me every year around the time of my birthday. I miss those days.

The music drew to its closing bars, and everyone began to gather ready to go through for supper. She looked around for Lawrence, as tradition dictated he should promenade with her into the dining room

Uncle Henry came to join them and looked at Isabella. "Are you ready? You can lead the way, and family will follow Lawrence and you." He looked around. "Where's Lady Moreton? She should join me in the procession. "

"Lawrence told me that she was taking light refreshments with Miss Dymchurch. I believe she will join us any minute now that the dancing has paused for supper," Isabella informed him.

"And Lawrence?" Uncle Henry asked with a level of agitation in his voice. "Where on earth is he?"

"He told me he needed to deal with some urgent business. It sounded like something which wouldn't wait. He was highly apologetic at abandoning me."

"I've never heard anything like it," exclaimed Uncle Henry in frustration. "At this rate he shall fail to turn up for the wedding."

He saw the look of concern on her face and took her hand. "I'm sorry, my dear Isabella. Forgive my words. I don't wish to worry you. I do believe he should have been here to escort you to supper though, and I'm not sure how we can deal with his absence. It's expected that you both will lead the procession through to supper."

"There's Lady Moreton with Miss Dymchurch," Isabella pointed as she saw them emerging back into the ballroom. "We're still missing Lawrence though."

Lady Moreton descended on their group with concern on her face. "Henry, I can't find Lawrence. He promised to return to my side well before supper. Miss Dymchurch has looked everywhere and there's no sign of him."

"I've searched every room and looked on the terraces," added Miss Dymchurch.

"He told me he needed to deal with urgent business," Isabella told them, everyone listening intently to her words. For the first time she felt a gnawing stab of anxiety.

I can imagine Lawrence abandoning me, but he is always conscious of society expectations, and this is his betrothal ball as well as mine. His mother expected to see him, and he is totally devoted to her welfare. Wherever can he be?

Uncle Henry, although obviously not at all happy, made a decision. "Very well. We shall delay supper for another half hour. "Peter, please go and tell the orchestra to play gentle music while we locate Lawrence. Penelope, ask Mr. Fletcher and Mrs. Finchley to encourage people to partake of the cold collation in the salon. Tell them to keep that punch bowl full and ensure there is still an air of celebration to the proceedings."

"They will probably just assume Cook has problems with the white soup or pot pies," declared Penelope.

"Don't worry," Uncle Henry said gently, looking around the group. "We shall find him. He's probably got involved with the minutiae of this business matter. Lady Moreton, I suggest that you withdraw and rest in the drawing room, there's a warm fire and one of the footmen will bring you tea. I think tea is most appropriate at a time like this. It's all I ever drink myself these days."

"Thank you, I do feel quite exhausted by Lawrence's absence. It's almost as though he's disappeared," Lady Moreton said distractedly.

"Come, Lady Moreton," said Everett, who still stood with the group. "We shall do all we can to find Lawrence. There is no need to worry."

Uncle Henry seemed calmer as he spoke. "We have a plan. The sooner we find Lawrence, the sooner we can take supper."

"Everett and I shall organize the household staff to search every corner of the house and gardens," added Lord Brownridge.

"Thank you, my boy," said Uncle Henry. "Now, Isabella, you will join me and we shall circulate among the guests while we wait for news."

I don't know whether to be concerned or infuriated. Lawrence abandoning me this way will create talk, and I would rather there wasn't gossip about our betrothal. He seemed as committed to marriage as I. Now I must smile and talk to guests to avoid speculation about his absence and stop wondering if he's disappeared because he wishes to end our arrangement. I can't think about that, as the public humiliation would be intense.

Stop making this into a catastrophe, she told herself. *Lawrence will appear any minute and smooth all ruffled feathers in his usual charming way.*

Chapter 5

Everett looked across the room towards Isabella. She stood alone with an air of fragility, but he recognized her central core of strength and resilience shining out. He saw the moment when she took a deep breath and moved across the room towards Lady Moreton, taking that older lady's arm in hers and guiding her out of the ballroom towards the drawing room. As they worked their way through, she greeted several ladies, smiling and accepting their congratulations on her betrothal.

In those moments Everett knew that there was still something between them, it was difficult to describe, but it smoldered deep inside, creating a feeling of warmth and comfort, accompanied by a flame of excitement.

He sensed Clarissa moving towards him to stand next to him.

"Are you well? You look a little distracted brother. I suspect our evening of celebration is at end. How strange that Lawrence should disappear this way."

Everett turned to look at his sister. "Oh, it somehow doesn't surprise me at all. I've known Lawrence for years, and I have to say that the man has always put himself before everyone else. There's something about this situation that is disturbing though. It really isn't like Lawrence to make a public scene and draw attention to himself in this way." Heavens! It must be so difficult for Isabella. This is her betrothal ball, and her betrothed has disappeared.

Everett looked around him. The majority of guests had not noticed anything different; anything strange about the absence of the future groom. Only the household staff and guests in the close family circle had that look of intense concern etched on their faces.

How could Lawrence treat Isabella this way? It wasn't Everett's place, but he determined he would say something to Lawrence when they finally discovered the man's whereabouts.

Everett looked at his sister, as he realized how much she had been looking forward to the evening. "I'm so sorry that your first ball has ended this way, Clarissa."

"Oh, I've had a wonderful time, and this is the first of many balls for me. I'm excited about this recital that you are holding at the Manor too, brother. I may encourage you to add a little dancing after the violin recital."

"I believe I might be encouraged to do that for you, Clarissa. I promised you a social season here in Hertfordshire before you left for London in the spring."

"So, a mid-winter ball, Everett?"

Everett laughed before replying. "Perhaps, I'm not committing to that yet though. And now I must go and join the search for the missing Baron Moreton. Can you go and check how Isabella is coping?"

"Of course, I think Penelope is with her, but I'll see if there's anything I can do to help."

He strode off to find Peter, who had thrown himself into the task of searching the house for Lawrence.

Everett found Lord Brownridge looking out into the dark. "How is it going?"

"The house staff know Drayton, and it seems to me that they know what they're doing. I don't believe the Baron is in Drayton Park."

Everett looked out at the grounds of Drayton. "I'm going to start organizing the search outside in the immediate grounds. I believe Lord Drayton has already sent for the stable hands and grooms to come over and begin assisting in a search. Isabella says that Lawrence seemed to be planning to discuss business in a quiet place, so it's possible that was outside."

"Well, I don't believe he is in the house, but we need to keep looking to be absolutely sure and also for appearances sake."

They ventured outside into the coolness of the moonlit night. Everett stopped and stood for a moment, looking up at the sky and noticing how bright the stars shone against the darkness on this wild winter's night.

"I believe you're right about him not being in the house, Peter, but I can't see him being out here either. It's turned far cooler, and there's a definite chill in the air. It's different to the temperature, even to an hour ago." Everett was preoccupied as he turned back to his cousin. "Do you think anyone knows who the business acquaintance he claimed to be meeting during a ball was?"

"No one has any idea, however Penelope heard something which may be of interest."

Everett looked at Peter. "She had something? Tell all."

Peter continued. "Indeed, she heard an interesting conversation. She was heading out to the terrace to look for Isabella when she heard voices. She didn't know who the woman's voice was at the time, but she believes she recognized it as Lady Moreton. The woman's voice sounded strident and commanding in tone, and she seemed to be telling the man that he needed to put a plan into place immediately. He seemed reluctant to act, but she persisted and became quite cruel in her choice of words."

"That certainly is interesting."

Peter nodded. "Yes, and if that was Lady Moreton, it is possible that after a heated disagreement Lawrence has made himself scarce. She is a very forceful woman."

"Well, I don't think there is anything else we can do but keep searching for now. Lady Moreton is certainly distressed at Lawrence's disappearance so I don't think she will be up to answering any questions about the conversation. It is always possible Penelope may be mistaken. I'll take the garden area and terrace. Can you take the park and the area going down towards the woods?"

Peter bowed his head in agreement.

"Right? We have a plan," Everett clapped his hands together.

Peter turned to Everett as he walked off towards the park and woods. "If he's here on the Drayton Park estate, we shall find him."

Everett himself moved towards the far edges of the terrace, scanning the bushes around him. The leaves were falling now as autumn turned into winter. It was lucky it was such a mild evening but he shuddered as a blast of north easterly wind blew across the garden, scattering the leaves around his feet.

Was that the wind, or a voice? He turned around and saw a figure in a woolen shawl hurrying towards him, with another figure scurrying close behind.

"Isabella," he called. "I thought you were with Lady Moreton?"

"Lady Moreton has Miss Dymchurch in attendance and seems to be coping, despite her protestations that she isn't. It's hard to tell with Lady Moreton." She pushed a hand through her hair, strands coming loose from their pins and hanging loose around her face. "I'm sorry, I am usually kinder in what I say about others. Lady Moreton is concerned about Lawrence, and I shall let that excuse her sharp tongue."

Everett looked towards her, thinking how this wilder lock of hair falling around her face suited her very well indeed. "I suspect that when you are married to Lawrence you will become exhausted if you try to keep thinking of excuses for that woman's sharp words and put downs. I predict now that it would be an impossible task."

Despite her obvious anxiety, she gave him a half smile in response and inclined her head in agreement.

"But what are you doing out here, you should be inside with your guests?"

"I'm certainly not going to sit in there. I need to join the search. Uncle Henry said it was acceptable, as long as Maisie came with me. I'm surprised he didn't send several footmen to guard me as well. I have promised not to leave the formal terraced gardens."

"Your Uncle Henry is right to be cautious, though I still believe we will find Lawrence and he has gone off on some private business and not told anyone he was leaving the estate. He will probably just turn up again soon and wonder what all this turmoil was about."

"His horse is still in the stable though," Isabella told him. He rode over to the ball, he didn't take the carriage with his mother and Miss Dymchurch."

Isabella turned to Maisie, who was obviously not used to running after her mistress. "Maisie, you can sit on that bench, over by the lantern and wait for me. You can see me at all times and I'm perfectly safe with Lord Kennington. He's a family friend."

A look of relief spread over Maisie's face. "Very good, Miss Isabella," she said as she panted.

"Don't be too sure that I'll be able to resist taking advantage of you," Everett said with a grin, despite being acutely aware that it was not his place to utter such words to another gentleman's intended. Should that bridegroom vanish amidst their betrothal ball—careless of his betrothed's sentiments or the impression it might make upon witnesses—then...

Isabella gave him a sharp look, and the coiled passion he felt deep within rose and then sank down again. He knew he had to focus on finding the missing Baron, and that was all that Isabella needed from him at this time.

He became serious as he asked her. "Are you sure he gave you no indication of where he might meet this mysterious business associate?"

Isabella shook her head. "If I'm honest I was somewhat irritated with him for scheduling a meeting during our ball and thought it could surely have waited a few more hours. I should have asked more questions, but I didn't."

"Why would you?" Everett told her, worried she might take the weight of this disappearance on her shoulders.

As they walked side by side, he felt thankful for the lanterns and sconces illuminating the garden. The breeze had quietened, and it felt warmer, though he noticed Isabella pulled her woolen shawl firmly around her.

He heard voices, the men shouting to each other in the distance, and knew the search had begun to widen beyond the immediate grounds. He was familiar with this garden from visiting so many times while growing up. They walked along all the paths, checking out secluded benches, gazebos and hidden arbors. He needed to help Isabella stay calm, but something about this whole strange scenario began to concern him. Something seemed very wrong indeed.

How easily we fall back into familiar patterns, he thought, as they walked together along a fragrant pathway. They didn't need to speak with each other as they searched every part of the aromatic herb garden, they moved in synchrony.

It's as though we've stepped back in time, and those years of hurt and formal distance between us never existed. I know my inability to cope with rejection caused that rift between us. I had to respect Isabella's decision that she didn't see us as anything other than friends. The sadness is that our friendship got lost in the aftermath. I must have been such a fool. I vowed I'd never ask her again a second time, like those men in gothic novels who keep trying until their lady finally admits their love.

"What's that over there?" he said out loud, though he had meant to keep quiet. He cursed himself when Isabella began hurrying across to where he pointed. The sight of her looking so fragile in her muslin ball gown made his heart ache. He hoped there would soon be news of the Baron to ease the distress he could see Isabella suffered.

He heard her call. "Over here?"

"Yes, there's something on the ground, I saw something glinting as it caught the lantern light. We should check it out."

Everett knelt down next to a rhododendron bush with a stalk almost as thick as a tree, its branches arched high and spilling over onto the lawn. He looked around. Something was partially hidden beneath the bush. He motioned for Isabella to stand back, out of the light and knelt down to scrutinize what was in front of him. He found a piece of fine cloth and reached down to retrieve it, emerging holding a handkerchief bearing Lawrence's monogram. He held it out of the light so Isabella could not see it clearly. Everett took a deep breath when he noticed a dark stain covering one corner of the handkerchief. It had to be blood. He'd been in enough situations to recognize a spatter pattern, and how that would affect Isabella if she saw it. She stood beside him, her shoulder against his coat as she leant closer trying to examine what he'd found.

It was not enough as Isabella had clearly seen the cloth. "It has to belong to Lawrence. He always insists on having that coat of arms monogrammed on all his handkerchiefs. He's hurt. He must be hurt. Oh Lawrence, what on earth has happened to him."

"We don't know that he's hurt," responded Everett gently, "we know nothing for certain. Everything that we're thinking here is merely guessing and is not definite. We need to keep calm and assume that he may have dropped this earlier today. I believe he's been staying here at times at Drayton Park, so it's entirely possible this is unconnected to his disappearance."

Isabella was not convinced. "But that's definitely blood. I can tell that's blood. Oh, what an earth are we going to tell his mother?"

He could see the rising panic In Isabella's eyes as she looked at the monogram on the handkerchief. Without thinking he reached out and touched her arm and drew her close, wanting to give her comfort in her moment of fear.

I want to make everything right, he thought*, but that's not possible. I suspected there was something strange about this situation from the moment that we found out Lawrence was missing.*

He stood and called out to Peter and Lord Drayton, hoping they would hear him. "We've found something, I'm going to be heading back to the house if you can join me?"

Everett turned to look at Isabella, their eyes meeting as he tried to impart confidence which he did not feel about this situation.

"You've been so strong. You need to continue to be strong for a little while longer. There are still guests at the ball, and it won't do Lawrence any good if more rumours start to spread around. Let us endeavour to maintain a discreet demeanour for the present."

"You're right," she answered. "None of us want this to become public and gossip to spread around *ton* circles. If you take that handkerchief back to show my uncle and Lord Brownridge, then I shall go and speak to the rest of our guests. Penelope can come with me, and we shall explain Lawrence had to leave due to urgent family business. I think that's for the best."

"It's a good way of dealing with it." he agreed, still looking intently into her eyes. He saw those tendrils of hair that had come loose and impulsively moved towards her to push a strand away from her eyes.

Isabella turned away and called for Maisie to follow as she made her way back to the house. "We shall find him," Everett told her.

He stayed a few more minutes, looking around the area, checking under the rhododendron bush and the area around it to see if there was any other sign of anything. He found a cufflink, which he thought might belong to the Baron, suspecting it may have been torn off in a struggle.

As he started to head back to the house, he heard footsteps coming behind him as Peter and Lord Drayton arrived beside him.

It was Lord Drayton who spoke first. "What have you found?"

Everett handed over the handkerchief and cufflink. "I didn't say anything to Isabella, but I suspect there's been a struggle here. I believe this stain on the handkerchief is blood. I'll know more when we get back to the house, and I can look at it in the light, but everything tells me that the Baron has been involved in an incident in this garden. It could be that he's gone off to deal with a wound and not cause his betrothed distress during their betrothal ball. We've got to hope that there's an explanation like that."

Lord Drayton agreed. "You're right, my boy. It doesn't look good. What on earth could have happened here this evening?"

"Whatever happened the Baron has disappeared without trace," added Peter. "Well one thing is for certain, I doubt very much that Lady Moreton attacked her son and caused this blood stain on the handkerchief. Penelope did overhear a quarrel, but it looks as though it isn't connected to his disappearance."

Everett nodded. "You're right, Peter. I had hoped that Lawrence, who we all know is very close to his mother, had run away after a fallout between the two of them. That looks increasingly unlikely, though it was a good theory."

"We need to find whoever insisted on meeting about business this evening. You know what I'm thinking," Lord Drayton looked from Everett to Peter.

"I believe I do," said Everett. "They say in town that debts are being called in with an increasing level of violence. Could Lawrence have a gambling debt? Has he made one wager too many?"

"There's blackmail too," suggested Peter. "It may be no coincidence that this happened at a betrothal ball. Maybe someone made a move to try to extract money for withholding information that the Baron didn't want to come out."

Lord Drayton shook his head. "It all seems very extreme. Are we thinking that one of his forgotten lovers was hiding, waiting to accost him from the bushes?"

"Maybe he has ruined a lady's reputation," added Peter, quickly retracting this statement at the sight of the expression on Lord Drayton's face.

Everett endeavored to bring a sense of calm to the situation before the speculations got any wilder. "The best thing we can do now is to go back to the house and ensure that Lady Moreton and Isabella are comfortable and try to get some rest ourselves. It's been a long night and we shall have to make an early start. We can return to the Hall, Peter as it's not far away, and we'll return before breakfast to help with the wider search."

"I shall send the head groom into Whitchurch village to ask around if anyone has seen the Baron. He's a man I can trust to be discreet." Lord Drayton told them. "Now let's go into the house and see how the ladies are faring."

As they walked towards the terrace door, Everett looked back to the wood, seemingly in the distance, but actually coming close to the garden. There was a path leading to an old carriage road which led to the Dower house. It would be easy for someone to abduct a person in this garden and take them at pistol point or knife point to a waiting carriage. But surely someone would have seen or heard something? It was a clear night, stars filled the sky, the moon light was strong. Yet if they asked the guests if they had seen anything, it would create more gossip. The thing they most needed to avoid if at all possible was a scandal which involved Isabella and her missing betrothed.

Chapter 6

As she saw Drayton Park looming up in front of her Isabella felt torn. Part of her wanted to return to the house and share the news, and part of her wanted to turn away in the other direction, and retreat to the safety of that walk around the garden with Everett. In her mind she saw his tall figure scanning the garden, and moving with quiet confidence, in that way which had always drawn her attention and made her feel comfortable.

Isabella made herself think about Lawrence. If she was being honest with herself she still felt angry with him for leaving their ball to meet someone to discuss business, no matter how important. At this moment though it was futile to think about that. Her pace quickened and entering the anteroom, she handed her woolen cloak to Maisie, who had just about managed to keep up with her. Isabella realized she hadn't even been aware that Maisie was still with her and it was just habit that made her hold out the cloak.

"I'm sorry, Maisie. Please can you take it back to my bed chamber?"

"Of course, Miss Isabella Don't worry, I'm sure that the Baron will come back soon."

"You're quite right, Maisie. We shall find him very soon. Uncle Henry will make sure that we find him, and he returns safely." Isabella took a deep breath. "Now I must go and say farewell to the guests and check on Lady Moreton."

As Isabella made her way towards the hallway, she took a long steady breath. This was not going to be easy, but she needed to keep up appearances.

Despite all her concerns about Lawrence's absence, she never expected they would find evidence suggesting harm. Yet she found herself drawing strength from Everett's calm presence rather than feeling the panic which a betrothed in this position should surely experience. She chided herself for seeking comfort from her old love, instead of focusing on the future with Lawrence.

Penelope and Clarissa joined her. "You can't go in there alone," insisted Penelope. "That isn't fair. We shall come with you".

Isabella was grateful for Penelope's strong friendship as she replied, her voice barely audible. "Thank you, Penelope, I'd be glad of that. And you too Clarissa."

"You know that Lady Moreton was not on speaking terms with her son. They'd had an argument earlier in the evening. I heard them in a heated conversation on the terrace. I pulled back to give them privacy, but I think they saw me and they stopped talking very abruptly," confided Penelope.

Isabella found herself feeling sorry for Lawrence's mother. "That must be so hard for Lady Moreton now. I wonder what the problem between them could be. I don't think I've ever heard them exchange words before, certainly never in a heated way."

Penelope looked thoughtful. "I keep thinking, worrying in fact, that it might have something to do with Lawrence's disappearance. Who knows, perhaps he stormed off full of anger needing time to calm down?"

"I'd like to believe that, but that can't be the case. We found a handkerchief stained in blood, and now I've heard Everett found a cufflink as well. It is beginning to look as though Lawrence may have met with an incident in the garden." Isabella heard Penelope and Clarissa take sharp breaths.

That blood stained handkerchief is changing how people think about this situation.

The next few minutes were tortuous. Isabella circulated among the guests trying to maintain a composed exterior and reveal nothing of her inner turmoil and anxiety.

Lady Carstairs was her usual, forthright, self. "And where is that handsome betrothed of yours?"

Isabella could only give her the answer she'd rehearsed in her head. "He's been called away on urgent business. I think there's a matter at the estate that needed dealing with and couldn't wait."

"Oh really? How surprising. You'd think he'd have a man who could deal with that sort of thing. It's not the done thing to disappear during one's betrothal ball you know!" Lady Carstairs was not one to withhold her opinion.

"It sounded very serious. I don't think he had any choice. He asked me to meet everyone and issue his apologies for having to leave so urgently."

Penelope was at her side and whispered in her ear. "You're doing really well. People feel that Lawrence has been somewhat rude, but that's all. There's no indication that any one has worked out that he's disappeared."

"I do hope he doesn't disappear on your wedding day," was the response of the Marchioness of Stanbury, before adding in a loud, strident voice. "Young men these days have no idea how to behave. I don't believe in these betrothal balls. A lot of unnecessary expense. Why not get married and have done with it?"

Isabella was becoming more confident with her answers, almost believing the story she was telling, wishing it was true. "It couldn't be helped, It was a very urgent matter, and he couldn't stay."

"And Clarissa," continued the Marchioness, looking at Isabella's young companion. "My dear, how delightful to see you at this ball. Is it your first-time out in local society?"

"Indeed, it is, your Ladyship," Clarissa, bowed as she spoke, unsure yet of social etiquette in these early days in *ton* society. "I shall go out in local society until I go to London for my season in the spring."

Isabella could see the Marchioness surprise Clarissa with her response. "It will be delightful to see you at balls and recitals. You do so remind me of your mother, you have her grace."

Clarissa inclined her head to thank this rather scary woman.

I'd rather someone like her who speaks her mind, than someone who gossips behind your back, thought Isabella.

Penelope whispered to Isabella. "We must go and find Uncle Henry." But Isabella wanted to let Clarissa finish her conversation with the Marchioness.

"Your Ladyship must attend our soiree at Kennington Manor. My brother, Everett is going to ask the violinist who played the solo this evening to do a recital."

The Marchioness looked delighted at the invitation. "Of course, my dear, I'd be delighted to attend any event hosted by your dear brother Everett."

And with that, they moved away. Isabella breathed a sigh of relief at seeing her Uncle Henry coming towards them. "My dear," he shouted in a loud voice which none of the guests could fail to hear. "Lady Moreton is quite overcome. I'm afraid we must end the celebrations a little earlier than expected."

He smiled at the assembled company. "We should like to invite you all again to Drayton Park for a midwinter ball. My apologies that we've had to end tonight's festivities early."

Isabella noticed several looks of confusion around the room. She wasn't convinced that the guests had believed Uncle Henry. Something had clearly happened to affect the evening, and she could see the guests talking and chattering between themselves. Could they avoid a major scandal? Possibly. This far from London in their local society they might manage to keep the reason for the Ball ending early to themselves.

The orchestral ensemble began to play quiet background music as the guests gathered in groups ready to leave. Carriages, summoned by Uncle Henry, began to arrive outside the main entrance of the house. As she watched, Isabella felt a pang of sadness, almost of grief, that the celebratory evening that she'd looked forward to had turned into such a dismal, anxiety ridden affair.

As the guests departed and Isabella nodded to various acquaintances from local society, she felt an increasing weariness and exhaustion overcoming her. This had not been the betrothal ball that she had expected. Uncle Henry, Penelope and Lord Brownridge stepped forward to assist with guest departures in a timely manner.

Isabella smiled to herself as she saw Penelope and Lord Brownridge working together, smiling and reassuring the guests that there would be a future ball in midwinter to look forward to, and the wedding of course.

They made such a wonderful couple, their complementary efforts showing a close connection beyond that of stepping in to help during a crisis, each anticipating the other's needs.

Certainly, they are in the beginnings of love, if not fully in love yet, she thought to herself. A warm glow of happiness for her friend and cousin filled her despite the misery of the evening.

In that moment she sensed someone beside her and turned to see Everett. "I thought you might need some support," he said gently and quietly. "Lady Moreton is quite settled with Miss Dymchurch, there's nothing to concern yourself about there."

As other guests moved towards her she stiffened. Everett must have noticed as he whispered to her that he would stay beside her, and he did indeed remain protectively near her while she spoke to various guests, all of whom enquired about

Lawrence and said how sorry they were that he was unable to take his leave of them.

Isabella felt a shared purpose with Everett creating a natural connection. Surely this was more than friendship? This evening, she no longer cared about propriety and the usual boundaries. She knew that she needed him there to get through this ordeal. *It's a strange, compelling comfort that I find in his presence. I know it's exactly what I need to be able to cope and deal with talking to all these people.*

I find his presence so reassuring during this crisis. It's almost as though we think together, we move together in tandem. And despite the years of formal distance, his support feels like a partnership. We're together, we're close, and I want that closeness.

Why didn't she have the same closeness with Lawrence. She worried that when they married, she would lose something of her independence and herself, but with Everett it felt like a partnership rather than the constraint she now feared from marriage. She knew that this was what she needed to create with Lawrence.

"Of course, Mrs. Elton," Isabella heard Everett say to a local Dowager. "I shall pass on your good wishes to the Baron. And remember there is no escape or excuses, we shall expect you at our soiree at Kennington Manor."

As the last of the guests left, only close family and friends remained. Isabella looked around the group, noticing the worry and concern, the grave expressions on all the faces. Uncle Henry looked around, expressing relief that all the guests had left and suggested they retreated to the parlor.

It seemed so strange to see afternoon tea set out in the parlor after midnight, and yet it was exactly what they needed. Mrs. Finchley intuitively knew what they needed to cope. Clarissa took it upon herself to move the table and began to organize the tea set and pour the tea.

When they had entered the room, Everett had moved away from her and now stood near the fireplace, his tall figure creating an anchor point to which she felt herself naturally drawn.

I will stay here. I may feel that pull to go to him to feel the shelter of his closeness, but I shouldn't be so aware of his presence, especially given the current circumstances. I'm betrothed to Lawrence, and he's disappeared.

But looking at Everett, she saw him as a tower of strength, and that only increased her admiration. She knew she was glad to have him back in her life, like a brother she thought to herself.

Lady Moreton sat near the fire with Miss. Dymchurch next to her. Clarissa went over to offer Lawrence's mother a cup of tea, which she took and held in her hands. Isabella could see they were shaking.

She looks so distraught, thought Isabella. *She's almost diminished in size. She seems smaller, somehow than she did earlier this afternoon. I know she had an argument with Lawrence this evening and no one is sure what it was about, but from what Penelope heard there certainly seemed to be an acrimonious situation between them.*

Isabella wondered if she would tell them about the argument. It seemed important that everyone should be truthful and put forward as much information as possible. It may give a direction to follow to help find Lawrence.

Lady Moreton looked up at Uncle Henry. "Is there any news?" she asked in a faltering tone.

Uncle Henry could only give one answer. "No, my Lady," as he patted her hand gently. Lady Moreton looks quite convincing, Isabella thought to herself. Yet for a fleeting moment she thought she detected a look of calculated precision in Lady Moreton's eyes despite her distress.

Isabella took her tea from Clarissa, thanking the young girl for stepping in as hostess. She held the porcelain cup in her hands, inhaling the fragrance of the tea, taking a sip feeling that it helped her stem the rising anxiety.

When they were all settled, and had taken refreshment, Uncle Henry nodded to Everett, who proceeded to take out the bloodied handkerchief and show it to them for scrutiny.

Lady Moreton gasped, and Miss Dymchurch put a soothing hand on her arm.

I'm not sure uncle has made the right decision showing that to Lawrence's mother, thought Isabella.

Uncle Henry tried to soothe Lawrence's mother. "My dear Lady Moreton, calm yourself. It is likely this is of no significance, but Everett discovered it in the garden, and it seems important to keep everyone informed about what's happening".

"I feel this should be reported to the authorities," said Everett, "without delay. As local magistrate I'm happy to submit a report and involve the sergeant and constables."

"I'm not sure we're ready for that level of involvement yet," protested Lady Moreton. "I don't think it's what Lawrence would have wanted. He may well arrive back at any minute, and we may find we have overreacted."

Lord Brownridge stepped forward. "The advantage we have," he said, looking around the group, "is that Everett is the local magistrate, which means that this can be kept within these four walls for now. We cannot ignore that bloody handkerchief, though, as Lord Drayton has said, it may well mean nothing at all."

At hearing these words, Lady Moreton began to weep loudly.

She seemed so quiet and controlled a few minutes ago but now her distress is extreme, thought Isabella. Perhaps it was the formal step of involving the authorities which had made her son's disappearance seem all the more real to her. She seemed determined not to involve the constables, and mention of the authorities had propelled her into this physical collapse. `She swiftly took across her smelling salts and handed them to Miss Dymchurch, who whispered her thanks.

Isabella knew her uncle well enough to recognize the troubled expression on his face. She suspected there was a conflict between the responsibility of requiring appropriate investigation, and a concern regarding the potentially damaging scandal which she suspected may even ruin her future. At this moment, her reputation, and any gossip attached to Lawrence's disappearance, didn't matter to her, but her Uncle Henry took his duties as her guardian very seriously indeed. He wanted to protect her from scandal if at all possible.

Isabella saw Everett exchange glances with Peter, and some silent communication passed between the two of them. Everett spoke next "I believe the decision is yours Lord Drayton regarding external assistance with the investigation. It is only pure chance that I'm here, involved, and happen to be the local magistrate. I would like to offer Lord Brownridge's and my support with this investigation, including the involvement of the local constabulary should you or Lady Moreton decide it is needed."

Uncle Henry indicated his thanks and moved to pour the gentlemen a glass of fine French brandy. Later, after Everett, Lord Brownridge and Clarissa had left for Kennington Manor, they retired to bed with heavy hearts. The sad sight of Lawrence's formidable mother leaning so heavily on Miss Dymchurch as she climbed the stairs was heart wrenching.

Lawrence where are you? Please return soon.

Later that evening, after Maisie had left her, Isabella sat a long time by the fire, closing her eyes, and trying to make sense of what had happened that evening. Where was Lawrence? Had he been hurt? Maybe he had gone into town to a business meeting without telling them he was leaving the estate, and the blood on the handkerchief was from a simple nosebleed, or a cut finger, and all would be well in the morning. And yet, deep down, she felt cold dread, and an impending sense of doom.

As she closed her eyes, leaning back in her chair, it was Everett's face she saw, remembering how they had exchanged glances, and that shared understanding, which had passed between them without words, a connection which strengthened as they had spent time together. She felt certain that he'd recognized it too, but it was something that they could never speak of. She was betrothed to another.

Even in the midst of the crisis his mind worked alongside mine.

Isabella mulled over what had been different in the way in which Everett communicated with her and suddenly in that moment the difference seemed crystal clear. *Instead of attempting to shield me from unpleasantness, he treated me as an equal partner.*

She had felt the comfort of a special closeness, a connection, and a feeling of true partnership. Isabella had struggled with what, at times, seemed a cloying, overwhelming, protective attitude from Lawrence, which she knew meant he cared, but which she always tried to evade.

She awoke early, watching the dawn, pale and wintry, wondering if there had been any news of Lawrence overnight. Poor Lady Moreton, her distress had been so extreme it had taken Miss Dymchurch and Penelope to help her to her room.

Everett and Lord Brownridge would return to Drayton Park soon and the search would begin again. Where could Lawrence be?

Lawrence, wherever you are? Whatever has happened, please return to us.

Chapter 7

When Everett and Peter arrived at Drayton Park the next morning, they settled their horses in the stable and walked across to the house.

Thoughts were passing through Everett's mind, and he suddenly made a decision. "Let's take a detour. I'd like to look at the place we found the handkerchief and cufflink again."

He looked at Peter as they walked side by side before expressing his concerns. "If Lawrence isn't located soon, and I have to take on my magistrate's role, I'm not looking forward to it, I can tell you that now."

Peter tried to reassure him. "Surely he'll be found today. He can't have gone far. I still think he owed money, or became involved with someone's wife, or daughter. He has always had that reputation."

"You're probably right. I'm increasingly convinced there must have been an abduction, with him taken by surprise. I can't see a duel happening in a garden during a ball. His own betrothal ball at that."

"Maybe the answer is that?" said Peter thoughtfully. "If he had been involved with another young lady and then offered marriage to Isabella. A betrothal ball would have been a time of high emotion to the jilted young lady and her family."

"It's also all supposition, but it seems a good theory. What we need to do is find the man and then deal with any scandal when we've got him back."

Large gray storm clouds loomed on the horizon, but the air was warm and the day felt pleasant. Peter looked up at the sky. "I hope that storm doesn't reach us. We lost too many trees in those dreadful Autumn storms last year."

They made their way to the place in the garden where Everett had found the bloody handkerchief and cufflink the day before.

"You didn't mention the cufflink to Lady Moreton?"

"Something held me back. It clearly pinpoints him as in the garden, and that shirt sleeve must have been ripped. I didn't think it the time to mention it."

Peter crouched down, examining the area with military precision. "None of the vegetation has been disturbed. I might have expected to see trampled grass. But no, there is nothing to indicate a struggle."

Everett nodded. "I agree. Usually when we find a clue, evidence dropped at the scene of a crime, there are signs in the surrounding area that something untoward has happened. I don't see that here. I wanted to hear what you thought before I gave my own opinion," he added. "There is something very strange here." Everett was thinking aloud. "A monogrammed handkerchief, stained in one corner with blood, and a cufflink on the ground beside it."

"You think he set this up himself?"

"I wouldn't go that far, but there's definitely something unusual here," Everett replied as he continued to inspect the area.

Everett stood up. "Let's go to the house and see if there's any news. We can then work out how best to assist with the search."

"And hope Lady Moreton hasn't risen yet," Peter added with a wry smile.

Mrs. Finchley, greeted them. "Is there any news?" Everett asked her.

"No, your Lordship. Nothing's changed. Mr. Fletcher and the footmen are out searching the grounds with the estate staff. "They've got down as far as the lake now, and it doesn't look good, my Lord. It's not my place to say so, but it doesn't look good."

Everett nodded in silent response. He wasn't surprised, but he'd really hoped for a different situation.

The housekeeper ushered them into the breakfast parlor where the family was sitting looking ashen faced.

The ladies remained seated as Lord Drayton stood up and came over to greet them.

"Everett, Peter. How good to see you again. We need you this morning. I admit I'm at a loss as to how to proceed."

"There's been no news then, your lordship?" queried Everett.

"None. Lawrence seems lost. Gone without a trace."

"How is Lady Moreton?" asked Peter.

"She's still in her room. Miss Dymchurch called the local physician, Mr. Noakes, first thing this morning. She was very concerned about her ladyship. He's given her a sleeping draft. We don't expect her to rise until at least noon. The physician will return later and give further advice. It's a sorry business."

Everett looked across the room towards Isabella and their eyes met. His heart went out to her, and he put as much sympathy and concern for a friend into his gaze as he could muster.

"I think it best your lordship if I take over acting in my capacity as local magistrate." Everett suggested.

"I'd be glad of that," agreed Lord Drayton. "I can't think of anyone I'd rather have overseeing this investigation, and I'm beginning to feel out of my depth."

"Clarissa will ride over later to see if she can be of any assistance in the house. We're less than half an hour away. However, if you'd like us to move in here while we're searching, we'd all be glad to do that."

"I'd like nothing better," replied Lord Drayton, relief filling his face. "I'll ask Mrs. Finchley to prepare bed chambers for you both, and for Lady Clarissa."

"I can easily ride home, or Peter can, whenever that's necessary. We'll certainly stay with you for a few days or at least until the Baron is found. Let's hope and pray that's today."

"We-none of us-have much of an appetite but do come and sit with us and take breakfast," urged Isabella.

Everett accepted a cup of tea from Penelope, who smiled faintly at him. He watched Isabella out of the corner of his eye. She looked as though she hadn't slept, and he felt a strong desire to comfort her and hold her close in his arms, but he knew that was inappropriate. He disliked the fact that she was betrothed to the Baron. He could admit that to himself this morning, but that didn't mean he didn't wish the man would return and respect the betrothal. The stress on this family today, facing fear and uncertainty was immense.

Isabella smiled in his direction but didn't make eye contact, before saying quietly, "I can't thank you enough for joining us." Everett noticed that she seemed so preoccupied she had retreated inside herself, which seemed quite natural in view of the situation. Her betrothed had disappeared during their betrothal ball. It may be that society would not gossip today, but there would inevitably be gossip by the end of the week.

Isabella might not face ruin, but no young lady of grace and favor needed to be talked about and pitied by the *ton*. Tongues would wag, and this verged upon scandal. He was unsure how much she cared for the Baron, but there must have been a closeness between them for her to agree to marriage. Perhaps she loved him. Perhaps it was a marriage of convenience. Whatever the case this was a traumatic time for Isabella.

"I suggest we meet in the library to decide how best to proceed today," Everett said in a firm but friendly way.

"Of course, my boy," replied Lord Drayton. "Let's agree to a plan of action."

Everett loved the library at Drayton Park. There was something about the room, with its high arched windows, which made it a pleasure to spend time there. He gazed out across the gardens and the parkland towards the trees in the distance.

They decided to divide into groups. Peter and Penelope would ride over to the village and make enquiries at the local inn. It was past the time of pretending that there was nothing amiss. Lawrence had disappeared.

"I think it best that you remain here," Everett suggested to Lord Drayton. "Just in case there's news which needs any action."

"It will be good if someone is around when Lady Moreton rises," added Penelope.

"I'll take the path nearest to the place where Lawrence disappeared," Everett told them. "There's a carriage path which seems a likely place for him to have been taken if he was abducted. However, there's also that path which leads down to the lake, and it's best if one of us goes down and checks that in daylight. I'm happy to do that."

Isabella spoke up immediately. I shall come with you."

"Are you sure?" Everett asked.

"Absolutely. I feel the need to visit the place where he disappeared."

"As you will be with the local magistrate investigating this case, and you've known each other since childhood, let's not worry about the need for a chaperone today," suggested Lord Drayton. "But I will send one of the footmen along in case you need assistance."

"Thank you," Isabella murmured, smiling at her uncle. "I know how much you are trying to protect me from gossip. I fear though, Uncle, that this incident may lead to my eventual ruin. But it is more important that we locate Lawrence. I never sought society life. If it becomes closed to me, then I'll still be content with my life here."

Everett could see the bravery in her face, the absolute look of conviction that she cared not about the *ton* society. He believed every word she said and he hoped they would find the missing Baron today.

A few minutes later, he found himself in the library with Isabella by his side. He took a large piece of paper and with her guidance, he made a map of the part of the estate where Lawrence had disappeared.

"I think we should search here," Isabella suggested, pointing to several places on the map. "There's a cart track here, which few people know about, and it meets the pathway to the lake. The advantage of using that would be that nobody would see any comings or goings."

Everett nodded. "That makes sense."

"If you give me five minutes I shall need to change if we're going down towards the lake. This muslin dress is not suitable."

He gazed out of the window down toward the woods, and the hillside in the distance, and thought how unchanged and beautiful was the landscape, contrasting with the atmosphere in the house where everyone was now existing in a state of total anxiety. He lifted the paper again, wishing he could feel there was some hope of finding Lawrence in the places marked on their map.

When the door opened again, he looked up and saw Isabella standing there, her chestnut curls glinting in the morning sunlight. She'd changed into the old grey dimity dress, one of her practical working gowns, which he remembered from several years ago. He felt his heart pull a little tighter as he recalled she'd been wearing that very dress on the day when he'd proposed to her and she hadn't accepted his offer.

"Let's go to the anteroom. I need my sturdy shoes and cloak, and that door is nearer to the garden where we'll start our section of the search."

In the anteroom he watched as she chose a simple straw bonnet with green ribbons and tied it under her chin.

Why did I leave her? I could have asked her a second time if she would marry me. I could have talked with her about why she rejected my suit. Instead, my temper flared and took the better of me and I left without a second glance. I know now that was the most foolish thing I ever did.

Lord Drayton, his estate manager, chief groom, and Mr. Fletcher stood outside on the carriage drive. His lordship issued instructions to his assembled staff about where to search for the missing Baron.

He noticed that the men gathered around Lord Drayton included men from the local inn and village, so news must have spread about the disappearance, and the local community had volunteered to be involved in the search. Soon, everyone had instructions about where to search, and it seemed a very comprehensive plan. Lord Drayton's army days had given him a flair for organization and command which Everett admired.

"You each have your area to search," Lord Drayton commanded. "Go in pairs so one of you can return and report anything unusual."

Lord Drayton must have seen Isabella walking past the rear of the crowd and nodded towards her.

He clearly cares for his niece" thought Everett. *That protective glance shows a genuine concern beyond the care needed by a guardian. He's a good man, he's concerned for Isabella's welfare and that involves finding the missing man to whom she's betrothed.*

Everett made himself study the map he held in his hands, though he knew where they were going and the route they would take, he needed to hide his facial expression and underlying feelings from Isabella.

"Shall we start here?" she asked. "There is a path we can take down to the lake". He leaned forward to look at the place she was pointing, his sleeve brushing against hers as they leaned forward to look at the wooded area leading to the lake. He felt a sudden surge of nerves firing together as they connected with his brain and he recognized the intense feelings he felt for this woman who stood next to him. Small, demure and yet so strong.

Her focus remains unwavering, even amid this crisis, he thought, watching her. *Few women would approach this dreadful situation with such clarity of thought.*

As they approached the place in the garden where he'd found the missing handkerchief, he heard Isabella drawing a sharp breath.

"Why would he come out here?" She asked, as if she was thinking aloud. "It makes no sense".

"I agree there's no logic to any of this. What we do know is that he told you he needed to meet somebody, and that it was urgent, but not the reason for that meeting. We also know about that heated conversation with his mother immediately before he disappeared. There are no answers in any of that, but it does show that he must have been preoccupied that evening".

"It's as though he disappeared without trace. And with all the arrivals and departures by carriage for the ball it gave perfect cover for someone to abduct Lawrence". Isabella looked down at the rhododendron bush where they'd found the handkerchief and he saw her look up to the sky, as though she was scrutinizing the distant horizon.

"Oh Lawrence, come back now. Your mother is under sedation. None of us know where you are. Come home."

He felt the strength and tenderness of her emotion.

She does care for him. I was wrong in thinking there wasn't that same emotional closeness between them. This is tearing her apart, at what should be a happy time in life.

Chapter 8

Isabella led Everett through a gap in the thick hornbeam hedge, which bordered the garden, to a path leading away from the house. "Not everyone knows about this path, but Lawrence would as I've walked it with him several times in recent weeks. It's certainly possible to get a cart and horses down here or a small gig, and I suspect that's how they took him away".

Everett looked at her. "You're thinking he's been abducted too?"

"I simply can't imagine Lawrence causing his Mama this amount of stress and anxiety. I'm realistic, and I know that he might not worry about leaving me in this difficult situation, but with his mother it's different."

She felt a sharp contraction, almost a pain close to her ribs somewhere in her stomach. As she spoke the words aloud, she realized she believed every word of what she had said. Lawrence would not have thought twice about leaving her to face humiliation and scandal.

"I see," responded Everett remembering when he'd first met the Baron at university. "He's always been extremely close to his mother. At Cambridge he would return home to be with her whenever he could. It was a bit of a jest amongst his friends."

She looked at him with an intense expression in her eyes.

Isabella knew she could trust Everett and so decided to share her thoughts. "None of you have said it to me, but I suspect he's either been blackmailed or has a debt he's struggling to pay. He certainly showed enthusiasm about marrying me and yet there isn't that level of connection or even close friendship between us. We get on well enough, and I believe that affection will deepen over the years, but for Lawrence this is an alliance as much as a marriage."

"I'm sorry to hear that." Everett spoke quietly, and reached to put his hand on her arm in a gentle reassuring touch. "You deserve a little love and romance in life."

She thought back to when he had brushed against her in the library while they gazed at the map. The jolt, the startle and intense reaction of her body responding to his touch had stunned her. She knew she needed to dampen down those feelings, hide them and lock them away deep inside her. Here she was, betrothed to Lawrence who had disappeared without trace, and this was not the time to experience rekindled feelings for her old love.

As he brushed against her again the same warmth spread out to the far reaches of her body, despite the gravity and seriousness of their conversation.

That connection between us is still there, it never went away. All these years it's been there and today I feel it strongly. Isabella knew now was not the time to be feeling this close, comfortable connection with Everett, regardless of her complicated feelings about her betrothal. Lawrence's safe return had to be her priority. That's where she needed to focus her full attention and effort. She could work out her feelings for Everett later. She had always felt sadness and regret about how things had been left between them, and she pushed down a growing awareness that those embers had been fanned into a steady, bright flame.

As she reflected on the intense emotions, she was trying to suppress something caught her eye.

"Look here," she pointed to the ground ahead of them. "We had wet weather last week, it rained a lot, and I believe I can see traces of tracks. I think the marks are from a small carriage rather than a cart, but I can't be sure."

"You're right," Everett said, bending down to examine the cart track. "These marks were made recently. We don't know if Lawrence was taken forcibly, against his will, or if he planned and had a man waiting to take him away. No matter, the important thing is still to find him."

"And alive," Isabella whispered, for the first time speaking of the dread she felt inside, that they might never see Lawrence again. She could not bear to think of the distress Lady Moreton would feel at the loss of her only son.

"We have to be positive," Everett reassured her." I'm going to ask your head groom, Simmons, to come down here and take a closer look. He might know which type of vehicle left those tracks."

They continued walking along the forest path and she distracted herself by looking carefully and analyzing any changes in the plants growing close to the track. "I love this path, it's where I first began to develop my interest in botany. I sometimes think I know every flower, every tree along the way, but there is always something new I see that can surprise me."

"I remember you recording details meticulously, even in those days."

Isabella caught sight of the first glimpse of the lake, glistening silver in the autumn sunshine, and thought how beautifully mysterious it looked. She knew they would not find Lawrence here; those tracks they had seen told a clear story. Had he been waylaid, bundled into a carriage during the ball? The evidence they had all seemed to point in that direction.

Every so often they heard a shout in the distance from one of the estate workers searching Drayton Park's extensive grounds.

"It looks as though there are a lot of people searching over towards the west, so let's take this path here and follow the stream down to the lake," Isabella suggested.

"I think that makes sense." Everett led her forward as they made their way along the path. They were forced to stop walking side by side and continue in single file as the path narrowed.

Isabella found herself wishing that they were sitting together having an alfresco luncheon at Drayton Park, instead of searching with an ever-increasing gnawing anxiety for her missing betrothed. It really was a beautiful day.

"We'll need to return by late afternoon," Everett told her. "I've asked Clarissa to come over, and we shall need to see if any of the other search groups have found anything of significance and report those tracks."

The high canopy of trees let sunlight filter through the leaves, and as he reached to offer his hand to help her cross a difficult piece of terrain, she noticed how the sun highlighted the strong line of Everett's jaw as he scanned the surrounding woodland.

Even after years apart, we fall into step together without effort, she realized, her awareness of him sharpening each moment they spent time together, despite the difficult circumstances.

The stream ran faster here, gurgling over smooth stones. "Do you remember?" he asked in a quiet tone.

"Of course," she responded, looking up towards him. "It's where we used to build dams when we were children. I also remember those summer days when we could bathe in the pool over there, where the stream widens before it reaches the lake."

"It's one of the most beautiful places I know, especially where the trees open up into that wide overhead canopy that resembles an ancient Roman temple. I often think of it," he added, with an immediate look that suggested he regretted the words as soon as they left his mouth.

Isabella crouched down kneeling at the water's edge, moving the foliage with one hand and peering at the plants around her. Her gloved fingers carefully brushing aside leaves as she searched. "The frost hasn't killed it yet," she said. "Here's that first rare orchid which we found together. I've propagated it, but I have a soft spot for this one, as it's one of the first plants that intrigued me when I began to have an interest in botany."

She stood and walked to a natural viewing point, and stopped suddenly as something caught her attention.

"This is strange," she said, her voice suddenly urgent. "Someone's been here, it's almost as though they've been hiding here in the woods."

Everett crouched down beside her, his shoulder nearly touching hers as they both leaned closer to examine some partial footprints, visible in the mud.

His proximity sent her pulse racing in a way she had to work hard to suppress.

"You're right," he muttered, his head low down, scrutinizing the tracks a man had left not many hours ago.

Isabella looked at him. "It may not be significant. It is unusual to find tracks here though. I spend many hours in these woods on my knees looking at different plants and I rarely find footsteps."

"It could be an important piece of the puzzle, or totally unconnected." He looked thoughtful before asking, "It isn't as though the village children are coming here to play?"

She shook her head.

"Or poachers?"

"We very rarely have poachers at Drayton Park, I think that's because uncle makes sure that the produce from the estate is shared fairly between those who live and work here."

"Well, someone has certainly been here. I'll get Simmons to take a closer look down here as well."

"Tell them to be careful with my plants," Isabella spoke without thinking. Realizing what she had just said she added, "I'm sorry, if it helps find Lawrence of course my plants can be trampled on"

Everett reassured her. "There's no need for that. They know you and rest assured they shall be careful."

It struck Isabella that Everett treated her as an equal. *His respect for my observations creates a space for genuine partnership,* Isabella thought, noting how Everett built upon her thoughts and ideas rather than dismissing them as less worthy than his own.

This difference with Lawrence's directive, somewhat autocratic manner stood out starkly in her mind.

She heard a familiar voice calling and looked around. Penelope and Lord Brownridge, with two of the grooms, came down the path towards them. And who was that with them? To Isabella's surprise she saw Miss Dymchurch.

Indeed, Lady Moreton's companion, dressed in boots and a borrowed attire, walked next to Penelope.

Isabella waved to them. "We're here. We've found footsteps dried in the mud. It seems strange, so we're going to get Simmons to take a look."

"Let me see," said Lord Brownridge, edging forward, being careful where he trod.

"It's curious, because Isabella often works in this area and has never noticed footsteps before," Everett told them.

Isabella turned to welcome Lady Moreton's companion.

"It's a surprise to see you, Miss Dymchurch," Isabella smiled at the lady who usually said very little.

"I truly could not stay waiting any longer. I saw Miss Penelope and Lord Brownridge from the drawing room window, and rushed to join them. At least I feel useful here, as we search for Lord Moreton."

"And how is Lady Moreton?" Isabella asked with genuine concern.

"She has been heavily sedated by Mr. Noakes. I admit that I dread her waking up and finding out that Lawrence is still missing."

"We've had no luck apart from the cart tracks and these footprints," said Everett.

"And we found nothing in the village either," added Lord Brownridge. "We asked at the tavern and called at the Rectory to see if the Reverend Garstead had heard anything. Nothing. No one has seen or heard anything."

"It's baffling," concluded Penelope, looking towards Lord Brownridge with obvious affection.

Isabella could see once again that something had developed between them. There was a flow, a sort of natural harmony.

Everett looked at Isabella. "I believe we should return to the house now. I am keen to take another look at that handkerchief and I want Simmons to come down here as soon as possible to give his opinion on the tracks and footprints."

Lord Brownridge nodded. "Let's go back now. I've asked Clarissa to begin recording anything that people discover or remember which seems significant. She'll note that in a book, so that we have it all in one place."

"An excellent idea. I haven't sent for the sergeant and the constables yet, as I wanted to wait a few more hours in hope that Lawrence might return."

"That's wise," agreed Isabella. She looked up to see the sun beginning to lower in the sky. The days were noticeably shortening now. She usually loved the last Autumn days, but today the increasing darkness felt so dismal and dispiriting.

They made their way back to Drayton Park mostly in silence. Everett and Lord Brownridge strode ahead and were almost blurry shapes in the distance. She walked alongside Penelope and Miss Dymchurch.

"Those gentlemen walk so fast," commented Miss Dymchurch.

"Well, they have sturdier footwear on longer legs but if there are any clues then we will be the ones to find them as we are looking around us as we walk," Penelope assured her.

"It's a good thing her ladyship isn't here," giggled Miss Dymchurch. "I don't believe she would approve of the mention of men's legs."

Isabella and Penelope exchanged a glance. It was Penelope who replied. "That sounds quite old fashioned. We must be modern women Miss Dymchurch."

"That sounds rather nice," said this prim lady who so rarely spoke. "You girls must call me Althea," she urged them.

Isabella looked at Miss Dymchurch hiding her surprise with a warm smile. "Althea, what a lovely name."

"It comes from the mallow, that pink flower we delight in during the summer. My mother said it linked with the Greek for healer too. She always said she wanted me to have an individual name."

"I like it very much. Would you prefer for us to continue calling you Miss Dymchurch in front of her ladyship though, Althea?" Isabella asked her.

"Perhaps that would be best." Miss Dymchurch seemed to make a decision as a look of defiance crossed her face. "No, my dears, continue to call me Althea. It's my choice what people call me."

"Then Althea it is," cried Penelope.

Althea, as she had now become, turned to Penelope. "I believe you are gifted musically?"

"It's true that I enjoy music and playing."

"I hope to hear you play while we are at Drayton Park. My own efforts at the spinet are not gifted, but I enjoy music very much. It so soothes the spirits."

"Which is what we all need at the moment," declared Isabella. "It looks as though Mrs. Finchley is already lighting the candles. At least there will be a warm fire in the hearth."

As they came up to the house a feeling of doom pervaded it.

It's as though someone has died, but they haven't, Isabella thought to herself.

Lawrence is such a larger-than-life character that I can't imagine him restrained somewhere, hurting in pain. She shuddered at this strange situation and her growing apprehension about her betrothed.

Mrs. Finchley greeted them as they entered Drayton Park Manor.

"I've prepared a hot collation for this evening. His Lordship thought that would be best. Lady Moreton will be taking dinner in her chamber."

Althea made her way towards the back stairs to join her mistress. She turned back to them before making her exit. "I'd better go and join her. I hope we can walk together again in the future, hopefully under pleasanter circumstances."

Isabella called to her. "Althea, there is no need for you to use only the back stairs. Please use our main staircase, you are a guest here."

Althea nodded in surprise and immediately turned and made her way up the main staircase.

"I told Peter that I'd meet him at the stables for a late afternoon ride," said Penelope.

"An excellent plan, although you need to be quick as there is not much light left in the day. You can blow those cobwebs out of your hair and find a chaperone."

"That's what we thought," Penelope replied with an embarrassed smile at Isabella.

I rather like the way Penelope has started to refer to 'we' when talking about Lord Brownridge. There is a definite romance blooming there.

The drawing room was empty, her uncle still being out searching alongside the staff. Isabella made her way to the library and, on hearing voices, tapped gently on the door. Everett's voice called a greeting, and she went in to find Everett and Clarissa standing at the table looking at a notebook. Isabella could see the stained handkerchief and cufflink were on the table too. The sight of the blood made her shudder, but they had to properly investigate what had happened to Lawrence, and Everett was the local magistrate.

Clarissa gestured to Isabella. "Come and join us, Bella. We're reviewing all the information gathered today."

"Is there anything especially significant?"

"Your discovery of the footprints and the tracks is the only thing so far," replied Clarissa. "I really am quite parched and shall ask for tea. You look as though you would benefit from a cup Isabella?"

Isabella suddenly realized how tired she was. "Indeed, I would. I am rather exhausted."

Everett looked at her and she could see concern in his eyes. He pulled a chair away from the table and guided her to sit down. "Sit there and rest for a few minutes," he urged gently.

"I can't rest," Isabella protested. "I have to keep going."

"Not for a few minutes. I can show you what Clarissa and I have been perusing, although I have to admit there is very little to go on. I'm so glad Lady Moreton has taken to her room. She is so very close to Lawrence and the lack of news will do nothing for her state of mind"

And I'm not, Isabella thought to herself. *I'm concerned for his welfare, but not in the way in which a bride-to-be should be. I can't think about that today though.*

Everett handed her the leather-bound book which Clarissa had opened on the table. As he leaned across, her arm brushed his and the brief touch ignited that same spark she had been hoping might just be her imagination ever since they had met again at the ball.

Despite her exhaustion she closed her eyes and relaxed, feeling the lingering, tingling sensation of his touch on her arm.

In the last of the sun's rays she watched as he examined the handkerchief carefully, turning it towards the light, holding it up to scrutinize the markings.

"It isn't a spatter pattern," he said, almost as though talking to himself. "And it isn't the pattern of something applied to the wound to stop bleeding. It's a strange shape and pattern. I can't work it out."

Isabella knew Everett was a talented artist and he had an artist's eye for detail. He tried to hide it as he had been discouraged from pursuing painting by his family but Isabella could see it as she watched his long fingers trace the monogram on the handkerchief.

She looked again at the handkerchief and a thought occurred to her. "It reminds me of the pattern after I've cut my finger."

"I believe you're right," Everett exclaimed. "That's exactly the sort of pattern. Clarissa noticed the stain had an unusual edging.

The door opened and Mrs. Finchley entered with a tea tray, closely followed by Clarissa and two footmen bearing candles.

Isabella closed her eyes, hoping that soon there would be some news, as she felt increasingly certain that something dreadful had happened to her betrothed during their celebratory ball.

Chapter 9

Everett could see how tired she was, her whole body showed the exhaustion which had overtaken her after the many hours of uncertainty, waiting to hear news of her missing betrothed.

Yet even now her composure remained intact even after a long day of searching. His admiration grew for the way that she had handled events, and how she'd focused on practical things such as making the map with him that morning. She had thrown herself into the search for Lawrence, when she could easily have sat at home in the drawing room waiting for news of her missing betrothed.

Even now when she sat in the chair too exhausted to stand, she looked eagerly at the leather book in front of her seeking information which might help find Lawrence.

He saw her watching him scrutinizing the bloodstain, determined to be involved in the quest to find Lawrence.

When he had stood next to her, moving the chair for her to sit, he felt overwhelmed by a warmth and her subtle floral fragrance, the scent of what had to be roses and jasmine distracted him. He needed to remember that the hunt was for her missing betrothed, and his feelings needed to be suppressed and locked away. There could be no prospect for how he felt, more a lingering melancholy that they encountered each other once more at a time when they could not advance in their pursuit of reunion.

He closed his eyes for a fleeting second and that subtle floral fragrance filled his senses.

She could also feel this connection, she could feel this pull, this strong magnetic force between them. Yet neither of them could acknowledge the feeling and its intensity.

His thoughts returned to the present as Clarissa began to make notes about the discovery of the footsteps in the mud near the orchid in the woodland. Everett forced himself to focus on his sister and her endeavors to record the investigation in detail. Sometimes when he held magistrate's court at Kennington Manor, she took on the recording, ensuring clarity in the record of the proceedings, aiding him in his duties as a magistrate. His little sister had grown into a competent efficient organizer of events.

Everett pulled open the heavy oak library door and asked a passing footman to go and find Lord Drayton and Lord Brownridge. Within a few minutes the two men joined them in the library and Clarissa asked if they'd like to take tea. He knew for a fact that Peter would have rather had a brandy but could tell that due to his regard for Clarissa he agreed to take the offered cup of tea. Lord Drayton took a seat nursing his own hot cup of tea in his hands, ready to listen to whatever Everett had to report.

When he'd finished describing all that had been found so far, he saw Lord Drayton look immediately to Isabella, his first concern being for his niece. "I agree it looks grave," Lord Drayton spoke quietly. "I wish it were otherwise."

"I've continued to hold back from involving the sergeant and the constables, but I don't think I'd be able to leave that another day," Everett informed them.

"Of course not my boy, you're the magistrate here. I'm long retired from that role. It's important that we follow your judgement and take guidance about whatever you feel is the best action in this dreadful situation."

Without realizing it, Everett found he had instinctively moved to stand closer to Isabella, taking a protective stance near her chair.

It's as though I need to protect her, he thought. In that moment he knew that in all the years he'd been apart his feelings for Isabella had not changed, and yet now when he could admit this to himself it was too late. She was not only betrothed to another, but in the difficult social situation of her husband-to-be disappearing. This was not the time to tell her how he felt about her. With any luck he would be able to suppress those feelings and in a week's time he'd be able to prepare to attend her wedding and smile as she was joined to Lawrence in matrimony.

Until Lawrence returned, he would protect and look out for Isabella in any way that he could.

Lord Drayton stood up. "It's almost twenty-four hours since Lawrence disappeared. The situation becomes more desperate with every hour that passes. I told you yesterday that I rarely drank anything other than tea, but I'm going to suggest that we open some of that fine French brandy. It may even help us to sleep tonight."

A sharp knock on the door interrupted the words that Lord Drayton was in the middle of delivering to the group. Mr. Fletcher entered the library carrying a silver salver bearing a single envelope addressed to Lord Drayton and Lady Moreton.

"One of the footmen found this letter by the door," explained Mr. Fletcher. "I thought it best to bring it to you as soon as possible, my Lord."

"Everett, could you?" asked Lord Drayton.

"It's strangely written," said Everett looking at the envelope. "Each letter is in a different style. it's almost as though someone has been trying too hard to disguise their handwriting."

A heavy silence filled the room, expressions of concern on every face as Everett opened the envelope and took out the letter from inside. He scanned the page, his expression darkening as he read its contents.

Everett handed the letter to Lord Drayton, whose face took on an expression of disbelief and then anger. He heard Isabella asking frantically, "Uncle what's the matter, please tell me what it is. Is that letter about Lawrence?"

Lord Drayton's hand trembled slightly as he passed the note to Isabella. Penelope stood close to her, and Isabella held out the parchment so her friend and cousin could read it.

"Surely this can't be the case. It seems someone has kidnapped Lawrence?" gasped Isabella.

"And they want five hundred pounds by tomorrow evening to return him safely," added Lord Drayton taking out a handkerchief and mopping his brow in disbelief.

"What do we do?" asked Isabella. "These are criminals, felons of the worst type. If we give them the money, then surely, they will kidnap somebody else next week. I wonder how many other men of *the ton* have been targeted in this way."

No one had heard the door open, or noticed Lady Moreton standing close to the doorway, listening as the letter was read aloud.

"I believe that letter is addressed to me as well as you, Lord Drayton", came her strident tones across the room.

"That's quite correct, Lillian," replied Henry. "If you sit next to Isabella, you can read the contents of the letter for yourself."

"I think not," she said less forcefully, with a look of bewilderment in her eyes. "Lord Kennington, kindly tell me the contents of that letter now."

"It's a demand for five hundred pounds by tomorrow evening. The money is to be taken to the ancient oak tree at the eastern boundary of the Drayton Park estate. The kidnappers stipulate that it should be Miss Drayton who comes alone with the ransom money with no escorts or protection of any kind."

"I see," replied Lady Moreton, her voice shaking. "Is there any more?"

"Unfortunately, yes, your Ladyship," continued Everett. "Isabella, Miss Drayton is to leave the payment, a purse of money beneath the fallen tree. They state that any sign of authorities or armed men in the vicinity will result in Baron Moreton's immediate demise."

Lady Moreton gasped in disbelief as Clarissa rushed to her side. "They're threatening to kill him. We need the authorities to intercept these people as soon as possible," she cried.

"They say they are watching our every move, and we have until sunset tomorrow," Everett told the assembled group.

"They have my son, and I have to pay for him to be released. I tell you now that I do not have that money. Even five hundred pounds is an amount I do not have to spare." She put her head in her hands. "What am I to do?" she cried.

"You can't let Isabella go to the forest on her own. How can we trust these people? They're threatening to kill Lawrence," Penelope pleaded with them.

"It's of no consequence," Isabella's voice was quiet, but firm. She handed the piece of paper back to Everett, and as she did so he felt a tremor, which she succeeded in hiding from the others.

Without thinking Everett stepped forward and put his hand onto Isabella's shoulder. "We shall find a way out of this situation," he told her. "No one will allow you to put yourself in that level of danger."

"Excuse me," came the strident tones of Lady Moreton. "I see no reason why Isabella, as Lawrence's betrothed, should not carry out these instructions. Surely that's preferable to having my son dead on our doorstep?"

Penelope spoke up, looking a little uncertain of herself. "We must keep calm. We all want the same outcome, which is the safe return of the Baron."

Everett was grateful for Penelope's intervention and picked up the thread. "We have the full force of local law and order at our behest. I serve as local magistrate, and in that position, I'm prepared to listen to whatever you'd prefer to do as a family."

He looked over towards Isabella exhausted and fragile.

I will not allow harm to reach her, his protective instinct rising with surprising intensity.

"We will work through this," he told them with a confidence he did not feel, relieved to see Isabella relaxing back a little into her chair and breathing what he thought was a sigh of relief.

"Work through it, work through it," Lady Moreton protested even more forcefully. "In my opinion the ransom should be delivered post haste."

"I'm not sure that's the best plan," Everett looked at her, keeping his voice calm to try to reassure her.

"I do not care if it is the best plan, but it is the plan we're going to follow. I absolutely insist on that."

"I am the magistrate here and I shall make that decision," he responded more forcibly.

At his words Lady Moreton cried out and transformed from ice cold control to a dramatic histrionic collapse, holding the small table near the library door for support. Her voice rose with theatrical intensity as she insisted that they had to follow the instructions precisely and that remained the only option for Lawrence's safe return.

As Everett watched her it occurred to him that this was not the first time Lady Moreton had used these strategies to get exactly what she wanted. However, he needed to tap into compassion, as her son had, it seemed, been kidnapped. He may well be hurt, as they had all seen that handkerchief spattered with blood.

They had a ransom note asking for a specific amount of money to be delivered in a controlled and specific way. Lady Moreton did, in these circumstances, have a right to her opinion about the next steps to take in this terrible situation.

As he watched her Lady Moreton continued to become more visibly distressed. She moved towards them, her arms stretched out before her, tears streaming down her face.

A small part of him remembered a similar performance he had seen in an opera as the main characters knew they were about to plummet into doom and disaster, but he pushed that away as unkind. This woman had always overseen her son, dictating his every choice in life, and suddenly he had gone, disappeared, and she would, of course do anything to have him returned to her.

"If you will not help me then I shall wear Isabella's cloak and bonnet and go with the money to this oak tree in the forest. I am determined that my son will be released," she cried.

Lady Moreton stared at Everett in distress. She was clearly used to always getting her own way. In this situation she had no power, or control and all she could do was beg for their support in meeting the kidnappers' demands. She held out her hands towards him, pleading for him to do exactly what the kidnappers requested.

Isabella stepped forward, moving towards Lady Moreton. "We must follow these instructions," she declared with quiet firmness. "Whichever way we look at this, and whichever moral course we take, Lady Moreton is right, and that we risk losing Lawrence if we ignore these demands."

"Thank you," said Lady Moreton in anguish. "Finally, someone understands that we have to do what these criminals ask."

"I've weighed the possibilities of success against the risks, and it doesn't matter whether I'm in danger or not, the reality is that we have to follow this directive and hope that it will result in Lawrence's release."

"Isabella, you cannot put yourself into danger", said Lord Drayton equally forcefully. "I won't allow it."

"I'm afraid you're all going to have to let me be the judge of what I can and can't do in this matter. I know I could not live with myself if we ignored these demands and something happened to Lawrence."

"Bravo my dear," cried Lady Moreton. "We might save Lawrence yet."

"And what if we give them this five hundred pounds, and then they backtrack and demand more money?" asked Lord Brownridge.

"Well, if that happens, we shall need to talk together and reconsider our actions. I'm inclined to think that we will refuse to pay any more money." Isabella looked around the room. "Listen, I believe we can pay this ransom and then later retrieve the money as well. It's a case of setting a trap, and planning our actions in minute detail."

Everett's jaw tightened as he realized he had a choice to make here. He thought there were many potential pitfalls with this plan, but in the end he offered no objection. Isabella was right, if they played their cards carefully then they might find a way to release Lawrence and capture the kidnappers in the process.

"My son must be saved. Surely that's the main priority," cried Lady Moreton, her voice again becoming increasingly hysterical.

"Very well," Everett agreed although he could not hide his obvious reluctance from his voice. "I suggest we agree to this demand, but make sure that Isabella is safe by positioning observers at strategic points, who could intervene at a moment's notice."

"So, I wouldn't go alone?" Isabella asked. "Surely that would break the conditions?"

"The observers stay at a safe distance, and other than having a supportive ring around you we keep to the letter of the instructions. I refuse to get involved in this if there are no safeguards to protect you."

Her courage is astounding, he thought. *She's been so astute in her analysis of this situation. She's even prepared to face potential danger alone.*

He felt a cold, icy dread in his stomach at the thought of her putting herself into danger, which stunned him with its force. *I'm frightened for her. I haven't felt this fear since I was behind enemy lines during the war.*

"We have a plan and can fine tune it before the deadline looms to handover the ransom money." Everett turned to Lord Drayton. "With your permission I'd like to tell the local tenant farmers and estate workers something of this situation. They can be our eyes and ears and may see or hear something important."

"Of course. I'll make sure they know that something is amiss."

If Isabella looked exhausted before, now she looked close to the point of collapse. He began to move towards her, seeing her sway a little, concerned she might swoon. Before he reached her Clarissa was there, offering Isabella her arm, and encouraging her to sit and take a cup of hot, steaming tea into her hands.

He felt proud of both these women. Isabella, who thought nothing of any personal danger to herself, if it meant saving Lawrence from captivity. Clarissa, barely out of the schoolroom and showing a maturity and calm confidence as she supported others.

He could see Clarissa speaking in hushed tones to Penelope who had stood and joined Isabella. Penelope spoke to Isabella. "Bella, I insist that you go to take a hot bath and retire to bed to rest. This has been an incredibly traumatic twenty-four hours for you. You can't carry on this way, especially now that we know there are further challenges to face tomorrow."

"Absolutely right," agreed Lord Drayton. He turned to Everett. "Could I ask you to accompany Isabella and Penelope upstairs? My niece looks exhausted and needs to rest and I'm worried she may collapse."

"Of course," Everett agreed. Penelope already had the door open, guiding Isabella away from the room.

"Bella, I'm worried about you," he heard Penelope say as they entered the hallway. "You haven't eaten anything since the ball, and this is intense stress. Your nerves must be on edge all the time, and now there is this ridiculous plan for you to take money and put it near some oak tree in the woods."

"I know," Isabella smiled weakly. "It seems the only thing I can do to help Lawrence and his mother too."

Isabella took a step towards the stairs, and at that moment she reached out to hold a side table for support and a vase of flowers went crashing to the floor. "Help her," cried Penelope. "She's about to faint."

Everett caught her as she began to fall backwards and without conscious thought lifted her into his arms. Her head rested gently against his shoulder, and she murmured something as Penelope waved smelling salts under her nose.

"I'm sure she'll be fine," re-assured Penelope. "We just need to get her to her room, where Maisie will look after her and make sure she rests."

"She seemed so brave and strong. I didn't realise just how much of a toll these events had taken on her," Everett apologized to Penelope.

"She is the most courageous person I know," said Penelope. "But if you think about it, she hasn't stopped since Lawrence disappeared, and I doubt very much that she slept last night. He's her betrothed and it's bound to take its toll on her."

He only half listened to Penelope's words, overcome by the sensation of holding Isabella in his arms. He felt her warm breath on his cheek and could swear he felt her heart beating against his chest. He found it difficult to concentrate on anything else.

"She needs that hot bath and a good night's sleep. I shall ask Mrs. Finchley to bring some more tea. Can you carry her to her room? Maisie will be up there waiting for her."

Penelope rushed towards the housekeeper's parlor as he began to carry his precious burden upstairs. He spoke to her as they climbed the stairs, and she murmured occasionally. As they reached her bedchamber, he knocked on the door and Maisie appeared instantaneously, pointing to the bed.

"Is she ill?" asked Maisie, concern filling her voice.

"Exhausted, and she needs rest. Miss Penelope is bringing some tea."

"We heard about the ransom note," added Maisie.

"How so?" he asked in surprise.

"Word spreads quickly in a house like Drayton Park Manor. Is it true Miss Isabella is to go alone to deliver the ransom?"

Everett nodded, as he gently placed Isabella on the bed. He felt this strange reluctance to let her go, craving that continual closeness, the feeling he'd experienced as he carried her in his arms.

"Then I shall accompany my mistress. A lady should never go anywhere without her maid," Maisie's voice suggested that she was determined and there would be no point in arguing.

"Well I …" he began.

"Frivolities, your Lordship. No one considers or takes notice of a lady's maid, and it would be impossible for a lady to go alone into such a situation. She would be risking her reputation. I shall follow at a seemly distance, but I won't need to hide."

"I see," he said thoughtfully. He could see some sense in Maisie's words but his worry was that the kidnapper might not see it the same way.

"There will be others hidden, waiting and watching for these rogues?" Maisie asked.

"Indeed, and I will be among them," he told her earnestly.

"Then I insist on accompanying my mistress."

"Maisie, I'll speak with Lord Drayton, but I think that this could be a very good idea."

Maisie let out a deep breath. "Oh, thank you, your Lordship. I need to make sure she's safe."

"As we all do, Maisie," he replied, as Isabella opened her eyes fully and looked up at him in confusion.

"You had a funny turn in the library. Penelope is bringing you a soothing tisane and Maisie is organizing a hot bath. We all agree that you need rest, and we should have noticed you were near to collapse sooner."

"I didn't dream about the ransom note then," she said as she moved her head back against the soft, feather pillow.

"I'm afraid not, but it's important you don't think about that now."

She nodded, and he turned to leave her. Something made him turn back and she still looked towards him with those glistening eyes. In a moment of sudden compulsion, he leaned over and kissed her gently on the forehead. He heard her gasp, alongside his own pulse thumping loudly in his ears.

"You need to rest now," he murmured. "Tomorrow promises to be a difficult and long day." And with those words he left the room.

Chapter 10

What on earth happened? Had she fainted? Surely not ... she'd never fainted before in her life.

I remember being in the library and agreeing to take the ransom money to the oak tree. Everything after that was blank, until she'd recovered half conscious in Everett's arms as they approached her bed chamber.

For a moment she closed her eyes and remembered that warmth, the comforting sensation of being cradled so close to the man whom she'd loved for so many years. In those moments, when she'd relaxed in his arms, she'd felt that silent support that she found so stabilizing amid the chaos of this strange situation in which she found herself. A bride-to-be with a missing betrothed.

Maisie had lit the candles and gazing at the flickering flames helped her to feel calm.

Why did Everett's presence provide more comfort than thoughts of my betrothed, she wondered.

She knew the answer to that question, but she had chosen to stay on her path of marriage to Lawrence. She had made a promise and would keep it.

Now, when it was too late, she could admit this to herself. Everett had offered her marriage, and she had turned it down. She had lived with regret and memories for a long time.

I never expected when I said I was uncertain about marriage that I wouldn't see him again for almost five years. When I saw him at the ball yesterday it was as though my heart which had frozen melted, and a warmth flowed through my body. The irony was that I met him again at my own betrothal ball ... a betrothal to a man I admire and like but have never loved.

I still care for Lawrence though. I'm committed to our marriage, and I don't wish any harm to come to him, even if that means putting myself into danger. I only had to take one look at his poor mother's face to know that he is loved, very much loved, just not by me.

I'm determined to make a positive marriage, based on companionship and a shared view of the important things in life. I need to remember that Lawrence is one of the few men who is prepared to support my working and continuing compilation of my encyclopedia of British wild plants.

Isabella heard Penelope's voice, and realized she had drifted off into a daydream, a sort of trance where she had been lost in a maze of thoughts. The bedchamber felt like a cocoon where she could hide and rest before returning to the world outside.

"Penny. Tell me what happened to me?" pleaded Isabella.

"I believe you swooned. You looked near to exhaustion; we were all very concerned. You agreed, and I still can't believe it, to deliver the ransom money to the oak tree. I think that took the last vestige of your strength. You moved towards the library door, felt dizzy and then you fainted."

"I see, and Everett carried me up to my chamber?"

"He did. He seems very solicitous of your welfare, Isabella. A kind, considerate and compassionate man; yet so decisive when he needs to take the lead in a situation. If I didn't feel so close to Peter I might have set my cap at him."

"Oh, he's one of the best men that ever lived," Isabella replied, soulfully.

"There's something between you, well there was something between you," mused Penelope. "I'm not going to ask you more tonight, but I'm determined to ask you when you feel stronger."

Isabella looked at her friend and took a sharp breath. "It's alright Pen. There isn't much to tell. We pretty much grew up together, in fact I was with Everett when I discovered my first orchid in the woods down by the stream. I believe I saw him as an older brother; he is just a few years older than me. I didn't realise he'd begun to see me differently."

"Ah, I start to understand."

"It seems he'd fallen in love with me. I was young sixteen years of age, just out of the schoolroom, and looking forward to coming out at my first season in town." As she thought back to that time, which seemed so far away it felt like another life, she felt a tear begin to fall down her cheek and raised a hand to wipe it away. Penelope listened silently, waiting for her to continue.

"One summer's day while we were walking in the woods, on that path towards the lake, he asked me to marry him. I was so surprised, so stunned if I'm honest, that I didn't know what to say. I turned him down. I said I wasn't ready for marriage and I was too young, and in all honesty, I don't believe I was."

She paused for a moment, gazing towards a candle flame as it flicked in the darkness.

"I thought perhaps he might suggest we married in a year or two when I was a little older and more certain, but instead he very politely and very formally withdrew, and within a few weeks he had left the country."

She remembered those days of confusion and unhappiness after he'd left. Eventually she'd reached a place of calmness and left for her season in town. She'd never met another man where she had felt that close friendship, alongside something more, and she now knew it had been the first stirrings of tender love.

"The last I heard he was courting Lady Viola Harrington. Although our estates border each other I only saw him again when he arrived with his family at the ball last night. I've seen Clarissa occasionally, but never Everett."

Isabella could see Penelope looking at her with sadness in her blue eyes. "I'm so sorry."

"And now it seems as if he's never been away, and all my regrets at turning him down all those years ago are whirling around in my mind. I didn't know how much I loved him until it was too late. I made my peace with myself about my decision, met Lawrence, and agreed to marry him, hoping that love between us would grow over time. With Everett it's different, I was too young to realise that I loved him."

"Oh Isabella, I had no idea. You lived with that sadness for so many years."

Isabella nodded and smiled weakly. "Love is a strange thing, Penelope. When you find it, seize it, for it might not be there when you look for it the next month. We think of men as strong, but their emotions can, it seems to me, be as fragile as ours. I hurt Everett when I rejected his proposal. I lost both a friend and the man I loved that day in the woods."

"And you walked those same woods with him today. How strange that should happen."

"A quirk of fate. Yet while we were walking together it was as though time had stood still, and we were back in that place five years ago."

"What will you do?"

"Nothing. I'm betrothed to Lawrence. I agreed to marry him and that's what I shall do. It's no different really, nothing has changed, and I still hope that a measure of love between us will grow over time."

She took the tisane which Penelope handed her feeling the warmth of the cup in her hands, sipping the tea filled with herbs.

"I'll leave you to get some sleep. You need to rest Isabella."

"I know," she said, smiling as her friend left the room.

She forced her thoughts away from tomorrow and the demands of the kidnappers. Soon she fell into the dreamless sleep of exhaustion and the rest that she needed.

***

Isabella breakfasted in her room before venturing downstairs to meet the others in the library to plan for the day. In a few quiet moments she studied the ransom note again, with her analytical mind weighing possibilities against risks. She knew the action she planned to take could be dangerous, but she could see no other choice.

Isabella, Penelope, Henry, Everett, and Peter gathered around the polished oak table where diagrams and maps were spread out showing the ancient oak tree's location.

She traced the paths approaching the tree with her finger, determined to show a composed demeanor after fainting and showing what she saw as weakness the evening before. The feeling of serenity she'd felt on waking had disappeared, and she needed to mask the rising tension in her body.

Everett seemed to sense her anxiety and came to stand next to her, at her elbow, talking to her in a very matter of fact way. This did the trick and helped her to reduce the rising panic she felt about delivering the ransom money.

When Everett occasionally brushed against her as they leaned forward to study specific details in the terrain on the map, she pushed aside the spark which flamed through her body.

Clarissa, accompanied by Mrs. Finchley, entered with morning tea. "Clarissa," laughed Penelope. "You're becoming quite the expert on tea."

"You're quite right," giggled Clarissa, "but I'm happy to relinquish the role if you'd like to take over."

"It's time to talk specifics," interjected Everett, bringing them back to why they were there. "We need to work out who will hide where, and the route which Isabella will take through the woods."

"I think it best if we take the shortest most direct path," suggested Isabella. "That means you have less area to protect as I walk to the oak tree."

"That makes sense," agreed Peter.

Isabella felt Clarissa standing beside her, as the young woman put her arm reassuringly on Isabella's in silent support. "You're so brave," she whispered.

"I'm not really," she whispered back. "I'd rather drink tea here than walk through a woodland on the way to deliver ransom money. But I'd never forgive myself if I refused and something happened to Lawrence, so it's something I must do, I have no choice."

"What time should we take the ransom money?" asked Uncle Henry.

"I think early evening," replied Everett. "The note stipulated before midnight, but nowhere does it say the drop off has to happen at midnight. I suggest we leave around three o'clock and get this out of the way."

"Have you got the ransom money?" asked Peter.

"I've drawn it out of the safe," Uncle Henry replied before lowering his voice. "As she isn't present, I think it's sensible for me to remind you that Lady Moreton has disclosed to me that she does not have sufficient funds for this ransom. It seems her financial affairs are in a dire state."

It occurred to Isabella that this was most likely the reason that Lawrence had been so very keen to marry sooner rather than later, even though he knew there was no true love between them. Isabella had suspected something, but it was now very clear to her that this was a marriage of convenience to access her fortune. She didn't mind, she just wished Lawrence had been more honest with her about his reasons for marriage.

Uncle Henry returned with the money and reluctantly began to count it into a leather pouch, each movement reflecting his internal conflict between Isabella's safety and Lawrence's potential peril.

"There that's all ready, and I've counted it twice, and they are not to get a penny more than they've asked for."

"Let's discuss the surveillance next," suggested Everett. "The main thing is that we need to allow clear observation of Isabella without detection by these rogues should they appear. I've marked on the map here the positions where we should conceal ourselves.

"I'm keeping this within our circle today, I've decided against involving the constables in this delivery of the ransom."

"Quite right, my boy", agreed Uncle Henry.

Isabella nodded with approval, her analytical mind appreciating the thoroughness of the planning.

As the others dispersed to prepare for the action, Isabella found herself momentarily alone in the drawing room, gazing out of the windows down towards the woods where the handover would take place.

She heard the door open and turned to see Lady Moreton standing in the doorway, her face showing the ravages of recent tears, despite her perfectly maintained appearance.

She always appeared so rich and sophisticated, one of the elite in the ton, thought Isabella. She knew the family was not as wealthy as it had been some years ago, but it now sounded as though they may be close to destitution if they couldn't afford the money for the ransom. The kidnappers were obviously unaware of this and must think the family is still very rich.

"Isabella, I hoped I'd find you here. I'm glad of the opportunity to talk," said Lady Moreton.

How strange, she seems uncharacteristically hesitant this afternoon, thought Isabella. *The bravado and her usual theatrical manner seem replaced with this quiet intensity. Lawrence's Mama seems genuinely vulnerable for the first time since he disappeared. I can't imagine the level of anxiety that she's experiencing.*

"It's difficult to say this," began Lady Moreton in hesitant, hushed tones. "I may seem possessive at times my dear, but Lawrence is all I have in this world."

Her trembling hand reached out to clutch Isabella's arm as she paused. Isabella placed a reassuring hand over Lady Moreton's.

"After I lost my husband James, so many years ago, Lawrence was my only family and my only purpose in life. I cannot bear the thought of losing him."

"It seems to me," Isabella tried to reassure her, "that all these criminals are interested in is money. If they harm him, they risk hanging, that's the reality of this. They are most likely cowards and will avoid risking that at any cost."

"Even in the last few hours I've felt lonely without Lawrence's company," confided Lady Moreton. "I hope you don't mind me staying at Moreton Hall when you're married. I know I should move to the Dower house, but I've got so used to seeing Lawrence every day."

Isabella didn't feel this was the right time or place for this conversation, so she murmured something reassuring, without actually agreeing that it would be an excellent idea for Lawrence's mother to stay holding the keys of Moreton.

"I need to thank you for your courage in offering to deliver the ransom yourself," Lady Moreton continued.

Isabella felt a little closer, more compassionate, towards Lady Moreton. She was glad she had come to talk to her. Lady Moreton was always so difficult to read with that careful social mask which she maintained most of the time. Isabella found her one of the most terrifying women of the ton. Yet today her gratitude seemed sincere, and she had given Isabella a glimpse of a frightened mother behind the elegant calculating woman that she had always seen Lady Moreton to be.

***

Isabella made her way up to her chamber to change for the challenge ahead. She stood before her mirror adjusting a simple work dress that she'd selected for delivering the ransom money. She reflected on how much she had changed from that young girl who rejected Everett's proposal. As she gazed upon her reflection, it appeared to her that her countenance was notably gaunt, yet resolute in expression.

I need to hide my fear, that determination to help Lawrence and Lady Moreton will carry me through what I need to do. I'll have Maisie close by, and the watchers strategically placed in the woods.

Next time I look in this mirror, it will all be over and hopefully Lawrence will be back where he belongs.

As sunset approached a small party departed from Drayton Park, with Uncle Henry carrying the leather pouch containing the five hundred pounds. She took strength from Everett's presence as he walked beside her to the garden gate, feeling that now familiar warmth boosting her resilience when his hand touched hers briefly as they separated out to take their designated positions.

Uncle Henry handed over the pouch and hugged her as he left. "Be careful, my Dear. Don't do anything foolish. I will never forgive myself if anything happens to you."

The ancient oak was about a half mile into the woodland, and as she approached, she looked up to see it rising high against the deepening twilight. She clutched the leather pouch in her hand, walking silently with Maisie a short distance behind her.

I shouldn't be afraid, she thought. *That oak tree is an old friend, and I've known it since I was a child when I attempted to climb up its branches. I know this forest, it's where I work and I've spent some of my happiest hours. I won't let these rogues spoil my enjoyment of this ancient woodland.*

Within a few minutes, she stood beneath the winter canopy of the oak tree towering high above. Her gloved hand held the leather pouch looking for the place where she had been instructed to leave the money. She was determined not to look around as she could easily give away the location of her friends who were hiding in the woods. She didn't want to look around for any sign of the kidnappers either, and forced herself to focus on putting the leather pouch in the tree.

The decision to follow these instructions still felt somehow wrong, despite the necessity to save Lawrence. Isabella didn't like it one bit, but couldn't see what other option there was. She placed the money inside a hollow log at the base of the tree and then turned to look at Maisie and smiled reassuringly.

The shadows of dusk began to fall in the forest around them. "We can leave now," she told Maisie.

"I'll be glad of that, Miss Isabella. It feels as if there is something evil in the woods this evening, and I'll be happier when we're home again."

Isabella shivered and wrapped her cloak around her, as they turned to return to the house. "I've seen no sign of Baron Moreton. Perhaps they didn't mean to release him here. Let's hope he's there waiting when we arrive back home."

Chapter 11

Everett felt a sense of heightened alert, similar to that he had felt when infiltrating enemy territory in his covert work for the army. He kept his eyes on the small, elegant figure walking towards the ancient oak tree, followed by Maisie a few paces behind. Their steadiness in this crisis only increased his admiration for both of them.

Isabella had a way of standing back from a situation, analyzing it carefully, and trying out solutions to find which was most practical and realistic. She had done that here today. Others would have been prostrated with anxiety at the disappearance of their betrothed but she showed true bravery in volunteering to put herself in danger and deliver the ransom money.

Kneeling behind nearby rocks, Everett stayed still knowing any movement could give away their presence and endanger Isabella. His gaze alternated between Isabella and the surrounding forest, looking out for signs of the kidnappers.

His hand rested on the small pistol concealed in his long leather coat, the weight unfamiliar, yet essential given the danger to Isabella. Peter, a short distance away, within hailing distance, was similarly armed. Mr. Fletcher, Simmons and trusted footmen and grooms were in position closer to the entrance to the forest with Lord Drayton.

Penelope and Clarissa waited back on the pathway outside the forest.

The strategic placement followed hours of careful planning to ensure that Isabella appeared alone, while remaining fully protected.

Ah, now he could see Isabella place the money in the hollow log, keeping exactly to the instructions directed in the note. She appeared to show no sign of fear, yet he knew her hands would be trembling as she deposited the money.

Such courage, he thought as she straightened up and moved to be with Maisie.

Good, they've turned back towards the house. I'd like her and Maisie to be out of this area of danger as soon as possible.

He almost missed the cloaked figure emerging from the dense undergrowth, looking carefully around before advancing towards the hollow log.

There you are. We've got you, he thought.

He stood ready to move, to intercept the figure, which snatched the pouch and instantly retreated back into the shadowy undergrowth.

Oh, curse it, he's getting away. "Peter," he shouted. "he's taken the money and turned back in the other direction."

They raced towards the oak tree, crashing into the undergrowth looking for signs of the vanished kidnapper. Isabella gasped in surprise as they almost knocked her over as they raced past.

Too late, he thought. *We've lost him.*

Within seconds, the party from Drayton Park Manor had gathered around the ancient oak tree with groomsmen and footmen fanning out to search the whole of the woodland area. Everett knew it was futile, but they had to be thorough. The man might have dropped something and left a clue as he raced away.

"There's no evidence we can find," said Peter, only flattened vegetation showing where he's forced his way through to the other side of the forest. We think he had a horse waiting there, as there are recent tracks and it would explain how he's disappeared so quickly without a trace.

"No sign of the Baron either," Everett added in frustration.

"I don't believe they ever planned to hand him over," replied Uncle Henry as he joined them. "We'd better return to Drayton Park and give Lady Moreton the difficult news."

As they walked back to the house, Everett found himself walking next to Isabella with Maisie close by. As they talked about the futility of the last hour Everett's hand closed over Isabella's briefly, assuring her that he would do all he could in his power to bring Lawrence home. He drew strength and comfort from the fleeting contact and hoped she felt the same. She smiled at him reassuringly. "Don't worry I knew there was only a faint chance that we would recover him this evening. I'm sure we'll hear from the kidnappers again soon. They're going to want more money, aren't they?"

"I suspect so. They have the Baron, and they know we need him to return safe and well."

Everett couldn't believe the irony of working so hard to return Lawrence to Isabella. He might never admit it to Isabella, but Baron Moreton was now his rival in love. He wanted this whole business to be over, so he might have the chance to tell her how he felt. Yesterday he was content to wish her well in her plan to marry the Baron. Today all he wanted to do was to convince Isabella to end her betrothal.

As they walked along the path, he looked forward to those moments where it narrowed, forcing them to walk closer together. Each time he experienced a moment of closeness, his feelings grew stronger with a certainty that Lawrence was the wrong man for Isabella.

I need to position constables around the perimeter of Drayton Park as a ring of protection. Isabella is right in that it is likely there is going to be another demand for money and perhaps that will give us an opportunity to catch them in the act of leaving another ransom demand.

He could see Peter walking ahead, and Penelope running towards him seeking information. *There's something close developing between those two, and I suspect there will be wedding bells ringing before harvest time. If only...*

His thoughts drifted to that brave small figure walking beside him along the woodland path.

***

Peter caught sight of the figure racing towards him and his heart leapt with joy as it did each time his eyes saw Miss Penelope Drayton.

He didn't know how he had fallen for her so deeply. He was in a rapidly evolving relationship before he even realized what was happening.

It was that moment when he had taken her in his arms to dance at the ball that he knew he was lost. He planned to make her an offer of marriage within days, but the Baron's disappearance meant he needed to put those plans on hold.

He knew she felt the same, but he would wait to talk about their future together until after this current crisis had been solved. He wanted to tell Penelope how he would open up Darton Manor. He looked forward to their shared life together on his country estate. He didn't know if Penelope possessed an inheritance or not, and it didn't matter as he was perfectly able to provide a comfortable life.

And there she was standing immediately in front of him.

"What happened?" she cried. "Is there any news? Did you find anything?"

"Slow down," he replied, smiling at her to reassure her. "I can't answer all those questions at once, and I won't have any answers that you want to hear. We saw the kidnapper when he emerged from the undergrowth, but he faded back into it so quickly that pursuit was futile."

"Oh no."

"I still have no idea how he managed to escape. It's as if he disappeared from the face of the Earth. We had men in position on both sides of the forest and nobody saw him leave, and yet there is no sign of him."

"How infuriating. I can't imagine how Isabella must feel." She looked up at him curiously." And there was no sign of the Baron?"

"No, I don't believe they ever planned to hand him over today. We think it's going to be another demand and probably for a lot more money."

"And it seems Lady Moreton has no money."

"She doesn't need to worry, your Uncle Henry, Everett and I will make sure that their financial demands are met. We hope to catch the blighter next time. We're just going to have to wait to see if there is another ransom demand."

"And are the constables to be informed?" she asked.

"Everett is going to station them around the perimeter of Drayton Park. This can't stay within the family any longer."

"That seems sensible to me. Poor Isabella. The stress of comforting Lady Moreton, along with concern about Lawrence's welfare is immense."

"Penelope," he began.

She looked up at him and he knew from the look in her eyes that she felt the same as him. "Yes," she asked, her voice almost a whisper.

"When this business is over we must talk about our future."

"Our future?"

"Indeed. Despite all the trauma of the last twenty-four hours, I have to tell you that you've captured my heart. I cannot imagine a life without you."

"Oh Peter, I shall wait for that moment with pleasure. It's what I've hoped and dreamed about."

She put her hand on his, and he felt the thrill of her touch coursing through his body.

Despite the seriousness of the evening, he took a quick look around and could see no one close to them. He took her hand and guided her a few steps off the path under the shade of an elm tree. There he took her into his arms and lost himself in those mesmerizing eyes.

He gasped as she reached up to his neck and guided his lips down towards hers and they sealed their love with a gentle kiss, committing to a shared future together.

"We should return to the house, as I know they will be wondering where we are," she murmured.

"We shall have lots more kisses, and much more time together in the future, my love," he promised. "We just need to catch this kidnapper and retrieve the missing Lord Moreton."

Chapter 12

As soon as they reached the house, Isabella raced up to her bed chamber, closely followed by Maisie. *She needed some time and space away from everyone, her head ached, and the feeling of exhaustion had returned.*

She needed to gather strength before she could speak with Lady Moreton and Uncle Henry. Everett told her he would explain what happened at the meeting point, and how they had failed to bring Lawrence home.

She went up to the window, looking out towards the woods and the lake shimmering like silver in the distance. She was thankful that Everett had taken control of the situation in his capacity as local magistrate. *His nearness gave me comfort, despite our failure to capture the kidnappers today. When I feel nervous, or apprehensive, it evaporates when he is close to me. It's an overwhelming sensation of warm contentment and a strong desire to stay close to him.*

Where are you, Lawrence? I hope they're treating you decently. If I knew there was something I could do to change this situation then I wouldn't hesitate, I would do it in an instant.

***

Later that evening, after a late supper, they gathered together in the drawing room. Isabella kept looking at Penelope, knowing that there was something different, something that she couldn't quite understand about Penelope this evening. It was as though she glowed with a luminosity.

She must be in love, thought Isabella. *I'm delighted for her.*

The fire light flickered across the concerned faces gathered around the hearth but Penelope moved to the pianoforte and began to play gently.

She's chosen just the right music to match this melancholy mood.

Lady Moreton settled on the settee near the fire, handkerchief appearing frequently whenever Lawrence's name was mentioned.

As Penelope completed playing a Mozart sonata, Peter left the room and returned with several old newspaper clippings about similar kidnapping schemes in recent years. "It looks as though this isn't the first of these abductions," he told them.

Clarissa assisted arranging the information chronologically, determined to add key points in the leather-bound book where she recorded all the information about their investigation.

Uncle Henry cleared his throat and addressed Lady Moreton in a gentle tone. "Lillian," he began. "we've known each other for many years. This might be difficult, but I need you to tell me as much as you can about Lawrence's recent business activities, and any events which are significant in his personal life. Did he have any strong commitments to anyone who might be distressed to hear news of his betrothal to my niece?"

"You mean did he forsake a young lady, or..." Lady Moreton looked around in embarrassment, "have a liaison with someone?" She shook her head. "I can assure you there's nothing I know about."

Uncle Henry continued to gently prod Lady Moreton for information. "This is a touch delicate, but I have to ask the question. How desperate is Lawrence for money?"

Tears began to stream down Lady Moreton's face. "He spent it all," she moaned quietly. "He follows that set in town who play cards at his club every evening. He has no talent for cards, and they know it and they've milked him dry over the last few years. Whatever I say he doesn't listen. I believe I'm on the verge of losing my house and becoming destitute." As she spoke Isabella could see the pain on Lady Moreton's face.

"Is that why marriage to my niece was so important to him?" continued Uncle Henry.

"Yes, we love Isabella. My dear, you're the best thing that's happened to Lawrence, but I will be honest and say that your fortune did make a difference in his decision making."

"Don't worry, Lady Moreton. I knew our betrothal was mutually beneficial for both of us, and we hold each other in high regard. We both wanted the type of marriage we planned, and Lawrence suits me perfectly."

Out of the corner of her eye, she saw Everett tense as he listened to her words. *I know I'm causing him misery, but he should know the truth.*

"He didn't tell me about his dire financial circumstances though. I'm glad you felt able to be honest with us about those difficulties. It may help in locating him."

"Could Lawrence be in trouble with money lenders? Or be blackmailed?" asked Uncle Henry, his tone still very gentle.

"I think it possible; he's been rather quiet and withdrawn in recent days. He barely spoke to me yesterday. It's most unlike him. I believe something has been worrying him."

Something made Isabella look towards Penelope who was still sitting at the pianoforte and was not party to the discussion. Penelope caught Isabella's eye with a subtle gesture, indicating that they should speak privately.

She moved across to the window looking out at the moonlight and shadows and Penelope got up and joined her.

"Bella is something wrong? Well, more wrong than Lawrence disappearing?"

"I just listened to his mother telling about his financial difficulties, and Uncle Henry asked about any relationships where he may have been subject to blackmail."

"I'm so sorry," gasped Penelope "that sounds dreadful."

"I want to look through his room. I want to search through his personal belongings," Isabella said with conviction.

"But you can't..."

"I see no reason why not," countered Isabella. "I just have this strong suspicion that somewhere in Lawrence's room there's information relevant to his disappearance."

"I suppose that might be the case," agreed Penelope. "Can't Peter or Everett or even Uncle Henry have a look through his belongings."

"They won't look in the way that we will Penelope. I need this to be a thorough search. There are things being said about Lawrence that I don't understand, and it doesn't feel like the Lawrence I know."

"Very well, I shall accompany you and we'll search his bedchamber thoroughly. If you get caught it will be easier if there are two of us undertaking the search."

"I thought that, thank you my friend"

"We need to make sure that his mother doesn't go to his room while we're searching it"

"I'll ask Clarissa to keep her entertained," Isabella, had already given this matter considerable thought.

Once Lady Moreton was involved in a game of whist with Clarissa and Miss Dymchurch, Isabella announced how fatigued she felt and that Penelope would accompany her up to her bedchamber.

They took their leave, moved quietly out of the room and made their way to Lawrence's bedchamber.

"This feels wrong," said Isabella, "but I'm not sure what else we can do. I'm convinced there's an answer somewhere in this chamber."

"Well then, we're doing what needs to be done? I don't think we have any other option," Penelope assured her.

"I'm determined to find out as much as we can about Lawrence's life and what led to his disappearance. There's something in this room, I'm sure of it." Isabella took a deep breath before opening the door and stepping into Lawrence's bedchamber.

This is more important than any concerns about propriety, she thought to herself.

"Let's look in the writing desk first," Isabella suggested. "I know that walnut desk has a hidden drawer. Let's see what we can find."

Between them they turned the room upside down searching in wardrobe, adjoining dressing room and oak chest. Nothing.

Isabella was getting frustrated, disappointed that they hadn't been able to find anything. "There has to be something, somewhere!" She looked around the room taking in every aspect, closing her eyes and imagining where she might have hidden something. Of course, she said as she knelt down to search for a loose floorboard. She found one within seconds.

"What is it? What have you found?" asked Penelope.

"I'm not sure," replied Isabella. "It seems to be a package wrapped in oil cloth. I'm going to reach down and pull it out."

"Be careful there might be mice or spiders down there," cautioned Penelope.

"There isn't going to be anything as scary as walking in the woods to put ransom money in a hollow log under an oak tree. Believe me I hope I never have to do that again."

She pulled and retrieved the package which she placed on the writing desk and stared at it before opening. This was one of Laurence's most private possessions, and he had hidden it away, never expecting her or anyone else to see what he'd been hiding. Yet in order to save him she had to know as much about him and his life and private affairs as it was possible to know.

"So that's it," Isabella said quietly after unwrapping the package.

"Gambling debts?"

"Significant and crippling gambling debts," added Isabella.

It was as if a hole had opened up in the ground in front of her and everything, she'd known about Lawrence seemed to have been a lie. He had courted her for her money and nothing more.

"This letter is from a solicitor," Penelope had picked up some of the correspondence contained in the package. "It looks like he'd lost his house, wagered it away, and it was only a matter of weeks before the property was repossessed by a creditor."

"It's so hard to believe. I don't think Lady Moreton could know anything about this. That poor woman, she is about to lose her home, and we know that failure to pay gambling debts is a matter of honour, and surely that will mean being ostracized from *the ton*. Her whole life is about to come crashing down."

Lawrence never mentioned financial difficulties, yet this would explain his increased attention to me and my inheritance. He's a fortune hunter. He said everything he thought I wanted to hear, including my desire to keep working on my botanical projects after marriage.

The saddest thing of all is that I'm not surprised at any of this. Her expression remained composed despite these revelations, though her fingers tightened noticeably around the package of papers.

"I believe we have to return to the drawing room, Penelope, and I really don't feel like it."

"When shall we tell Uncle Henry?"

"I think this will wait till the morning. I believe the gentlemen had already started to wonder if Lawrence might have debts, or be entangled in a liaison with a woman, which could have made his engagement to me difficult."

"I never thought of a liaison." Penelope looked shocked.

"Well, it looks like that plain old, boring, financial ruin was what drove him to marry me."

"Oh Bella, I'm so sorry."

They returned to the drawing room, Isabella exclaiming that she felt much better after a breath of fresh air. Lady Moreton approached her and Isabella took a deep breath, reluctant to engage in conversation with Lawrence's mother this evening.

She breathed a sigh of relief when Peter created a conversational diversion, intercepting Lady Moreton as she moved towards Isabella. She heard him asking about the latest opera season in town, clearly captivating her ladyship with his gallant manner.

As the evening drew to a close, Everett and Uncle Henry conversed in muted tones with heads close together near the drawing room door.

Isabella watched Everett from across the room, awareness growing of his steadfast character and ability to put others first throughout this crisis. This contrasted sharply with Lawrence's increasingly questionable behavior towards her.

This uncomfortable comparison was making her question her chosen path. Yet even if she wanted to walk away from her betrothal, she would have to maintain appearances, and duty and propriety prevented her from acknowledging such thoughts even to herself.

***

The next morning Isabella rose early and joined with Penelope, seeking out her uncle in his study, to share their discovery of the hidden documents.

They entered the room to find Everett already present, discussing potential next steps and search strategies with her Uncle Henry.

"I need to share something with you, Uncle Henry." Isabella hesitated, still feeling guilty about how they'd found the papers hidden under the floorboards.

"Come over here and sit beside me and tell me about it, my dear," suggested her uncle.

She showed him the pile of letters. "Penelope and I found this correspondence in Lawrence's bed chamber. I'm fully aware that propriety should have prevented me from searching his room, but I had a strong conviction that there would be something there which might help us to find him."

She placed the pile of papers carefully on Uncle Henry's desk, and Everett moved across to look over Uncle Henry's shoulder.

Isabella was ready to wait for them to trawl through the information before she offered an opinion.

Uncle Henry's expression darkened as he noted the amounts involved. "I can't believe this. These amounts are astronomical. Lawrence faces losing everything."

"Several hundred pounds owed to multiple creditors and even Moreton may be lost," commented Everett. "There are several from Mr. Elliott, a solicitor in central London."

"And the tone is increasingly threatening," added Penelope.

"This has to be connected with his disappearance," concluded Uncle Henry banging his hand on the table in frustration. "What was the man thinking of? He's run up debts which are off the scale." He looked towards Isabella with concern. "My dear, I'm so sorry it has turned out this way."

"The content of these documents tells us that Lawrence may well have fallen victim to unscrupulous creditors," suggested Everett. "We know there's been an increase in violence and the use of extreme measures to secure payment. The man must have been desperate trying to keep up appearances in society, and fearful of retribution at any point."

Isabella looked at him. "I see what you're saying Everett, and as time passes, I'm increasingly concerned about Lawrence's character. These debts are crippling and he's continued gambling, placing ridiculous wagers until just a few weeks ago when his source of credit appears to have dried up."

"Only because he had no more assets on which to secure the loans," added Penelope.

Uncle Henry turned to Isabella with a mixture of sadness and anger in his eyes. "I can say this because Lillian, Lady Moreton isn't in the room, but I now have severe misgivings about your marrying Lawrence. We all hope for his return unscathed, but we're discovering things about the man which greatly concern me."

Isabella could only nod in answer. There was nothing else to say. She caught sight of Everett looking towards her with a concerned expression, and she felt grateful for this strong but silent support, which went far beyond a mere investigative partnership.

Perhaps we will regain a level of true friendship after this dreadful time. I'd like to think we could be close again. She smiled gently to show she appreciated his care for her.

Peter had entered the room and had caught the last part of the conversation. He handed Uncle Henry the leather-bound book where Clarissa kept those careful notes. "I have some information from the village which links to this. It seems Lawrence has been a frequent visitor to the Talbot Tavern. The landlord, Tom Bassett, is one of our tenants and he was away yesterday visiting his mother. When he heard we were asking about Lawrence he sent a message to me. It seems Lawrence met an unknown gentleman at the inn a few hours before he disappeared."

Peter looked around the group and paused, and Everett urged him to continue his story.

"Tom Bassett noticed this intense conversation in the far corner of the room. It seems Lawrence stood suddenly, knocking over his mug of ale, before storming out of the Tavern."

"At last, we have some useful information," cried Uncle Henry.

"And it supports what we know of his financial situation. Could this have been one of his creditors?" asked Isabella

"That seems likely," agreed Everett.

"Isabella are you alright?" asked Penelope looking at her cousin with concern.

"This just gets more complicated every day. All I can think about is poor Lady Moreton, who has no idea about the depth of their financial difficulty, and loves her son. Not only is he missing, but now his character is under scrutiny, and I admit that I don't like what I'm learning about Lawrence."

Chapter 13

While the others kept talking, Everett took the ransom note and studied the handwriting on the letter with an artist's eye.

Something about this isn't right, he thought. When he sketched, he knew the importance of precision about fine details. He tried to convince himself he was wrong, but there were subtle similarities between the notes they had found under the floorboards and the ransom demand.

The way certain letters were formed with a specific curl and flick of the pen, and the way the text stood bolt upright, rather than leaning a little to the side. Only an artist's eye would notice a possible resemblance in the style of handwriting. Surely not? It must be a coincidence.

I learned to write in copper plate, as did Peter, and it can be difficult to tell our letters apart.

He decided not to mention these observations to the others, as his impressions were intuitive and vague. There was no need to add to complications until Lawrence returned.

The door leading from the study to the terrace was open, and he saw Isabella leave the room. He followed her outside, glad of the reviving cool morning air on his face. Isabella stood close to the terrace wall looking out across the parkland towards the woods and lake.

"I wanted to check you were all right," he said. "You were so exhausted last night."

"I'm a little better today." She smiled at Everett. "And I must thank you for your gallant actions yesterday when I fainted."

"Please there's no need, I'm glad I was there and able to catch you as you lost consciousness. You should thank your uncle, he suggested I escort you and I think he realised just how close to collapse you were."

"Then I am very grateful to you both."

Everett looked out across the park. "It's a beautiful morning. I love seeing the autumn mist clearing across the valley."

"It looks magical on days like today, as if we've stepped into another world."

"Is that the major oak I can see standing tall in the distance?" he asked.

"Yes, it rises above the other trees. How spectacular it looks in this morning light."

She turned to face him, her eyes shining brightly in the morning sunshine. He returned her gaze and smiled. This felt right, this connection between them. He had avoided her for so many years and was glad they were friends again.

A voice deep inside him whispered that surely, they were more than friends, but he pushed it further down as now was not the time to think about such things.

"You remember?" he asked.

80

"Of course," she replied smiling at a shared memory.

"We spent almost an entire afternoon beneath that tree sheltering during the summer storm. We were children. How old was I? It must be about eleven years ago." He paused reflectively. "Sometimes, Isabella, I feel very old."

"No, not you, never," she declared.

"Can you remember how we ended up in the wood in a rainstorm?"

She looked a little sheepish at those words, as memories flooded back in. "I believe I'd just developed my interest in botany but at rather a young age and that summer I was determined to find as many varieties of daisy as I could."

"Bellis perennis! What better flower to inspire Bella than Bellis," he laughed.

"You remembered the Latin name!"

"And that project still continues," he laughed. "Though you moved from daisies to orchids."

"I still have an interest in all British wildflowers. My encyclopedia will not be about those hot house flowers, but the flowers that grow in the hedgerows, meadow and woodland."

"I shall be on the front row when you lecture to the Royal Society."

"Oh, that will never happen," Isabella replied laughing.

"I wouldn't be too sure," he challenged. "You need to have more confidence in your own skills, Isabella. You're a remarkable scientist."

"Perhaps we could collaborate, and you could do some sketching, even better some watercolors as illustrations for my encyclopedia."

"That sounds an excellent idea. I'd be delighted. I don't get my palette of paints out often enough these days."

Isabella looked surprised. "I don't believe I was serious with my suggestion, but if it encourages you to get your paints out again then I'd be delighted. You are a very talented artist, Everett."

Everett's heart jumped at the enthusiasm in her response. Perhaps that's how they could take this relationship forward, at a professional level, with him contributing artwork for her scientific encyclopedia.

"I probably should be more cautious. You may have to sign something swearing that I won't get wet through, sheltering from a summer storm under an ancient oak tree for a whole afternoon," Everett told her with mock seriousness.

"Oh, I know more now than I did then. It was quite dangerous for us to shelter under that tree in an electrical storm. As I recall the thunder crashed around us and the forked lightning flashed high in the sky. The tree could have been struck by lightning."

Everett laughed at the memory. "We were living dangerously."

"Yes, and a cow from Home Farm was struck by lightning during that storm."

"The perils of botanical research." Everett looked thoughtful for a moment. "I believe we compiled a small encyclopedia that summer. I wonder what happened to it?"

Isabella knew exactly where to find that precious encyclopedia. They had given it to her mother as a gift, and, when her mother had died, she'd put it safely in a box of treasures where she kept objects which linked to special memories.

"I have it still," she admitted.

"I'm glad. It's important to compile keepsakes of special times in life."

"We were such good friends then," she said thoughtfully.

"I believe we're good friends now," he replied. "I'm sorry it didn't stay that way and we've had this gap of several years."

He put his hand up as she started to speak. "Hush, there's no need to talk about it. I was wrong to ask what I did. You were barely out of the schoolroom. I think life was changing around me, a new world, I craved stability, and I couldn't imagine a life without you. It's long gone, past history now, and I believe we can be very good friends in the future."

He saw a strange expression in her eyes and had an inkling that there were things that she wanted to say but couldn't find the words.

"I felt comfortable with you then Everett, and I do now. I've always known that you value me and encourage my studies and research."

"You would have received a first-class honours degree at Cambridge. I've no doubt about it. I see no reason why women cannot study at the university. I'm convinced that one day that will change. You have a scientific, analytical brain which is second to none, and I'm proud to know you Miss. Drayton."

"Why thank you," she said quietly. "That means a lot. I believe we should put our brains into action analyzing the evidence, searching for patterns connecting Lawrence's financial difficulties to this current situation. I'm bemused by events. It does seem likely that he was unable to pay a creditor, and they've kidnapped him to recover their money." She shuddered. "It's a dreadful situation. He may have mismanaged his finances, but that's no reason to deprive him of his liberty."

"Let's go through Clarissa's notes again and see if we can gain any insight."

They went back into the study in time to see Lord Drayton stand up, clapping his hands decisively, clearly on the verge of making an announcement.

Had there been a development?

"I've just spoken to Mr. Fletcher and Cook," Lord Drayton began. "We're into our second day of anxiety about Lawrence and looking around this room earlier I could see the toll it was taking on all of you. The good thing is that we have contact with the men who have kidnapped him. We've responded to one ransom demand and I'm expecting another imminently."

"They're certainly going to want more money," agreed Peter. "You're quite right, another note could appear at any time."

"As head of this household it's my responsibility to look after the welfare of everyone living or staying at this Manor. So, instead of staying in my study pouring over more maps and documents, which you've all looked at several times already, I propose a walk in the morning sunshine."

"What a lovely idea," said Clarissa. Everett wondered when she had joined the group but was pleased to see her there.

"I'll understand if anyone chooses not to join us, and you all know that I don't underestimate the seriousness of this situation. However, I remain convinced that fresh air and exercise will help our thinking and planning when the second ransom demand does arrive."

Isabella looked delighted. "I think that's an excellent idea, Uncle Henry."

"And I haven't quite finished yet. Cook is preparing a light luncheon, and as the weather seems unusually clement for this time of year, I've asked Mr. Fletcher to set up picnic tables next to the lake. We shall dine alfresco."

Everett looked at Lord Drayton in admiration. What a splendid idea.

"Now if you will excuse me, I need to go and speak with Lady Moreton. I doubt very much she'll join us on this expedition, but I'd like her to know my reasons for proposing it."

"Althea, Miss Dymchurch, enjoys walking," added Penelope. "I believe she would join us if her ladyship allowed it."

"I shall be back in ten minutes. So, you all have a quarter hour to gather cloaks, bonnets and sturdy shoes and meet me at the anteroom door."

Chapter 14

Isabella saw her uncle approaching and was glad to see he had persuaded Althea to join them.

Uncle's right she thought, it's a beautiful crisp autumn morning there are still some leaves on the trees, and the forest path will be alive with sunshine. It will do us all good to go out for a walk on an autumn day."

They set off towards the path leading down through the forest to the lake. They passed Ned, one of the grooms, driving a cart laden with tables, heading for the longer route which led round to the other side of the lake where they were to take luncheon.

Isabella smiled as she noticed Penelope and Peter walking a long way ahead in the distance.

That romance has blossomed surprisingly quickly, she thought to herself. *And I'm happy for Penelope, who had almost given up on finding love. When Thomas died two years ago, of the morbid sore throat, she'd withdrawn from society.*

Thomas, the local rector, had seemed so healthy and vibrant, but lost his fight for life with an illness caught visiting sick parishioners. It had been hard for Penelope to lose him just weeks before their wedding. Since then Penelope had focused on her music and become quite serious minded. To see her lightness of spirit gradually return as her love for Peter deepened was wonderful to watch.

I wonder if he's made her an offer yet. That might explain the glow of happiness around her.

Uncle Henry walked with Althea, solicitous for her welfare. Isabella found herself thinking that they made rather a lovely couple. Uncle Henry had brought along Hermes, his spaniel, and she heard Althea throwing sticks and calling to the dog.

Clarissa had started off walking alongside Everett and her, but soon abandoned them, squealing in delight at the antics of the tiny young spaniel chasing sticks.

"He's a lovely dog," commented Everett. "I miss having a dog around, and with being away so much I haven't been able to take on a new gun dog yet."

"Hermes is special, and Uncle Henry has an interest in breeding those middle-sized spaniels. He's kept most of the litter from the summer, so I'm sure he'd let you take a dog if you wanted. His only stipulation is that they go to a good home."

"I may well speak to him about that," replied Everett, wistfulness in his voice. "Maybe I should commit more to life here on the estate. I hope to return to the vineyard in Portugal one day, but that's not going to be for a couple of years and dogs can travel. I miss having the company and always enjoyed training dogs."

Isabella pointed ahead. "We're walking past some of the sites where I have my experiments. You may have to stop me from dropping out of the walk and checking how each specimen is doing," she added lightly.

"I do remember this being one of your favourite walks."

"Indeed, it is. I love the sound of the stream rushing by next to the path, and as we near the lake, seeing glimpses of the water through the trees. In summer the lake has a beautiful green blue color, and at this time of year it changes to shades of pearly gray. It's my favourite place in all the world."

"I've travelled a fair bit as you know, but I agree this place is very special. I like this hilly, woodland part of Hertfordshire. We are lucky to have estates here."

"I agree. I find it hard to leave."

"But you will be leaving in a few weeks' time when you are married?"

Isabella wasn't sure what to say but until Lawrence had been found and confronted over his secret life, she decided it was best to believe that nothing had changed. "It's only a short journey away and I can drive a gig along the cart track. I'll be married so chaperonage won't be such an issue. Lawrence is keen for me to continue compiling my encyclopedia and research studies of plant habitats."

"That's very generous of him. I'm not sure his mother will agree with that plan, but that's a bridge for you to cross in the future, Isabella."

"She is rather formidable, which makes it all the sadder that she looks so diminished this week."

"We have to remain confident that it's only a matter of time before Lawrence returns. Once they have enough money, they'll let him go, I'm sure."

Isabella shivered visibly, caused by anxiety and not the cold. Everett had obviously noticed and he put out his hand and touched her arm wanting to give her that quiet confidence which came from the connection between them.

She drew in a sudden, sharp breath at his touch and she asked herself if he felt the same sensation that she did, whenever they had contact.

"This is all so strange. I couldn't have imagined anything like this happening last week. Lawrence kidnapped? It seems like a plot from a gothic novel, and yet here we are, he's held prisoner somewhere and they're demanding money for his release."

"We will catch them; the local Constabulary are out making enquiries on my behalf as we speak. No stone will be left unturned."

Isabella looked at him. "I have to believe that. I already have full confidence in our local magistrate too."

"Who will do his best to serve you at all times," he told her with a smile. She knew now that he meant every word of it.

Chapter 15

Everett watched Isabella veer off to scrutinize a plant she'd noticed, and he felt glad she'd distracted herself from those melancholy musings.

"Look," she cried, "it's jasmine. We'll have to wait till springtime to see if it's white or lilac coloured."

"I think I know the plant you mean. Tiny flowers against dark green leaves."

"That's the one. You know more than you think." Isabella looked around and up towards the canopy of the trees, glorious in their Autumn colors. "I've missed being here. In the last month I've been busy with preparations for the ball, fittings for the dress I'll be married in, consulting with cook about the celebratory supper. I've hardly had time to just walk in the woods."

"Your Uncle Henry was right; we'll think better after clearing our heads with a walk."

"And there's the lake," she said leaving his side to move quickly forward to look at the lake through a gap in the trees. "Even though it's gray, it's sparkling in the weak sunshine."

"Everett where are you?" he heard Clarissa's voice.

"Over here Clara, watching the lake," he called back.

"Lord Drayton says they have a rowing boat which they use on the lake in the winter. Should we have a boat on our lake at Kennington Manor?"

"You mean can I buy a boat?" Everett laughed," I see no reason why not, unless you expect me to row you around the lake every day."

"I shall row myself," Clarissa replied brightly.

"Then we shall get a rowing boat. We may even have one at the back of the old boat shed. I remember Papa used to fish in the lake".

"Hurry up Everett, the footman is unpacking the picnic lunch, and Miss Dymchurch is setting it out. We're nearly ready to eat." Lord Drayton greeted them as they entered the clearing next to the lake. The water lapped gently against a small pebble beach and Hermes was splashing gently at the water's edge.

"He hasn't swum before, but it's fair to say he's taken to it like a duck to water," smiled Lord Drayton with pride in his voice.

"Everett might be interested in one of the spaniels from the summer's litter," he heard Isabella telling her uncle.

"I'd be delighted for you to have one of them, my boy. There are three left. One midnight black coloured, one black and white, and one roan like its mother. They make admirable gun dogs."

"When this business is over, I'll take a look," he told Lord Drayton.

Soon they settled into the business of taking luncheon in the unexpectedly warm sunshine next to the lake.

Cook had surpassed herself in providing slices of cold roast beef, two roast foul, several venison pot pies and baskets of late season salad from the hot house. After the savory courses there were dishes of stewed fruit and plain biscuits, plus several of Cook's famous jam puffs.

As he put the cold beef on a plate, he reached for the bottle of mint sauce, sharp with the taste of vinegar and mustard. Breaking with tradition Lord Drayton provided quart bottles of ale and ginger beer all brewed on the estate from Drayton Park's own hop yard.

Such a delightful day, he thought to himself as he looked around the group. *It's doing Clarissa the world of good to get out of that house, filled with all that sadness and anxiety.*

His eyes rested on Isabella, delighted to see her smile at the antics of Hermes chasing sticks into the lake for the first time, proving to be a natural swimmer.

His thoughts drifted to the need to have more picnics at Kennington Manor. They could even swim in the lake. The trouble was that Isabella featured in every picture in his mind when he thought about future picnics, and in those daydreams, he didn't see her as a friend, but something more.

His thoughts drifted to that summer when he'd turned nineteen and words of love had escaped his lips during that walk in the woods at Drayton Park. He'd been wealthy, so why shouldn't he become betrothed when he chose, instead of waiting to be introduced to a fine young lady of the *ton*. He'd known then that Isabella was the one he loved.

What had she said? Thinking back on it she hadn't rejected him outright; she'd expressed surprise and the desire to keep their friendship always. She seemed confused, not yet out in society and he reflected it had been very early in life to commit to a lifetime marriage.

I can see her now telling me we should always be friends wherever life might lead us.

After that conversation he'd pulled away, and eventually moved on, sealing away his feelings and locking his heart behind friendship's safer boundaries. Within months he'd escaped abroad to the continent and taken an intelligence role in the army in the fight against Napoleon. The reality was he couldn't face being close to her and only a friend back then, and he doubted that had changed.

The idea of seeing her married to Lawrence, a marriage which, from what she said, was based upon convenience, chilled his heart.

Something must have made her aware of Everett's gaze as she glanced up suddenly catching him watching her. She didn't look away; her eyes met his as they connected briefly across the table.

My heart aches when our eyes meet like this. I will conquer this. I will remain her friend. I won't desert her again if she marries.

And she hasn't married Lawrence yet. We've only just met again, and maybe there's the possibility of a future between us. I shall hide my feelings, but I shouldn't give up hope yet.

Chapter 16

Dusk and dark shadows were gathering when they arrived back at the house. Isabella felt even more confused about her feelings for Everett. At this time when all her thoughts should be focused on Lawrence, she again found them drifting to her childhood friend.

She felt so uncertain about the future. She truly couldn't see herself marrying Lawrence. Yet what other choice was there but to remain loyal until he returned safely, whatever he had kept secret from her and his mother. Isabella prayed he wasn't hurt and locked in some dismal cellar. She felt the anxiety returning and wondered how Lady Moreton fared awaiting her son's return.

That great lady joined them for afternoon tea in the drawing room. The lively lighter atmosphere of the picnic was now replaced by silence. Lady Moreton was clearly, unsurprisingly, in a state of severe nervous anxiety.

"Would you like me to call Mr. Noakes again," asked Althea.

"He left me several sleeping drafts, and I may take one later, thank you," replied Lady Moreton curtly.

Everyone was silent, the only sound the quiet clink of silverware against the fine porcelain. Everett was seated across from Isabella and she could see his attention drawn repeatedly towards her.

Uncle Henry broke the strange silence by attempting conversation about the weather, but his forced cheerfulness fell flat in the tense atmosphere. Everyone knew a second ransom note was overdue. None of them had considered until that point what might happen if there was no further communication from the kidnappers. Lady Moreton clearly felt the strain, and Isabella thought it valiant of her to join them to take tea.

Penelope was doing her best to respond to her uncle's attempts at conversation, backed up by Peter who added observations about how the pleasant weather would help the constabulary in their search for Lawrence. And there they were, back again at the subject which preoccupied all their minds.

There's no escaping it, if only we had news, she thought. *This waiting is putting such a strain on us all.*

Isabella looked up and caught Everett's gaze. Every time he looked at her, she felt the butterflies fluttering deep inside.

She didn't understand why his mere glance affected her so much. It had been so long since they had grown up together, but something had shifted inside her after his reappearance at the ball and Lawrence's disappearance.

She quickly turned her attention to her barely touched plate of caraway seed cake. How long could they go on like this?

A knock sounded on the drawing room door and Mr. Fletcher entered bearing the silver salver and a single letter. Now that it had arrived Isabella very much wished it hadn't. What demands would the letter hold this time?

Mr. Fletcher's normally impassive professional expression revealed concern as he presented it to Uncle Henry. The butler turned to leave the room, but Uncle Henry stopped him telling him to wait and listen to what was in the letter, as there would no doubt be immediate action to take.

The heavy seal broke with an audible crack beneath her uncle's fingers. Isabella watched him closely, never taking her eyes off his face. Color drained from it as he read, and she saw his hand tremble as he passed the note to her.

She took the paper, her composure showing only the smallest flicker of distress as she read this second ransom demand. One thousand pounds, double the previous amount. The money was to be taken by Isabella that evening to an abandoned water mill east of Drayton Park. She gasped at the sight of a lock of hair matching Lawrence's distinctive shade attached to the letter.

She read the contents out loud to the others. "There's a warning this time against any attempt to follow the man who collects the ransom as happened during the previous exchange."

"And they promise Lawrence's return within the hour if all instructions are followed precisely," added Uncle Henry.

Everett moved immediately to Isabella's side, their shoulders nearly touching as they both examined the note.

The sound of hysterical sobbing from Lady Moreton took all their attention. "I don't have a thousand pounds," she sobbed. "What am I to do?"

Isabella wished she could help Lawrance's mother's distress. Lady Moreton raked her hands through her hair, tears streaming down her ashen face.

She had changed from the composed matron of high society to this disheveled shadow.

Lady Moreton clutched the arms of her chair for support and Isabella could see how her knuckles whitened at the force of her grip.

"You must not worry, Lillian," said Uncle Henry. "We will make sure that the ransom is paid."

"But how can I ever repay you?" she cried.

"My niece is marrying into your family, there is no need for concern about money," he told her firmly.

"I don't think Isabella should be put in the position of taking this ransom money again. It's too dangerous," Penelope declared forcefully.

"I don't think I have any choice."

"We absolutely must follow the kidnappers' instructions exactly," shrieked Lady Moreton.

"Well, if Isabella has to do this then I'm going to disguise myself as Maisie and join her," Penelope insisted. "I'm not staying behind again."

Isabella reached out and took Penelope's hand in hers. "Thank you," she whispered

"We're not going to let you go alone," Everett was equally insistent. "The fact that it's a water mill in the valley this time makes it easier to keep surveillance".

"We need to look at the plan of the area as soon as possible," Clarissa added.

As the planning continued, Lady Moreton suddenly pressed her fingertips to her temples, her expression transforming to pained distress as she announced the onset of a severe megrim. Miss Dymchurch immediately moved forwards with her smelling salts in hand, helping Lady Moreton to her feet.

Peter stepped forward when Lady Moreton almost fell heavily against the door frame. She turned to face them. "I'm sorry, I must leave you and go and rest."

"Should we call Mr. Noakes?" asked Clarissa, already standing, ready to go to the door and arrange for a message to be sent to the physician.

"There's no need for that," replied Lady Moreton with surprising firmness. "I don't wish to bother the physician unduly, and I already have a sleeping draft. I often suffer with these megrims."

I'm rather relieved she's gone, thought Isabella. *I'd like to ease her pain, but when she's with us the level of anxiety heightens to an unbearable level.*

They moved as a group together to the library, where Clarissa and Peter spread out maps showing the water mill and the surrounding countryside.

Uncle Henry explained the situation. "The estate manager has maps of every area on the estate. Everley mill has only been deserted for two or three years, and there are plans to redevelop it with a new water wheel. Here is the route in," said Henry pointing with his finger tracing the path from Drayton Park to Everley Mill. "It will be easier to place men observing the drop off this time."

Penelope stood close beside Peter, suggesting observation points. "I know the inside of the mill and the attached cottage. I used to visit the family who lived there," she told them. "I know that cottage well."

"With any luck we'll catch him, and this nightmare will be over." Isabella could see that Everett was trying hard to reassure them but he was not as confident as he sounded.

Uncle Henry continued his description of the site. "The Mill is centrally positioned in the middle of that valley. You can access it from above and make your way down the sides of the valley to the mill, but not many people know that route. The beauty is that it's under the cover of trees all the way. My great grandfather believed in trees and wanted an income from timber for his family in the future, and that may help us now in this crisis."

"You mean along here?" Everett asked.

"Exactly. The downside is that the mill's position offers multiple escape routes for the kidnapper."

"You may remember, Everett that we used to play in that valley as children. The forest which is close is quite thick there and we used to call it the enchanted forest in our games," added Isabella.

"I do remember it," he said thoughtfully.

"There are numerous streams in the winter trickling down to the river at the foot of the valley. It's a beautiful place". Memories momentarily distracted Isabella from the gravity of their current situation. Even now, she found comfort in shared recollections of simpler times with Everett, when their greatest concern was returning home before sunset with a bag filled with interesting specimens.

Uncle Henry looked worried. "I don't like this at all. I didn't say anything in front of Lillian, but this increased ransom amount suggests that they might not stop anytime soon. Why wait an hour to release Lawrence after we've handed over the ransom? I've never heard anything like that, not that I'm an expert on kidnapping people. However, my impression is that the victim is usually handed over when the money is given."

"That's quite right," agreed Everett.

"It's not looking good for Lawrence. I can't imagine what the poor man is suffering." Uncle Henry looked towards Isabella. "The longer this is prolonged the more likely it is that news of this situation will begin to spread among *the ton*. I agree to you going with this ransom my dear, but after this rendezvous the priority becomes preserving your reputation. It sounds harsh, but women have a difficult time in society, and I don't want your reputation ruined because Lawrence has built up such huge gambling debts."

"That's of no consequence Uncle Henry," she assured him. "Lawrence's life has to be our top priority, my reputation is insignificant in comparison with that".

"And can the constables be used again?" Uncle Henry asked Everett.

"Of course, the sergeant and constables are absolutely at our disposal. They're conducting searches as we speak."

"I'd like a whole dragoon of constables patrolling my estate," said Uncle Henry, but I know that isn't realistic."

"It's best if we keep it as quiet as possible," agreed Peter.

"I know, I know, but it all seems so futile," said Uncle Henry. "I still believe they'll release Lawrence soon. If I'd captured him, I'd release him within hours. The man is so damned argumentative."

"Uncle!" cried Isabella shocked at his words.

"I'm sorry Isabella, but what I say is quite true. You can't disagree with me."

She nodded her head slowly. "You're right, it will be excellent if Lawrence's argumentative character means he gets released from captivity soon."

Chapter 17

Everett looked towards Isabella.

She still seems so composed, her betrothed has disappeared, he has huge gambling debts, and society gossip may mean she is ostracized from the ton. I'm in awe of how well she's coping.

Even though she appeared so capable, Everett had a strong desire to take her away to a place of safety and protect her from any danger. He realized he needed to focus on the rendezvous at the mill as that was the best way to protect her right now.

"Let's look again at the map and fine tune our positions," suggested Everett.

This time he stood close to Isabella, no longer caring what anyone thought while they examined the map. His arm brushed against hers as he pointed to the landmarks on the eastern side of the valley. Even a brief contact sent warmth spreading through his arm into his body, and the strength of the sensation distracted him momentarily from the tactical discussion.

"Penelope, are you sure about going in disguise as a maid?" he asked.

"Absolutely, nothing will stop me," confirmed Penelope.

"I'll be glad to feel your company," Isabella was quietly grateful.

"Maisie accompanied Isabella last time when we just assumed the kidnappers would think nothing of it, so I don't believe there will be any difficulties," continued Penelope.

"I'm not confident about this," said Lord Drayton. "There are too many escape routes surrounding the mill. But it's what we have to work with, and we shall do our best to bring Lawrence home."

***

Dusk settled over the abandoned mill; its weathered timbers silhouetted against the deepening purple sky. The path through the meadow and down towards the mill through the woodland seemed surprisingly quiet.

Everett watched their arrival from his position in the branches of an oak tree close to Everley Mill. Peter and a footman also watched from their positions near the deserted mill. Estate staff from Drayton Park were scattered throughout the forest trails. The constables kept surveillance at every entrance to the valley.

And still I'm not confident that we'll catch the kidnapper, he thought to himself.

He'd attached a rope to the branch so he could swing out of the tree at speed if that became necessary. Everett looked towards the shadowed ruins of the old mill house twenty yards distant, determined to keep an unwavering watch. He trusted his eye for detail and past experience in the army to look for details that others might miss, the shifting shadows, a patch of disturbed vegetation and the subtle movement of branches against the evening breeze. His fingers brushed against the small pistol concealed inside his long leather coat.

He could not allow harm to come to Isabella, knowing that his protective instinct grew stronger with each passing moment spent in her company.

I should have persisted five years ago when I told her about my feelings, Everett acknowledged to himself, his gaze never leaving Isabella's figure. She looked so fragile, and yet within her was a central core of valor which meant that she would put her life in danger in order to return Lawrence to those he loved.

He reminded himself again that Isabella was betrothed to another, and in a matter of weeks she would be married and belong to another.

She isn't married yet though, and I haven't told her how I feel. I don't believe she loves Lawrence; she's acting out of a sense of duty.

The plan was for Isabella to again follow the ransom notes' instructions precisely, and he watched as Isabella and Penelope neared the deserted mill. Isabella stood near the crumbling entrance, the leather pouch containing one thousand pounds held tightly in her gloved hands.

He saw Isabella look around before she placed the purse of money in a hollow log close to the entrance of the mill.

This location wasn't chosen randomly, he realized with sudden clarity. *Someone knows local landmarks with historical significance beyond common knowledge - the mill hasn't operated for over eight years, although it was occupied more recently, and yet they selected the hollow log where children play games and leave messages.* He remembered that Mr. Thompson, the miller had never minded them doing that.

He noticed a sudden movement behind Isabella, as the cloaked figure approached from the west, not the expected eastern path. He prepared to swing down to intercept the rogue once he'd taken the leather purse.

The figure moved swiftly as if he'd rehearsed this, snatching the pouch in a single efficient motion, before swiftly retreating into the dense forest.

He isn't taking the path, realized Everett. *None of us expected he would return to the depths of the forest where there are no trails.*

Descending from the tree, he drew near enough to the gentleman as he sped toward them. A sudden pang struck his left arm when the man seized him with the blade of a knife, yet he pressed on in his hurried retreat toward the thicket.

Damn it, he thought as he felt the soft sticky blood running down his arm. "We've lost him again," he shouted to Peter.

"He knows what he's doing," cried Peter. "We didn't have a hope of catching him."

Everett made his way to Isabella, who stood waiting with Penelope close to the mill wheel.

She raced towards him. "You're hurt," she cried.

"It's only a scratch, a mere surface wound," he re-assured her.

"But there's such a lot of blood. It needs bandaging quickly before you lose any more," she insisted as she reached down to take her petticoat firmly in her hand and tear a strip to make a basic bandage.

She held his arm as she wound the bandage and tied it securely. "There, that should do temporarily until we reach the house."

"Thank you. I can't believe I let him wound me."

"He's deft, and he knew exactly the route he planned to take for his escape. It's never the one we expect. It's infuriating," Isabella's frustration was plain to see.

He noticed Peter standing close to Penelope, and saw his friend take the young lady in his arms, and hold her close.

He's going to have to offer for her now, he thought to himself, but he knew Peter was very happy to spend time with Miss Penelope Drayton.

They returned to Drayton Park Manor along the narrow woodland path leading out of the valley to meet with Lord Drayton and give him the news that they'd failed again.

Isabella found herself once again walking besides Everett along the narrow path and they began a discussion of the evening's events, and what they could do to improve next time. She kept looking towards him with concern in her eyes.

"I'm fine, please don't worry, Isabella."

"You shall be well, and I'll be glad, when we're back at the house and your man can wash and treat the wound."

"He's somewhere in the forest with the estate workers. He's used to military action, so I couldn't leave him back at the house."

When their hands accidentally touched as he lifted a briar to clear the way for her, he noticed that she didn't immediately withdraw from the touch. She seemed to welcome it.

As they left the forest he heard an exasperated shout, and one of the constables pointed to a figure on the horizon, riding at high speed. "That's him. He must have had a horse tethered close to where he entered the valley. He's prepared for this."

They arrived at Drayton Park's entrance where Lord Drayton awaited them with an anxious expression. Penelope waved in greeting, as he came running towards them, concern etched on his face at the sight of the bloody bandage.

"It's nothing, just a flesh wound, and it looks far worse than it is," he assured Lord Drayton. "Is there any sign that Lawrence has been released?"

"I'm afraid not, Everett."

"Then it appears that it hasn't ended. We were right, Lawrence should be handed over in exchange for the money. Have you told Lady Moreton we failed again," he asked Lord Drayton.

"I've tried, but she's nowhere to be seen. I've sent Mrs. Finchley up to her room with a message. I have to be honest I expected her to be waiting here for your return."

"It does seem a little strange," agreed Isabella, "but we all know she hasn't been herself ever since Lawrence disappeared."

"I haven't seen her since she retired to bed with that megrim. I keep meaning to take her some tea," said Miss Dymchurch, who had been waiting for their return at the garden gate.

"Ah, here's Annette now," Miss Dymchurch turned to speak to Lady Moreton's French lady's maid, who Lady Moreton had brought along to help her."

"How is Lady Moreton," asked Isabella. "Does she need anything, a cold collation perhaps?"

"Non," said Annette, "my mistress has retired for the evening and does not wish to be disturbed about anything."

"Even if we'd found Lawrence?" exclaimed Lord Drayton in surprise. "How very odd."

"I confess I'm a little relieved she won't be joining us for supper," Isabella said quietly. "I find she rather drains my energy."

"You're going to have to find ways of dealing with her when you live at Moreton house," commented Lord Drayton, obvious concern in his voice. "We need a conversation about this marriage as soon as the Baron returns."

Everett looked closely at Lord Drayton and Isabella. *It seems Lord Drayton may be changing his mind about the suitability of this match. I believe I'd feel the same in the circumstances.* He pushed aside a feeling of hope that perhaps Isabella might not marry Lawrence after all.

"Come Miss Dymchurch, you must join us for family supper. Your mistress has taken to her bed, and I won't hear of you eating alone in your chamber," Uncle Henry invited her but in a tone which accepted no disagreement.

Miss Dymchurch smiled. "Thank you. I'd be glad to eat with you," she agreed. "Her ladyship won't need me till tomorrow."

Chapter 18

After supper Isabella asked Maisie to build up the fire in her room, chose a book by Mrs. Radcliffe, her favorite author, and curled up in a chair needing to feel the warmth of the flames. She'd felt chilled to the bone since standing outside the ancient, abandoned mill.

Thoughts of Lawrence, thoughts of Lady Moreton and thoughts of a certain rather handsome Viscount Kennington whirled around in her head.

She closed her eyes, knowing she needed this time alone to clear her head.

However much I try to look confident, it's all an act, and underneath I'm desperately afraid. I hated taking that ransom money. I don't think I could have made it today without Penelope beside me.

She'd managed to fool Everett and her uncle, but Penelope had seen her fear.

As she'd walked towards the mill the load, she carried weighed heavily both physically and mentally. She feared the kidnappers were growing bolder.

She had never imagined her betrothal would lead to clandestine meetings with criminals, remembering how she willed her body not to shake with fear as she surveyed the shadowed landscape.

I stood there, risking my personal safety and reputation for a man whose character grows increasingly questionable. I would have felt better if they'd been honest about these gambling debts.

She had pleaded a headache and left the others in the drawing room to play cards and drink fine wine. At supper she'd sat next to Everett, and she was now acutely aware that every contact sent warmth spreading through her fingers and it had nothing to do with the mild temperature, as the warmth felt comforting and exciting at the same time.

What shall I do when this investigation reaches its conclusion and Lawrence returns? She no longer trusted Lawrence, but she still intended to fulfill her promise to marry him...

Yet when she finally fell asleep in the chair by the fire it was Everett she met in her dreams, walking along a path beside a glistening silvery lake, arm in arm.

***

Isabella rose early after a fitful sleep, and made her way downstairs to the library, determined to start working on arranging the evidence they had collected. She wanted to see if she could determine any connections or find any information they might have missed.

Clarissa had put the documents in a wooden box on the long table in the library. The notebook, where she kept meticulous notes, was also there. She took out the ransom notes and laid them side by side, avoiding opening the envelope which contained the lock of Lawrence's hair.

Isabella took a deep breath as she organized Lawrence's gambling correspondence into chronological order.

There must be a pattern I'm missing, she thought, stepping back to survey the documents. It was all here, Lawrence's debts, his disappearance, maps of the locations chosen for ransom delivery with everything pointing to complex, intricate, planning. This was far beyond a simple, opportunistic crime.

She startled when Everett entered without knocking. He apologized immediately saying he hadn't expected anybody to be in the room this early. He carried an armful of estate maps on which he'd drawn lines to every nearby building, putting a star next to those with stables.

Clarissa followed closely behind him with additional reference materials. Their three heads bent close over the maps spread across the large oak table, their shared concentration creating a bubble of connection which isolated them from surrounding concerns.

"I'm missing something." Isabella raked her hands through her hair. "The answer has to be here somewhere."

"Could there be another ransom note today?" asked Clarissa.

"I don't know whether to hope for that or not. I find this uncertainty, and the kidnapper always specifying it has to be me that delivers the money, very difficult."

"That's a good point," agreed Clarissa. "Why does it always specify that it has to be you delivering the ransom money? I can see no reason for that. As long as they get their money what do they care who makes the drop off?

Everett moved closer to Isabella. "You're fatigued. I can't believe you slept last night."

"You're right, I fell asleep in the chair and then tossed and turned for hours."

"You need to drink something and take breakfast. I'll ask Mrs. Finchley to bring something in here. I haven't forgotten how you fainted only two evenings ago."

And I'll never forget returning to consciousness cradled in your arms. She felt acutely aware of Everett's nearness; the sandalwood scent of his shaving soap, the warmth radiating from his tall muscular frame, the way his hair fell across his forehead when he leaned forward to concentrate on something, the sound of his voice so soothing in tone.

"Are you sure you're alright?" came that smooth baritone voice. "Clarissa has gone to ask for some tea and breakfast for you. I think even a little bread and butter would help. You barely ate anything at supper last night."

Isabella closed her eyes, breathing in the scent of sandalwood and luxuriating in the warmth radiating from his body. She felt him move towards her and hold her in his arms. "I'm worried you're about to faint again," he told her, his voice hoarse with an emotion she didn't recognize. "I wish I could take this load from your shoulders," he whispered, so faintly she had to struggle to hear his words. "Dearest Isabella."

She began to open her eyes as she felt the faint touch of his lips grazing her forehead. She gasped, feeling the closeness and never wanting this moment to end.

He heard the footsteps in the hallway at the same moment she did. He stood back, his eyes meeting hers with an expression of loving concern. He guided her to a chair near the hearth. "Sit here and forget about this business for a little while. Clarissa and I will keep searching for answers in the information we've collected. You need to keep your strength up."

Had she imagined it? That light touch of his lips on her forehead. She knew she hadn't, and that she would treasure that moment for the rest of her life.

Chapter 19

Everett knew he needed to be strong in overcoming his feelings for Isabella. He felt the connection between them growing stronger each time they met, but he could not believe there was a future for them.

How could he ask her to forsake Lawrence after the Baron had endured such a traumatic time and commit to Everett instead?

I can take action. I need to stop myself noticing details which I should ignore. The way a lock of hair falls across her cheek as she leans forward, that rather wonderful, determined set of her jaw when she is concentrating and determined to put forward her own point of view.

Everett glanced across at her sitting near the fire, holding a porcelain cup of tea, and remembered the graceful movement of her hands as she arranged papers on the table.

Her mind matches her beauty in a rare combination, he thought, appreciating her strengths of compassion and courage.

He was lost, not knowing how to pull away from her. He wasn't even sure if that was actually possible. All he wanted was to be close to her. At times it seemed the only thing important in his life.

And yet she was betrothed to Lawrence, a man Everett disliked intensely and had never trusted. That didn't matter though. It appeared Isabella and Lawrence were committed to each other.

He forced himself to focus on the documents in front of him on the table.

"Clarissa, come and look at this," he called quietly across to his sister. "What do you think?"

Everett placed a piece of folded paper on the polished oak table. A detailed sketch of the hooded figure's silhouette.

"It's very precise. You've used your artist's eye very well in compiling this sketch. It's as if you've brought the posture, the stance of the kidnapper to life."

"There's another one here." He placed a sketch of the man running away on the table. "He's in motion here."

"You've captured the subtle details of posture and movement, which if we ever catch this man should prove useful in identifying him."

"That's what I hoped. I need Penelope and Peter to look at it as well, as they were close to that hollow log, and may remember more than either of them realise."

Isabella rose from the chair and came across to look.

"I wanted you to stay resting by the hearth," Everett told her, gently.

"I heard what you said, and I would like to see the sketches."

Everett watched Isabella's reaction and saw her eyes widen at the quality of his artwork. "You've captured the essence of the man perfectly. I can see him moving when I look at that second sketch."

She paused for a second or two, deep in thought, and he noticed that quirky positioning of her jaw again. "You know, on reflection, I think he had a rather individual gait. There was something strange about the way he walked and then ran from the scene."

"That's an important piece of information," Everett told her. "I'll get that circulated to the constables immediately."

Isabella looked at Everett. "You have a very special talent, you really shouldn't keep your artistic abilities hidden away."

"That's what I'm always telling him," exclaimed Clarissa. "I think Everett should hold an exhibition of his work. His sketches and watercolor paintings are wonderful. You must come to Kennington Manor and visit the art room."

"Oh no, that really isn't necessary," Everett protested. "I'm very much an amateur."

"Nonsense," insisted Clarissa. "There are amazing landscapes, several of which remind me of the walk through the woods to the lake here at Drayton Park. He's got an eye for character and can catch the essence of a person in a portrait."

"I will look forward to visiting and seeing those paintings," Isabella assured Clarissa, ignoring Everett's objections.

Everett didn't know what to say. He kept his artwork to himself. His father had despised his sketching and painting. Gentlemen had to spend their time in pursuits such as shooting and fishing. He felt uncomfortable under Isabella's admiring gaze, yet he knew that he lived for his artwork and discomfort mingled with pleasure at her appreciation of something which he'd kept hidden away for so long.

"He was always sketching when we were children," Isabella told Clarissa. "He sketched my portrait every birthday until I was seventeen. I still have that collection of portraits."

Clarissa's eyes lit up. "Really! I must see those."

"I shall find them for you," promised Isabella.

Their conversation ended as Penelope entered the room with Peter, and Everett breathed a sigh of relief that attention had been drawn away from his artistic skills.

Mrs. Finchley knocked and entered the room. "I'm sorry to disturb you, but his Lordship has requested that you join him in the drawing room. Apparently, Lady Moreton has risen early and wants to talk with everyone about what happens next."

Penelope answered for them. "Very well Mrs. Finchley. Please tell Uncle Henry we shall be there in a few minutes."

Why on earth does everything have to revolve around that unpleasant woman, Everett thought to himself. *She always seems to make herself the center of attention.*

They all walked together to the drawing room, joining Lord Drayton with the visibly pale Lady Moreton reclining on a chaise longue, sipping what was from the aroma, a brew of hot chocolate.

Once they were all seated, Lady Moreton began to lament the loss of Lawrence, clutching an embroidered handkerchief in her hands, trembling as she expressed the hope that her son would be released soon.

Everett began to tell the story of events at the rendezvous the previous day. Lady Moreton didn't listen for long and pressed her fingertips to her temples. "I'm afraid I must retire to my room. The megrim has returned, and the pain is quite severe. Miss Dymchurch, can you send for Annette to help me prepare to retire to bed?"

"Of course, Lady Moreton. I shall do that straight away."

After Lady Moreton had retreated to her bed chamber, Clarissa stood up and announced that she would very much like to go out on the lake in the rowing boat.

"That sounds like an excellent idea," said Miss Dymchurch, who seemed to be growing in confidence as the matron of the party. "We need to keep doing things to take our minds off this dreadful situation."

"Uncle Henry, could we ride over to the lake today? I could do with some fresh air to blow away the cobwebs," asked Penelope.

"I absolutely applaud that suggestion," agreed Lord Drayton. "I called you here to allow Lady Moreton to express her opinion on what should be the next steps. As she is no longer with us, I believe a change of scenery would be beneficial in improving everyone's spirits. It's a little late to ask Cook to organize one of her picnics again, but we could eat in the conservatory when we return. We don't use that room enough and it has a lovely atmosphere."

"I like that idea very much," added Isabella.

"Can we take out the rowing boat?" asked Clarissa. "It's a perfect day for being out on the lake. There's barely a breeze in the air."

"Of course, if I can remember where I put the key to the boat house, laughed Lord Drayton.

"I wonder if that raft is still there. We had such fun sailing that on the lake," recalled Isabella, her thoughts far away as she remembered what now seemed idyllic childhood adventures.

"I believe anyone who comes on this expedition should dress in old clothes," advised Lord Drayton. "It is entirely possible that everyone will get very wet."

The party set off at remarkable speed, with everyone desperate to leave the confines of the house.

"Althea, would you like to take the gig?" Isabella suggested. "Maisie can ride with you."

"You know I have a strong desire to ride on horseback to the lake. I did enjoy riding, and it has been a while as I haven't ridden since I joined Lady Moreton's household."

"Of course you can. I'm sure we will have some suitable clothing that will fit you." Isabella hurried off and, after a short time, returned with one of her mother's riding habits which fitted the lady's companion beautifully.

The cavalcade set off less than half an hour after Clarissa had suggested the idea. A coachman drove the gig, piled high with flasks packed in straw to keep the tea hot, and blankets for warmth if anyone fell into the lake. Everett smiled at the sight of Hermes, the spaniel, riding in the gig. *He's too young to run next to a horse yet, and he looks so important sitting there as if he's a prince.*

After Lady Moreton had retired in a state of extreme distress Lord Drayton had sent for the Reverend Barrington to come and sit with her. He'd arrived in haste to be told the good lady did not require support from the clergy. Lord Drayton had immediately insisted that the Reverend James Barrington join their expedition, and he'd accepted the invitation.

Everett rather liked the look of Reverend. Barrington. He appeared unassuming, yet thoughtful of the welfare of others. He could hardly be more than twenty-four years old, but he had that distinguished air that seemed to be essential for a country rector.

Everett managed to ensure that he rode next to Isabella, with Penelope and Peter taking the lead, followed by Clarissa riding with Reverend Barrington.

Miss Dymchurch and Lord Drayton brought up the rear of the party, and he could see that the conversation between them seemed to flow continually. Could there be a spark igniting between them? Everett wasn't sure, but they certainly found pleasure in each other's company and were forming a fast friendship.

He had waited for Isabella before riding out of the stable yard, remembering a time when Isabella had ridden every day, wearing breeches, just so she could ride faster and take jumps with confidence.

She had ridden up to him, smiling and greeting. "It's so wonderful to be riding again, and what a glorious day to be out in the sunshine."

"An excellent suggestion by Clarissa. I'm not so sure about the rowing boat side of it though. Your uncle seems unsure if the boat is still watertight."

"Well, I certainly don't remember us rowing on the lake since my father died," admitted Isabella. She smiled at him, her eyes bright in the sunshine. "But don't worry, I know you can swim," she added with laughter in her voice.

"I may decide to stay with my feet firmly rooted on the shore."

"Nonsense," she exclaimed. "You must row the boat."

"Well, my passengers will have a lovely time then going round in a circle," Everett said smiling.

Chapter 20

Isabella felt a sudden urge for speed. "Let's race to the lake," she cried. "I'm riding side saddle, so it's only fair that I should have a head start." And with that she clicked her heels, noticing how Melody her bay horse responded immediately. She knew the bridle paths and the route to the lake and took the decision to take a slightly different route.

She took the fork to the left and knew she would reach the lake before the others. "Come on girl, we can canter along here." Her feet gently gave the horse directions as they made progress along the track.

She wasn't alone. A rider had followed her and within seconds was riding alongside.

It was Everett, as she'd hoped it would be, and now they rode together. The path was narrow for two horses, so Isabella slowed her speed and he followed suit.

"Isabella, what on earth possessed you to go a different way? Your uncle might think you've been kidnapped as well! At least now they will know we are together."

"I didn't think," Isabella admitted. "I just wanted the speed of the ride, and I knew I'd reach the lake first. I know these woods better than anyone."

"You're reckless, and it's a good thing I followed you."

"I often ride alone," Isabella protested.

"But not in the middle of a kidnapping crisis, when everyone is on tender hooks and the anxiety levels are high."

"You're right. I wasn't thinking clearly. If we are missing together then they won't worry."

"They might make me marry you though," Everett said with mock seriousness on his face.

"We've been alone together too many times for that to happen," she replied lightly. "Uncle Henry regards us as brother and sister." She took a deep breath and looked up at him. "But we're not, are we?"

He looked back at her with equal intensity. "No, far from it."

"Would you protest if they made us marry?" she asked.

"No, not at all," he said, as he stopped and dismounted in a clearing in the woods where a stream raced down to the lake. A blackbird sang in a tree above and combined with the sound of water it felt calm and tranquil.

He held Melody's bridle and helped her dismount.

"Would you marry me if they insisted on it? Only to save your ruined reputation of course."

"I would," Isabella said simply, her heart singing at the closeness between them.

"Isabella ..." he began, his words faltering.

She took a step towards him, her eyes meeting his, and gently touched his arm.

He raised her hand to his mouth and gently kissed it. She felt as if the world began to spin around her with the intensity of the emotion that this had stirred inside her.

"I might have to marry you now," he murmured gently.

"If only you could," she replied, as tears began to stream down her cheeks.

He leaned forward to brush the tears away and drew her gently towards him into a gentle embrace. "I know. We can't commit to each other as you are bound to Lawrence."

"I'd end our betrothal in a moment. He's lied and been deceitful, and there never was any love between us. Yet I can't walk away while he is missing, perhaps lying injured in a cellar somewhere. I have to keep to my agreement with him."

"And I admire you for that," he told her, his hand gently caressing her cheek. "I'm allowed to dream of it being different, to hope that there might be a future for us."

"I dream of that too," she told him and raised her head to look at him, knowing that she would soon feel his lips on hers.

His kiss gently brushed her lips, yet set her pulse racing, a promise of tender love and commitment. She'd never experienced anything like this in her life before.

She let the sensations settle, sighed and stepped backwards, putting a little distance between them.

"We should go and join the others, my lord."

"Indeed, that is the only option open to us, Miss Drayton."

They returned to the horses, and he helped her mount the bay mare. The now familiar warmth glowed throughout her body as he lifted her and she settled in the saddle.

I need to lock that memory away somewhere special. I cannot know what the future holds for me. I'm expecting a life with Lawrence who does not love me. His mother will rule the household with an iron rod, and I will busy myself with my research. There are many who have far worse lives. I will find a level of contentment.

Yet if I could take a different fork in the road I would without a moment's hesitation. I'm in love with Everett, Viscount Kennington.

***

The sun sparkled across the lake surface as they unloaded the blankets from the cart. Miss Dymchurch and Uncle Henry settled to talk and watched the lake.

Uncle Henry gave Everett and Peter the key to the old boat house, saying that all should be well, as some of the estate workers had gone ahead to check and tidy out the boat house, and it seemed the rowing boat was still in good working order.

Clarissa ran eagerly towards the boathouse, followed by Isabella with Penelope. Memories of that unexpected interlude in the woodland glade were all that filled Isabella's thoughts.

Clarissa's enthusiasm proved infectious, and they all worked together to pull the rowing boat down to the lake. Everett lifted Clarissa into the boat and indicated that Peter and Penelope should join her.

With laughter, and some shrieking the boat set off towards the middle of the lake, Peter rowing and Clarissa and Penelope trailing their hands in the water.

"It's a welcome relief from the tension at the house," Isabella said to Everett as they stood watching the boat row away.

"I believe your uncle is relaxing a little too."

"Poor Uncle Henry. He's been trying so hard to stay calm and act as the head of the household, but I know he'd rather have a quiet life in his library."

"He seems to enjoy spending time with Miss Dymchurch," observed Everett.

"Oh, you mean …" she stopped, startled, as realization dawned. "You think perhaps …"

"I do," he nodded. "I hope I'm right. They both seem to have lived empty lives without romantic entanglement for several years. We all need companionship."

"But it's Uncle Henry," she said in confusion.

"Who is a man who is far from elderly. You might even describe him as being in the prime of life."

"I forget that," Isabella admitted. "But Miss Dymchurch?"

"A calm and sensible lady of quality, even if she is forced to work as a companion to Lady Moreton. She shares many of the same interests as your uncle, including training an unruly young spaniel."

"I hope they find happiness. I cannot imagine the challenge of being a companion to Lady Moreton."

"Do you remember that time when we attempted to build a raft from fallen branches."

"I do, we returned home soaked to the skin."

"I recall I was unsure about the raft, but you were determined to proceed."

"I prefer to remember that as being a joint decision," Isabella said laughing.

How naturally we fall back into our old patterns, Isabella thought, watching Everett skim a stone across the water's surface. *This ease between us feels more genuine than any conversation I've ever shared with Lawrence, despite our formal betrothal.*

Lawrence does have an unfortunate tendency to direct and instruct, whereas Everett listens and takes notice of my thoughts. I feel valued, it is that simple.

Where Lawrence focuses on my appearance and social standing, Everett values my character and spirit.

Life is so complicated and there is never any certainty. We choose a path and hope it's the right one for us.

Everett's voice interrupted her thoughts. "I think I shall take a walk along the lakeside."

"I'll stay here. I enjoy watching the rowing boat, and so far, it hasn't gone round in circles. I'm a little fatigued, I will value a few quiet moments. Enjoy your walk."

I'd usually offer to join you, but after that interlude in the woods I feel I need to regain my balance before we spend time together alone again. I think we'll both benefit from a little time apart.

Isabella noticed a leather-bound book on the blanket beside her. It was the notes related to their investigation into the kidnapping. Isabella decided that she would have another look to see if anything occurred to her. She was still convinced the answer was in there if only they could find it.

The sun shone in her eyes as she reached for the book. She opened the page but soon realised it wasn't the notes from the investigation. This must be Everett's sketchbook. She felt intrusive, but with an overwhelming curiosity to see more of this hidden artist's work.

These landscapes, they're so romantic and idyllic. I know that's the stream where we played as children, and that's the ancient elm tree marking Drayton Park's eastern boundary.

I can almost feel I am stepping into these places.

Curiosity drew her in, and she turned the next page.

It's me. it's my likeness. He so talented. I feel as if my eyes are looking back at me from the page as if I'm looking in a mirror. He's caught my character too, I'd like to think I have the strength and intelligence of the woman staring at me from the page, she thought half smiling to herself.

Everett sees me as I truly am, she realized with shock, her heart racing as she studied the portrait.

She couldn't take her eyes off the sketch, it felt mesmerizing.

She was drawn into a world of make believe, different interpretations of the landscapes which she knew so well. She became engrossed and stopped watching the boat, losing track of time. Isabella was startled to hear Clarissa's voice beside her.

She made a move to put the book down. "Don't," said Clarissa. "I can see you are as impressed with Everett's talent as an artist as I am."

"Indeed, I've been quite lost in the landscapes."

"And the sketches of people?"

"They are so realistic, and yet they hint at the inner person as well. He's truly talented."

"In his studio at Kennington Manor he's filled many books with sketches over the years. Sometimes he turns them into watercolors which are ethereal and yet capture the true essence of the place or person. I believe there's a portrait of you on the studio wall. I hadn't realised that until today."

"We were very close until the season when I came out, and he left to join the army. I mentioned that he gave me a sketch of myself every year on my birthday. His style has changed though; these have a remarkable quality, a contrast between the likeness and an impression of what's underneath."

"That's it exactly," agreed Clarissa. "I believe when he was in the war zone, often undercover in enemy territory that his art gave him an emotional release from the heavy weight of duty as a soldier. And now it's the same with the responsibilities of a viscount."

"That pull to duty can make people rather ... boring. He's a magistrate as well, so he's involved in difficult situations every week."

"Our father didn't approve of his art. As soon as he returned to Kennington Manor, he set up a studio in an old hunting lodge at the far side of the estate. I believe he can be himself there. "

"How could your father not see the talent?" asked Isabella. "I'm astounded."

"My father was an army man through and through. He believed in doing your duty. Everett never expected to be the viscount, he was the youngest son and he talked of going into the church and taking a living after leaving the army. I think he's doing an amazing job stepping into our brother's shoes, particularly in such sad circumstances. The land on the Kennington estate made a profit for the first time this year, and it is due to his innovations in farming."

"I can believe every word. I've never known anyone more thoughtful of others. Everyone on the estate will know that he cares about their welfare."

"I believe the death of our mother and my father's rejection caused him to hide his artistic nature. He is the most sensitive and compassionate of brothers, and yet so often he needs to hide that side of him in order to function in society."

"Society can be quite governed by strict regulations. I know I fully expect to be ostracized when news of Lawrence's disappearance becomes widespread."

"Surely not? You can't help the fact that he disappeared."

"It will make no difference. There will be something unusual, an intrigue surrounding me, and there are some women of the *ton* who will not like that."

"I've always known there's something sad in my brother's life, beyond my father's harshness. He courted Lady Viola Harrington, but never committed to marriage. We all expected an announcement of a betrothal and instead the relationship dwindled over time. I liked Viola very much, and she's happily married to the Duke of Barnstaple now. I always believed that something held Everett back from committing to her." Clarissa paused as if she was searching for her words. "I have to ask you this, Isabella. Are you the mystery lady in my brother's life? Is it you that he's been pining for all these years?"

Isabella took a deep breath, unsure how to reply. She looked down for a few seconds before raising her eyes to meet Clarissa's. "I didn't know till today, but yes, I think I am. It won't help for you to know this, but I think I've been carrying the same candle inside for your brother ever since I turned down a proposal he made when I was very young. I believe I've regretted that ever since."

"I'm glad you felt able to share that with me," replied Clarissa quietly. "I'd hope for a happy ending, but you're betrothed to the Baron, and now he's disappeared. It's a dreadful situation."

Isabella nodded sadly. "All we can do is hope he will return soon safe and well from this ordeal."

Penelope joined them, crouching down on the blanket laid on the grass, peering over Isabella's shoulder at the sketches. "Those are amazing," she exclaimed. "That portrait of you somehow captures your personality. It's quite remarkable."

"It's Everett's sketchbook, and I looked at it quite by accident. You mustn't tell him that we've looked through it."

"I won't," agreed Penelope. "He shouldn't keep a talent like this hidden away though."

"Here he comes," cautioned Clarissa, and the book was quickly returned to where Isabella had found it.

Everett walked towards them smiling at his sister. "Do I still need to purchase a boat for our lake?"

"I think you know the answer to that brother," Clarissa replied laughing.

"Very well, we shall buy a rowing boat?"

"It really was lovely out there in the middle of the lake, so quiet and peaceful," Clarissa told him.

Isabella could see the moment when his gaze latched on to the sketchbook. He frowned and reached down to retrieve it immediately.

Isabella determined she would be honest with him. "Indeed, I thought it was the book documenting our investigation, so I opened it. I'm entranced by your work. You're truly talented."

"I enjoy sketching, nothing more," he countered, and fell into silence.

The silence was broken by Uncle Henry as he approached with Miss Dymchurch and Hermes leading the way.

"We should return to Drayton Park Manor. I wish we could stay all afternoon, but circumstances are such that we'll have to plan to return to the lake another day. I for one feel better for a break from the house."

"Do you need help pulling the boat up to the boat house?" asked Penelope.

Uncle Henry shook his head. "No, all we need to do is pull it out of the water and leave it on the gravel beach. It won't come to any harm, and it will be there for us if we return later in the week."

"Well, there isn't much to pack up, so we'll be there and ready in a few minutes," Isabella told him...

***

Later, entering into the conservatory, Isabella gasped with surprise. The fire had been lit and this, combined with the heat of sun on glass, made the room feel pleasantly warm.

Mr. Fletcher had utilized a temporary table in the central area; it glistened with crystal glasses and decorative porcelain.

"It's a simple menu of salad, pot pie and lemon posset your lordship, but I thought that would work well in the conservatory."

"You have worked wonders Mr. Fletcher. It looks exactly what we need to distract us from this dreadful business." He smiled around the group. "Sit down everyone and enjoy a late light luncheon. There's no needful formality. The important thing is that we all enjoy a good lunch."

Isabella looked around the conservatory, deciding that she spent too little time here. There were few flowers at this time of year, but the green leaves of the evergreen plants provided a lush tranquil atmosphere.

No one mentioned it, but everyone's mind was on when the next ransom note would arrive.

As they finished their lemon posset Mrs. Finchley arrived in the room, looking breathless and worried. Miss Dymchurch stood up and went across to her immediately. "Please take a seat Mrs. Finchley, it's obvious to all of us that something's wrong. What do you need to tell us?"

"It's her ladyship, Lady Moreton. Annette just found her collapsed on her bed chamber floor. I've already sent a message to the stables to ask one of the stable lads to ride and fetch Mr. Noakes immediately. That poor lady, it's all been too much for her."

"Calm yourself, Mrs. Finchley," Miss Dymchurch said gently. "You've done the right thing in sending for the physician. I shall come upstairs and check she's comfortable."

The two ladies hurried off, leaving the group staring at each other in disbelief.

"I'll ask for tea to be served in the drawing room," said Isabella. "This waiting is quite tiresome. If anyone would like to take an afternoon siesta, then please do so."

Everett and Peter retired to the library to continue scrutinizing documents, searching for solutions about where the Baron might be held. It had to be somewhere close to Drayton Park. Uncle Henry had decided to walk down to the stables.

"Come along Clarissa," Penelope urged Everett's sister. "We can't do anything to help find Baron Moreton, so let's go and look at some fashion plates. We can still hope that there shall be a Midwinter ball, and we can meet to instruct the seamstress about our gowns."

"Oh Penelope, I'd like nothing better. It is also very dismal. I know it can't be otherwise, but I had been looking forward to experiencing local society."

"And you've just come out of mourning and attended your first ball," continued Penelope. "That hardly seems fair. I did think Reverend Barrington seemed rather attentive. I wonder if you might have made a conquest already?"

Clarissa blushed a rather fetching shade of coral pink, and Penelope smiled in delight. "I knew it! I am never wrong about these things."

"He seemed very nice. He has always seemed a little austere and dull when he gives a sermon, but he seemed very different when we talked."

"Of course he did," smiled Penelope. "Come along, after we've looked at the fashion plates, we can go upstairs where we have a room filled with vintage gowns, lace ribbons and hats. We could spend some time there if you like."

Isabella laughed listening to the conversation. "I think you two are going to have a wonderful afternoon!"

Penelope smiled at her. "Will you join us, Bella?"

"Not this afternoon, I have some household tasks to accomplish. Enjoy those fashion plates."

News came that after Mr. Noakes had examined his patient, he had given strict instructions that she should remain on bed rest, with a calming herbal tisane. Miss Dymchurch would sit with her until she fell asleep.

Isabella found herself drawn back to the conservatory, and the warmth and peace, seeking momentary solitude. *I love it here, the green is so restful to the eyes, and even in the last days of autumn we have a few scented flowers.*

It had been three days now, and they were still no closer to Lawrence returning, she reflected, as she ran her fingers along the wavy frond of a fern.

Surely, we must hear something soon.

Her thoughts though continued to drift to Everett rather than her absent betrothed. Those few moments in the woodland glade now felt like a dream.

I'm there in his sketchbook, I'm curious as Clarissa says there's a portrait of me on his studio wall. I'm sure he loves me. Yet we can't be together.

She found a willow woven seat in the corner of the conservatory and relaxed into it closing her eyes in an effort to regain more strength. *I'm tired of waiting for the next demand. I truly don't want to deliver another ransom to a hollow log.*

***

She must have fallen into a light sleep, as the sound of someone entering the conservatory made her sit up with a jolt.

"Who's there?" she cried.

"It's Everett."

"I'm over here in the far corner. Is there any news?"

"Not yet," he told her.

And so, it continues, she thought to herself.

Chapter 21

Everett opened the conservatory door quietly and entered thinking it likely that Isabella was still there.

He hesitated, not wanting to disturb her, knowing intuitively that she craved solitude.

She called out, and he reassured her that he was alone. She replied telling him that she was in the far corner close to the warmth of the fire.

As he turned the corner, he saw her sitting almost in a bower of plants, looking like some sort of Greek goddess. She gestured for him to join her, and he felt hesitant, a little nervous after that enchanting interlude in the forest.

"I wanted to explain about the sketchbook," he told her.

"There's nothing to explain. Such a lovely collection of very special artwork. I'm proud to be one of the sketches in that book." She smiled hesitantly. "I still have all those sketches you gave me every year on my birthday."

"I've improved a little since then," he told her. "I had no idea that you would keep them all."

"I do have one question. When you're so talented, why have you kept your art a secret, why did you hide it away, as if you're embarrassed about it?"

He looked at her with relief in his gaze. "You remember my father?"

Isabella nodded.

"He didn't approve of my art. I think he made me feel it was something to be embarrassed about, almost unpleasant."

"Well, thank goodness other well known artists' fathers didn't feel that way," replied Isabella, "or the world would be a darker place."

"I began to paint again when Charles, my brother, died. Sketching or painting gave me a feeling of calmness, I suppose you could call it solace. I had painted a lot after I was injured in Spain too, while recovering during those months on the family estate at Portugal. It helped me to heal."

"I can see how that would be the case," she whispered.

"And then there was Viola." This time he touched the leaf on a tree, his fingers tracing the edge of it, his mind preoccupied and a long way from the conservatory. She waited for him to feel ready to continue.

"One day I showed Viola my studio, and it filled her with horror. I can describe it no other way. She ridiculed my artistic nature, when I explained how it helped me to cope with life, she dismissed that as over sensitive and impractical, and added in warning that in her opinion dreamers made poor husbands."

Isabella gasped, surprised at this callous attitude to something as special as art.

"She told me that I'd make a poor provider, and she did not wish to marry me. I hadn't asked her at that point, but we had been close, I'd been courting her for several months and I was on the verge of making her an offer. I know now that I didn't really love Viola, but at the time it hit me hard."

"What did you do?" Isabella asked gently.

"I stopped painting for a couple of months, persuading myself that my love of art had ended my relationship with Lady Viola. I buried that part of me beneath practical estate management. Since then, I've only shared my artwork with Clara, and today you saw how you still feature in my sketches."

"It was an accidental discovery," Isabella assured him. "I truly thought that leather book was Clarissa's notebook, and I wanted to go through the evidence again."

"I should never have left it there. It was my error."

"Everett, listen to me. You have true talent. Each of those sketches gave an indication of a wider depth to the place or person. You brought each sketch alive. That's a rare talent."

"All I know, Isabella, is that painting does me good. When I sketch, I sit with my palette and watercolors and I feel at peace with the world. That's true even in a battle zone."

"Lady Viola cannot have been right for you. Anyone who can look through your sketchbook and be so derisory about the contents has a very shallow character."

"Thank you, those words mean a lot to me."

"Could I sketch you again?" he asked hesitantly.

"Of course. I was struck by how you represented me in the portrait. I felt as though you saw my character beneath the outward appearance of my face."

"I hope I conveyed the beauty of your features too?"

"You did," she assured him.

His gaze met hers as their eyes met, and he knew every word she spoke was the truth.

She does admire my artwork, he thought. *Isabella is the most beautiful woman I've ever met. Yet more important than that is this strength of character and strength in adversity. That's so much more important than the conventional beauty I was so attracted to in Viola.*

He smiled, losing himself in the reflective colors of her eyes.

"I believe you've done me good this evening, Everett. I confessed to feeling a little low in spirits. I know you spoke the truth; it wasn't just empty compliments. I've had enough of those to know the difference."

"Surely Lawrence tells you how he feels about you?"

There was a long silence, Isabella seemed to be deciding whether to speak or stay silent.

"Lawrence would never speak to me in this way. He considers me an appropriate match, and I now realise that my fortune was the big influence in his making me an offer of marriage."

Isabella paused, obviously choosing her words carefully before continuing. "But nothing is different to when we spoke this afternoon. I accepted his offer. We marry within the month. He's going to need me even more when he returns. I can't imagine the horror of being kidnapped. I have to be there for him, even if I sometimes wish I could wind back the clock and make different decisions."

"I understand," he said simply. "You are betrothed, and to you it's a binding contract."

She nodded.

How could Lawrence not value this wonderful woman. She knows he does not love her. He's clearly never spoken of love, and perhaps it has no value for him. Everett's heart bled for her as she was prepared to enter into an arid, emotionless desert of marriage for the sake of duty.

Isabella was so much more than many young women. An outstanding knowledge of botany with an ability to hold a scientific argument equal to any man he'd ever met. She will play her part in being a Baroness, but he should love her mind as well. Surely that's what's important in any marriage.

Everett felt a weight of sadness, convinced that Lawrence never even looked beneath the surface to discover the incredible depths of Isabella's personality and intelligent mind.

Everett would support her all he could, and make sure they had an enduring friendship. His gaze held hers for a moment longer than propriety allowed, strengthening that connection that transcended any formal *ton* relationship.

Now they had met again, he hoped he would always have Isabella in his life, to know that she was well, what she was doing in life, and be there to support her through difficulties in any way in his power. The idea of going back to the previous years where he might occasionally catch a glimpse of her in the distance at a large ball, but never speak with her, filled him with the chill of fear.

We used to be friends, her uncle regards us almost as brother and sister, or cousins. It's that level of relationship I need to work hard to develop in the weeks ahead.

Chapter 22

The words Isabella had just spoken to Everett were some of the most difficult she'd ever uttered in her life. She had to keep true to her commitment to Lawrence. Once he'd returned home, and they knew he was safe, then maybe she could make different decisions, but at this point in time she had to keep things steady.

I wish I didn't feel so confused. Everyday my feelings seem to become more complicated. It's hard to keep that steady even composure, especially when I'm close to Everett.

He was close now, and the awareness of his presence, the fragrance of sandalwood, and the intent expression in his eyes, was almost more than she could bear.

I must stop comparing Lawrence and Everett. The only way to cope is to see Everett as a friend, and he's proved himself to be a good friend to me. It doesn't help that Everett genuinely appreciates me for who I am, and treats me as an equal partner, whereas sometimes with Lawrence I feel he's directing me and wants to change how I think. Space and freedom to be yourself in a relationship has to be firmly set into the foundations.

And while I'll stay loyal to Lawrence, I can't ignore the growing evidence that my betrothed values my fortune more than my mind or spirit.

She stood and smiled at Everett, determined to put him at ease. He had nothing to apologize for, and she knew she could have put down the sketchbook as soon as she realized it wasn't linked to their investigation. Instead, she had been drawn in, fascinated by the sketches, and the talent of the man who had kept his artwork hidden from the world.

As they prepared to rejoin the others, she noticed that Everett seemed to be on the verge of saying something but struggling to find the words. She smiled encouragingly waiting for him to speak.

"I wonder, I'm hoping, that once Lawrence has returned you might visit my art studio. You could of course bring Penelope, and Clarissa would be there, I couldn't keep her away if I wanted to. I converted a hunting lodge in the far reaches of my estate into a studio. I think you will like it, it's in the forest and it's a very tranquil place to spend a few hours."

"I'd be delighted." *And I won't need Lawrence's permission to visit an old friend.*

As they walked together towards the door Clarissa appeared at the conservatory entrance.

"Clarissa what's wrong?" asked Everett who read from her face that something had happened.

"Nothing unexpected, Everett. You're both needed in the drawing room, another ransom note has arrived."

Isabella saw Clarissa look at them both with a questioning expression. *She's noticed something different between us. I hope no one else does.*

Isabella felt her body go numb, as she dreaded hearing what would be expected of her this time.

"Tell Lord Drayton we shall be there momentarily," Everett told Clarissa, before turning to Isabella, who stood rooted to the spot.

"I know how much delivering the ransom money to these remote locations is taking out of you. I also know, that even though it's making you ill, you'll still agree to put yourself in danger."

She nodded, glad to see he understood how she felt.

"Whatever is requested, you won't face it alone," he promised, and took her hand gently in his to give reassurance.

"We should make haste," she said quietly.

She knew from the subdued looks on the faces of the household staff, as they walked through the Great Hall that the news of a new ransom demand arriving had spread.

"Ah Isabella, Everett, you're here. Come and join us," urged Uncle Henry.

"Can I see the letter?" asked Everett. "Is it a similar demand to last time?"

Henry handed Everett the letter, and Isabella stood close to him reading it over his shoulder.

This time there was a promise that Lawrence would be delivered the following evening and left close to the eastern lodge.

And I'm supposed to go to an isolated location with an additional payment of eight hundred pounds. If we involve the authorities, then Lawrence's safety will be compromised.

"They claim this will be the final exchange, this time promising that Lawrence will be returned once they have received the money, as long as no one tries to stop them," Peter told them after Everett had let him see the letter.

Uncle Henry took one look at Isabella, immediately pulling out a chair and ushering her to a seat. He gestured to Penelope to go and find some tea for Isabella.

He paced the length of the drawing room, eventually stopping and turning to face the group of family and friends. "And who is to say it will stop this time. Lawrence was supposed to return within the hour after the last rendezvous. They know we are a source of money, and I doubt they're going to stop any time soon."

"We have little choice," said Isabella quietly, worried that her calm uncle had lost his composure.

"Oh, Heavens, Isabella. These demands are an obvious game, designed to extract the maximum payment. The authorities are aware of this situation, Everett is a magistrate, and the constables have been involved since the first drop off. They know we have no alternative but to keep paying the money and hope they keep their word."

Miss Dymchurch stood and went to Uncle Henry's side, placing a gentle hand on his arm. "Henry, you've done as much as you can, and we'll keep doing whatever is necessary in order to save Lawrence's life. We're all exhausted by this business."

"Thank you, Althea. I needed somebody to remind me of those things, and my becoming angry isn't going to improve this situation."

The library door opened, somewhat dramatically, as Lady Moreton entered the room.

Isabella, who had stood to greet her possible future mother-in-law, instead stared open mouthed at the state of the good lady. She was pale, almost deathly pale and she was clinging to Annette as if she was unable to walk unaided. It's been quite a change in three days from the formidable matron she'd been on the evening of the ball.

"Settle me here, Annette," Lady Moreton commanded, before turning to them. "I understand there is another ransom note. I have no idea why no one came to inform me!"

Uncle Henry handed her the ransom letter, and they waited for her to read the contents.

"We shall of course ignore that stipulation not to inform the authorities, Lillian. They're already fully aware anyway, as Everett is the local magistrate."

Lady Moreton rose to her feet, the chair crashing to the floor behind her. "My son's life hangs in the balance; you have to follow the instructions to the letter and do exactly as these people demand."

"We've done that with the first two ransom demands," an exasperated Peter told her, "and it has made little difference."

Isabella sat back in her chair her hands held tightly together. It was difficult to see this once proud woman pleading and clutching at Uncle Henry's arm as she tried to persuade him to change his mind.

"Lillian, Lady Moreton, please calm yourself. No decisions have been made. You look ill, and I suggest you sit and take tea while we discuss this together."

"I shall accept nothing less than our following these instructions to the letter," she wailed.

Everett stepped forward from his position by the fireplace where he'd been standing quietly. He spoke with quiet command. "I am the authorities, Lady Moreton. I'm also a friend of the family. I have a suggestion."

"Come on my boy, out with it," cried Uncle Henry.

"I will accompany Isabella at a safe distance. I'm used to working undercover and can promise that no one will realise that she isn't alone. It also means she will be fully protected. We can try delivering the ransom money one more time before handing this case fully to the authorities."

Isabella looked up, thanking him with a smile, and met his unwavering glance, the intensity of his regard creating that familiar warmth which spread through her, despite the feeling of chill she'd had when she read the ransom note.

Lady Moreton had moved to stand immediately behind Everett and the expression on her face intrigued Isabella. For a moment Isabella had thought she glimpsed a rather calculated look, but it quickly changed back to maternal anguish. She dismissed it as surely, she must have been mistaken.

"What Everett suggests makes perfect sense," reinforced Peter. "We need to position ourselves somewhere which allows full observation without detection," he added, as he moved to scrutinize their estate map. "Look, here and here," he said pointing out potential hiding places. The advantage is that it's a heavily forested area. I vote we do what we did that first time and position men high up in the trees."

Uncle Henry stood beside him considering the suggestion. "We need to put more thought into how we capture the kidnapper," he mused. "The drop off isn't until tomorrow, so we've got time to go and look at the site and decide the best position for observers."

"Let's go there now," said Everett. "They won't expect us to go anywhere near that site today, so we can do reconnaissance in preparation for the rendezvous tomorrow."

***

I look so gaunt with shadows under my eyes, Isabella thought as she looked in the mirror. *I'm dreading my third encounter with these rogues, but I know I have to keep to the plan.*

"Shall I do your hair now, Miss?" asked Maisie.

Isabella nodded. "Yes, and I'll wear my hair coiled simply and securely so I don't even have to think about it."

She turned on hearing a rap on the door and Penelope entered the room. She had dressed in one of Maisie's gowns, with her hair in the same style as the maid.

"You didn't think I'd let you walk to the drop off place alone? I know Everett will be close, but he wasn't far away last time, and neither was Peter, and the rogue still got away. It's as though he melts into the darkness."

"It's quite a phantom kidnapper we have," agreed Isabella. "What if this exchange proves as fruitless as in previous attempts?"

Isabella opened a wooden box on her dressing table and took out a small knife and asked Maisie to help her attach it to her cloak. "I need to be able to access it quickly," she explained.

"You're going to be armed?" Penelope couldn't hide the shocked expression on her face.

"I keep wondering why they insist on it being me bringing the purse of money. I admit I'm afraid that they might take me prisoner too. I asked Ned, the footman, to find me a weapon. I'd hoped for a pistol, but he found this small knife."

"This has gone on too long," agreed Penelope. "It has to end today, but if you go armed you will be in more danger!"

"I will only use the knife if I absolutely need to. I promise. My mind is crammed full of so many thoughts, all swirling around, that I can't concentrate," admitted Isabella. "I keep pushing away the thought that Lawrence may never return. We have no guarantee that they will ever release him."

"You mustn't think that way."

"I know, but it's the reality. If he never returns, I'll be left mourning a man I never married, who lied to me throughout our betrothal."

"We need to hear his explanation of events," cautioned Penelope.

"There might be no end for me. After discovering his only motivation for marrying me was to clear his gambling debts, then I believe I'd be quite justified in calling off our betrothal. He isn't here though. How can I call off an arrangement, because that's all it is, with a man who's been kidnapped?"

"You'd end your betrothal?"

"In a moment," Isabella added decisively.

"Is it Everett, Viscount Kennington?" queried Penelope.

Isabella swallowed and raised her eyes to her friend. She nodded. "Yes, he's been a good friend and more. I know the reason for his unwavering support is because he loves me. It's a dreadfully difficult situation. I'm discovering that I care about him, when I'm betrothed and committed to another man."

She pulled on her thick woolen cloak and regarded herself in the looking glass. "Even though Lawrence has behaved despicably, I can't desert him at this point."

"Oh Isabella, I can't imagine what you're going through."

"it's best if we don't talk about it, Penelope. There's little I can do to change the situation. Now distract me and tell me about Peter."

"I was going to wait till all this was over."

Isabella wasn't to be put off. She wanted something to take her mind off what lay ahead. "I can't wait that long to find out what's happening. You have to tell me now."

"I think I'm almost betrothed," whispered Penelope.

"You are? Now you really do have to tell me everything," replied Isabella, surprise and delight in her voice.

"He made a declaration when we were walking to the lake. He told me he loved me and wants me to marry him. I've never met anyone like him before. I try to think back to Thomas, and whether it feels similar to when we were planning our wedding, but the reality is that it's more than that. I respected and admired Thomas, and we would have been content together, but I love Peter."

Isabella came over and took her friend in her arms. She could feel tears welling in her eyes." Oh, Penelope I'm so happy for you."

"I wish you could be as happy. You seemed content, but never truly happy with Lawrence. I know you're in love with Everett, your path forward seems obvious to me."

"If it wasn't for the kidnapping, I believe I would know what to do next," admitted Isabella.

"I believe it will all become clear once Lawrence returns, and we have to keep believing that will happen. I came to the conclusion after Thomas died, that we should not wait if we see the opportunity of happiness in the road ahead. It seems to me it would be wrong of you to continue in a betrothal when you no longer respect the man."

"If only that were true," sighed Isabella. "It seems simple, but it is so very complicated."

"I believe true loyalty needs us to be honest about our feelings, and there are changed circumstances here. Even if Everett had not returned, I believe you would have had misgivings about marrying Lawrence after the events of the last few days."

Isabella thought this over before nodding. "You're right."

"And you made the commitment to marry Lawrence without fully understand the situation. It would have been different if he'd been honest about his financial difficulties. I'm glad that you discovered about his character before you exchanged vows in the chapel."

"That's true as well."

"And in what we know about Lawrence, from finding that correspondence, one thing stands out, and it's that he hasn't been truthful with you. I believe that fact alone gives you permission to reconsider and choose a different path." Penelope paused. "And this is a very unladylike way of putting it, but to perdition with what society might think. Happiness in life is more important."

Isabella looked at her friend, knowing she was right in what she said. "There's a lot to think about. At this moment I want to cry, and I'm going to push that aside and focus on taking this purse and hoping that means Lawrence is finally freed."

Several hours later, as the full moon rose high in the sky, Isabella approached the ancient stone marking on Drayton Park's border. She grasped the leather pouch containing eight hundred pounds, the weight heavy in her hand. Would it secure Lawrence's release.

She wished she had more confidence that she would see her betrothed's face within a few hours.

Chapter 23

Isabella was so close Everett he could almost hear her breathe, as he followed concealed in the dense undergrowth.

He would gladly place himself between her and any harm as he watched her composed figure stand beside the boundary stone.

Penelope, disguised as a maid, stood close to Isabella who followed the note's instructions precisely, placing the purse of money beneath the massive oak tree beside the boundary stone.

Everett thought back to their visit here the day before. He could see it had been chosen with care. There were multiple escape routes for the kidnapper with dense undergrowth all around. It did tell him that the kidnapper knew the estate very well indeed.

An owl hooted high in the tree above startling him. What was that movement in the shadows. They were expecting the kidnapper to approach from the west, but Everett discerned a figure moving towards Isabella from the north.

He got ready to spring forward. The cloaked figure reached the collection point and Everett could see he wore a mask to hide his face.

He signaled to Peter as he stepped forward, calling to the figure to drop any weapons and stand still. The cloaked figure immediately took a step backwards before retreating back into the thicket.

Everett could see the look of desolation on Isabella's face. They had failed for a third time. This nightmare wasn't over yet.

They all looked around bewildered, unsure what had happened. Peter summed it up for them. "He moves unpredictably. He chooses places where he can disappear in a split second."

"I'm going to remain here in case he returns for the money," Isabella told them, her voice empty of emotion. "We didn't involve the authorities, but no one could have expected me to come here without protection."

"He won't return now," Everett assured her.

Isabella was tired but insistent. "I know that's likely to be the case, but you've got to let me do this."

Everett did not wish to argue with her, he could see it would be useless. "As you wish, Bella. I'll stay close by in case they do return. Unlikely as it may be, seeing you on your own here may tempt them and I wouldn't want you to be alone."

Penelope wanted to stay with them, but Everett insisted she return to the house with Peter. There was nothing to be gained by her remaining.

After an hour in which Isabella stood near the boundary stone, Everett approached her again and was able to persuade her that they should return to the house before complete darkness made the return path treacherous.

His quiet presence, so close to her offered comfort despite their total failure. As they walked together to the waiting horses, she felt her pulse steady, and the feelings of anxiety recede.

By now Isabella was exhausted, and when she stumbled over a branch lying across the path, he was quick to catch her. She relaxed into his arms and in that fleeting moment they seemed alone together in a world apart. She sighed and pulled away, and he offered her his arm as they continued towards the house.

"Let's go in through the back door," Isabella suggested. "Look, what's that there? she asked with dawning horror, reaching down to pick up a single piece of paper, folded and secured under a stone. Her fingers trembled as she held the letter. "It's from the kidnappers. I'm stunned that they have been so close to the house. How many of them are there? I feel as though they have eyes everywhere."

"I've just about had enough of this," he said angrily. "There will be a constable on every door until we catch this gang of ruffians."

"Let's take it inside to read, the light will be better there. I am struggling to make it out here, and indeed it seems to be from the kidnappers."

The others came out, and Penelope looked at the note in Isabella's hand in horror. "They were arrogant enough to come this close to the house?"

Peter began to search the surrounding area, but Isabella called for him to stop. "Leave it. They're long gone."

"Unless they have a contact in the household," added Penelope.

"Or that actually lives in the house," added Everett.

Isabella was shocked. "I hadn't thought of that!"

"Surely not, the household staff have all been here for many years!" Penelope was clearly startled by his words.

"Nevertheless, I suggest we are cautious in future about being overheard when we discuss our plans," Everett told them, his tone grim.

Isabella looked close to tears. "Oh my head hurts. I hoped against hope that this would be over tonight, and now we have yet more waiting and uncertainty."

Once inside Everett held up the lantern while Isabella scrutinized the words. "It's what we expected, and it isn't good. We need to find Uncle Henry and make sure he knows about this."

"So, they now want fifteen hundred pounds by tomorrow evening, because we failed to follow the specific instructions. It seems it's the final chance to keep Lawrence alive." Isabella's composed manner wavered as disappointment and frustration overwhelmed her careful control.

"It's Everett's appearance which seemed to be the problem. They seem to have totally ignored your presence Penelope," commented Peter.

Everett's hand covered Isabella's briefly, offering wordless support before they moved on to find Uncle Henry. They found him coming towards them with an anxious expression covering his face.

"I know the attempt failed and he got away, but I need to know the specifics. Mrs. Finchley has tea waiting in the drawing room. She asked me about supper, but I didn't know if you'd feel like eating anything."

"Maybe Cook could serve a cold collation in the drawing room," suggested Isabella.

As they entered the drawing room, Everett could see the look on Isabella's face as they saw Lady Moreton seated there. *It's terrible of me, but I'd hoped she would be sedated upstairs.*

The shadows danced around the walls of the drawing room as Isabella explained about the failed exchange.

"And there's more," she continued, handing the letter to Uncle Henry.

"They've increased their demand, and death threats against Lawrence. This is a nightmare with no end!" Every word from Uncle Henry's mouth came out full of frustration.

Instead of bluster and argument, tears streamed down Lady Moreton's face. Miss Dymchurch sat with her, trying to ease her distress with soothing words.

They all stared at each other, lost for words, feeling the reality of failure and knowing they faced the same thing again.

It was Clarissa who spoke first as she stood up. "I'll pour tea." For some reason this sent Isabella off into the fit of giggles. It was quite inappropriate, but she could not stop once she had started.

Lady Moreton sat up straight in her chair. "How dare you laugh," she cried. "I told Lawrence you were no fit bride, and to look for another Baroness." The look she gave Isabella was venomous.

Isabella's fit of laughter continued, despite the fury on her future mother-in-law's face.

Uncle Henry came across and put his hand on her shoulder. "It's alright, Isabella. Take some deep breaths. I'm not surprised the tension has got to you eventually. Hysteria is a natural reaction to what you have been through."

Isabella tried to speak, but her breath was ragged. "I'm sorry," she tried to say.

"Despicable girl. I shall tell Lawrence of this when he returns. Mark my words you shall be sorry. I believe it was your failure to follow instructions precisely which has endangered my dear Lawrence. And now you laugh..."

Uncle Henry began to speak in an attempt to calm the situation, but it was Everett who spoke up in Isabella's defense, his voice icily cold. "You should apologise immediately, your Ladyship. This is clearly a hysterical, distressed reaction. Your lack of compassion is astounding. Miss Drayton has put herself at considerable risk on three occasions. She's been closer to the kidnapper than any of us, putting her life in danger, knowing that she could be taken too. I'm surprised she's kept going this long. She can be allowed at least one bout of hysteria. Some in this group have already had several."

Lady Moreton looked as though he'd slapped her in the face. "I still maintain that laughter is an inappropriate reaction, and as soon as my son returns, I'd be suggesting that he ends his betrothal."

Isabella took another deep breath and looked up at the woman who could be her future mother-in-law. "I believe that we will all be different after this has ended. I will discuss with Lawrence whether we marry, or not. You should certainly apologise to my uncle for your harsh words towards me, Lady Moreton. He has parted with a considerable amount of money in order to secure the release of the Baron, then you claim I'm not a suitable wife for your son."

Something changed in Lady Moreton's countenance. She put her hand across her forehead and collapsed back into the chair, as she began to wail hysterically. Miss Dymchurch patted her hand reassuringly, and then Uncle Henry went to stand next to her, telling her they all felt anxious and exhausted, and they had to be compassionate with each other.

"My patience with this situation is wearing thin. My niece has put herself at risk three times now, and it's taking its toll. I'm not sure if I will allow her to be involved in another drop off."

"But you must," wailed Lady Moreton. "Lawrence is all I have."

"It's all right. Of course, I'll deliver the next ransom," Isabella assured Lady Moreton.

Lady Moreton looked at Isabella. "I expected nothing less of you. The only important thing is to ensure Lawrence returns to us. Now if you will excuse me, I shall retire to my room."

Annette and Miss Dymchurch assisted Lady Moreton to her bedchamber. She seemed so small, and vulnerable as she leaned heavily on her companion's arm.

Everett paced to the window and then back to the hearth again.

Something isn't right in this situation. Peter's right. We're missing something, and this does not feel like a kidnapping. I begin to suspect that there is someone linked to the kidnappers within Drayton Park. There's work to do and urgently. I need to closely analyze all the letters in terms of parchment and the style of handwriting.

Everett shared his concerns. "There's something strange about these repeated demands. They could have taken the money this evening and returned Lawrence. This begins to feel like calculated extortion, far more complicated than kidnapping. I believe kidnappers are glad to receive the ransom and run, knowing capture will mean imprisonment or deportation."

"You're right," said Peter. "There's something very strange about this situation. I just can't put my finger on it."

"I want to examine the handwriting on the ransom notes again," said Everett. "I noticed something about the writing the first time but put it to the back of my mind. It's one of the few clues that we have, and now we have four notes to compare."

"The evening is young, and I'll find it difficult to sleep. We can spend as long as you want on those letters," agreed Peter.

Chapter 24

After Lady Moreton had retired to her chamber Isabella began to apologize for her outburst. Uncle Henry came to take a seat beside her.

"I thought it quite a natural reaction. You are tired, this has been going on for days, and it's you my dear who delivers the ransom money and puts yourself in danger. We all hoped it would end tonight, and it continues to yet another meeting with these criminals. No young lady should be faced with such a dreadful situation."

She smiled weakly, just about managing to mouth a thank you.

"It's all of us who should be saying thank you to you for your ability to keep going under such pressure. Lillian was wrong to speak with you as she did, and I believe that she regrets her words. I hope you will forgive her as she is under a terrible strain."

Uncle Henry paused, as if struggling to put his thoughts into words. She looked around the room and noticed the others had left. Penelope and Clarissa had gone to assist with Lady Moreton and Everett and Peter had retreated to the library to talk about how to approach the rendezvous the next day.

"We're alone, the others have all gone about their business. I am truly sad, Isabella, that the days leading up to your marriage are so miserable. Even before this despicable kidnap I had an inkling that all wasn't well. I have to ask this. Are you sure you wish to marry Lawrence? I know there is nothing that can be done until he returns, but as someone who loves you, I need to ask you the question."

Isabella looked at him for a long time, aware of a stray tear falling silently down her cheek.

He smiled gently. "I think you have given me an answer to my question."

She nodded, the smallest of movements. "I don't love him. It was very much an agreement between two people who respected each other. I thought him honourable and caring. He stood up for me against anyone who criticized my studies and interest in botanical research. I thought we could suit each other very well."

"And that's changed?"

"I didn't know the extent of his financial difficulties. I thought he was comfortably wealthy. The gambling debts have been a surprise."

"Well, none of us expected that development."

"And, if I'm honest with myself then I believe I love another."

"Ah, I wondered," Uncle Henry said quietly. "All I can say, Isabella, is that I am glad if you have found love. It's the most important thing in life in my opinion. I still miss your aunt very much. I knew she loved me, and I loved her more than life itself. If in the middle of this darkness you have discovered a spark of love then nurture it, and let's hope it can fan into a flame when we've retrieved the Baron."

"Whatever my feelings, the most important thing is to return Lawrence to his Mama. I have to hope that it will happen tomorrow."

"Stay calm, Isabella, and trust that love finds a way to take root and grow if we let it." He patted her hand. "You love Everett?"

She nodded. "I believe I've loved him ever since I turned down his proposal when I was about to embark on my first season in town."

"Ah, I see."

'I saw him as a friend, and only when I'd rejected his suit did I realise I felt something stronger than friendship."

"He's a good man, brave, and a true friend to this family."

With those words he patted her shoulder and told her he needed to speak with Viscount Kennington and Peter.

She put her head back and closed her eyes. *Could she have a chance of love with Everett? There was no possibility of thinking about that while Lawrence was held captive.*

The door to the terrace stood open, and she walked out into a chill evening.

I believe we might have the first frost tonight, she thought. The air felt crisp with a sharp still cold. It was exactly what she needed to help calm her body and clear her mind. Dear Uncle Henry, he cared for her and intended that she should be happy. *I'm lucky to have him and Penelope in my life.*

I wish I had a studio, a place of my own, where I could be myself, and read or swim in a lake without worrying about the proprieties. Maybe one day that's something I can make happen for myself. A place to write and compile my research into that encyclopedia. A door to close on the world and all its complications.

The clear sky showed the stars of the late autumn sky shining brightly overhead. Was Lawrence able to see the stars tonight, or was he kept captive in darkness? She shuddered, wishing It had been different today and he'd been released.

Each rendezvous brought a further demand for more money and no resolution. Had it been planned this way? It seemed likely, and they were so focused on planning for the next handover that they had no time to think about who the kidnappers were, or where they were holding Lawrence, and if any specific creditors in London were responsible for kidnapping him.

I believe Everett is right. If this had been about a debt of honour, with a gentleman paying what he owed, then Lawrence would have been returned by now.

Her head hurt, as she looked out onto the shadows of the tall trees in the distance.

She heard footsteps on the flagstones and turned, expecting to see Uncle Henry or Penelope come to check on how she was faring.

Everett smiled at her and came to join her.

"It's a lovely evening. I like these clear skies. Somehow the stars seem brighter than in the summer. Peter and I have been reviewing the ransom notes, and I wanted to see how you were coping after Lady Moreton's words."

"I shouldn't have laughed," she said quietly.

"It was the reaction of a person under great stress. I've seen it happen on the eve before a battle. The mind and body have limits, and laughter and crying are basic human emotions."

"I believe you're right. It just happened and I didn't have any control over it."

"You, more than anyone, have carried the load of this dreadful situation, I understand how you feel. You've been braver, and through more, than anyone else, and don't forget that."

"I'll try to cry instead of laugh next time, people might understand that better."

"We can't always predict what will happen, Isabella. I wanted to ask if you thought there was anything strange about this whole situation. I keep going back to why they haven't released Lawrence, and that the driving force behind their actions isn't paying gambling debts, it's about extorting as much money as possible."

"You know I've been thinking all week that this situation reminded me of something, and I couldn't put my finger on it. Just now, staring at the stars, my head clearing in the cool autumn evening I remembered what it was."

"You can't leave it there; you need to tell me."

"It seems so ridiculous, but I will share it with you. It reminds me of a novel I read by Mrs. Ann Radcliffe, and we all know her gothic style."

"Go on," he urged.

"It's the story of a duke who falls on hard times and must keep up appearances of grandeur. He tries to find a rich bride, but before the marriage can take place a creditor tells him that he needs to pay a debt immediately or he will be outed in a scandal sheet. *Ton* society has no pity for those who cannot pay their debts."

"There are a lot of similarities," he agreed.

"There's more. The duke arranges his own kidnapping, knowing that his rich aunt will pay for his release. He writes his own ransom demands and hides in a place close to his aunt's estate."

"I see, and you think there might be similarities here?"

"A few days ago, I truly thought that one of the creditors had kidnapped him to retrieve their money. If that had been the case, then surely, they would have released him by now."

"I'm inclined to agree with you, but this is Lawrence, Baron Moreton. It's rather a stretch to think of him arranging his own kidnapping."

"I know, and I can't imagine him setting this up himself. However, the extortion of the money, the notes, and the positioning of the ransom notes reminds me of this gothic novel."

"Is there a happy ending?" he asked.

"Oh no, far from it. The duke is ruined and has to sell his estate and leave the country. His life in society is over at the end of the book."

"A sad tale. I can't see Lawrence masterminding a scheme like that. And I can't see him reading Mrs. Ann Radcliffe and gaining the idea from a novel. However, I believe I shall read this book myself. Have you a copy?"

She nodded. "Penelope and I are both avid readers of her books. I plan to re-read one of her books again."

"I'll read that as well when you've finished, just in case we have another mystery in the future," Everett told her with a smile.

He looked preoccupied, as if he wasn't sure whether to speak or stay silent. "There is something which might be connected. It is probably coincidence, but I remember being intrigued by the handwriting on that very first letter. I'd forgotten about it until this evening, and when you look at Lawrence's handwriting and the way the letters are made on the ransom note there are certain, very distinct similarities. I'm not saying that Lawrence wrote the notes, absolutely not, but I feel it likely it's someone who studied his handwriting, as there is some very distinctive lettering."

"Oh, the complications never end," Isabella sighed. "It has to be somebody who knows his writing, and perhaps even someone who shared the same tutor, or went to the same school."

"I'll put enquiries in motion, it may lead us somewhere," Everett agreed.

"Was that a shooting star up there?" she cried out in surprise. "As I looked up a star just seemed to fall from the sky. I've never seen a shooting star before."

"I believe you're supposed to wish on a star," he told her.

"Wishes, dreams, so far from reality," she whispered, gazing upwards at the night sky. All that matters is that he returns. I'm so afraid for the future, and all the uncertainties. Something's changed, and I believe it's connected to trust and honesty."

Everett didn't reply immediately, unspoken feelings creating a tension between them.

Isabella continued. "Whatever happens I can't see a positive outcome for me. I can stay here and live quietly with no opportunity to spend time in society and marry. I can stay on course and marry Lawrence, but I no longer admire him, and I suspect that I need to walk away from him. I can't do that when he's held captive."

"Just move forward taking one small step at a time," Everett suggested. "I believe you'll know what to do when you see Lawrence again."

"I sincerely hope so. I'm struggling if I'm honest. This whole situation is draining me of energy."

Suddenly she was in his arms, he drew her close into a brief embrace. She felt that familiar warmth coursing through her veins. *I'm like a ship finding shelter in a safe harbor,* she thought. She leaned into the embrace, allowing her head to rest against his chest, his arms providing a sense of security she had not felt for a long time.

His heartbeat sounded steady and so close she found its rhythm comforting amid the chaos of her life.

She stepped back, moving slowly away, wanting the moment to continue but knowing how inappropriate it would be to rest longer in his arms.

Everett let her go. "I shall leave you now to go and read more of the work of Mrs. Ann Radcliffe. I believe we're as likely to find the solution to this case in a gothic novel as we are in my meticulous analysis of the style of the letters."

Isabella laughed gently. "Well then, I'll go and oblige and read several chapters by firelight. Perhaps in the morning all will have become clearer."

"Sleep well, Isabella," and with those words he bowed and left her gazing at the stars.

***

The next morning Isabella again awoke early, watching the sunrise and the rays of morning light streaming through the window. She'd stayed awake until the early hours, trying to think if there was anything they'd missed in their investigation. She had indeed read Mrs. Radcliffe's novel by candlelight until her eyes began to close, and she woke suddenly as the book dropped to the floor.

We're missing something. I know there's some crucial piece of information which is staring us in the face.

She'd slept fitfully, waking after a dream where she'd stood within Everett's embrace. It felt like coming home after a long journey.

She was no clearer about knowing what to do. The sense of duty towards Lawrence was significant, and yet her feelings for him had changed, and the trust between them had evaporated.

Although she knew Lady Moreton's words were unjust, she kept returning to the fact that they hadn't followed the kidnappers' instructions exactly. Everett had been close by her during the last rendezvous. Perhaps Lady Moreton had a point.

She rose and dressed in her riding habit, hoping a canter in the early morning air, through the meadow, would prepare her for the day ahead. She crept downstairs knowing the rest of the household was still asleep.

A noise startled her, and she turned, feeling a claw of fear, only to smile at the sight of Hermes up and waiting downstairs for his master. "You scared me, but I'm glad of your company. Will you join me on a walk to the stables?"

Hermes followed her as she walked along the path to the stable yard. Ben March, one of the grooms, saddled her bay mare quickly and efficiently despite the early hour.

"Have you seen anything strange?" she asked Ben.

"No, Miss, and it's all we talk about. We all hope Lord Lawrence will return soon."

"Nothing at all? Nobody has seen anyone strange, or found anything unusual?"

"Come to think of it, Miss, Adam found a linen handkerchief near the eastern boundary. We thought it might belong to you, or Miss Penelope."

She felt a stirring of excitement at these words. *Could this be a clue?* She knew that neither her, nor Penelope, had carried a handkerchief to that rendezvous. *Could it be significant?*

"I'm going to ride up to Home Farm and ride in the meadow. Can you make sure to give me the handkerchief when I return?"

"Of course, Miss."

She took the familiar path skirting through the far side of the woods towards the meadow at Home Farm, easing Melody into a trot and then a canter.

Isabella rode, and with the breeze in her hair, and the freedom of the ride her head cleared. She knew she needed to focus on the present moment and nothing else. The important thing was to secure Lawrence's release. Until then, she had no future to think about.

All I need to do is live each minute and not be drawn into thinking about anything else.

As she helped Ben the groom to cool down Melody on her return, she remembered to ask him for the handkerchief.

"You're quite right; it does look like a lady's handkerchief. I'll take it to show Uncle Henry." Isabella took it and kept thinking how strange it was to find a lady's handkerchief near the thicket. "Has Hermes been alright at the stables while I've been gone?"

"Absolutely, Miss. He thinks of the stables as his second home. His brother and sister still live here."

"I'd forgotten that. Now, I'd better go back for breakfast, before they start to worry about my whereabouts, thank you for your help, Ben." She called for Hermes, and they made their way back to the house.

Penelope smiled in greeting as she entered the breakfast room. She could tell from the expression in her friend's eyes that she had been worried about Isabella.

When the footman left to collect more coddled eggs from the kitchen, they found themselves alone able to talk.

"It did me good to have a ride. I should do it more often."

"I shall come with you next time," Penelope told her.

"And you say Adam found a strange handkerchief near the lodge?"

"Yes, it definitely belongs to a fine lady. It is strange it was found so near the rendezvous."

"Maybe one of the local ladies had an assignation," suggested Penelope with a smile.

"I don't believe any of the ladies around here would know what that word actually means," laughed Isabella.

"I saw you on the terrace with Everett last night. You seem closer each day. It must be so difficult knowing which direction to take."

"Oh, I have no idea which direction to take, but while out riding I decided that all I can do is concentrate on each moment and not worry about the future," and as she spoke the words, she knew this was exactly what she needed to do to survive the next few hours and days.

"An excellent plan."

Isabella sighed. "I believe we are to spend the morning in the library looking at maps and documents."

"You're right, that seems to be the plan. I do so wish we could go into town, or even the village, but until this is resolved it seems we are isolated here at Drayton Park Manor."

"It can't go on like this with money drop offs every day. Uncle is right about bringing in the full force of the authorities."

"And Lady Moreton is determined that won't happen," said Penelope.

"In the end it will be the local magistrate's decision, and I don't think he'll let Lady Moreton choose the direction of travel," added Isabella.

Chapter 25

"I don't like the look of those clouds gathering over there," Peter told Everett as he gazed out of the library window.

Everett looked up from his scrutiny of documents covering the long table. "Maybe we'll have a storm. That's just going to add to the difficulties with any drop off."

"Do you think we'll hear from the kidnappers today?"

"I'd be surprised if we didn't. There seems to be quite a routine pattern now. They were very quick to leave that note near the back entrance last night."

"We don't seem to have any luck in catching them," Peter's frustration was evident. "Poor Isabella, she's worried about Lawrence, putting herself in danger delivering money and you can see it's taking a toll on her."

"There's little else we can do except keep going with following the instructions as closely as we can. Heavy rain isn't going to make it any easier." Everett's thoughts drifted to Isabella, thinking back to the close moments they had shared on the terrace the previous evening.

I should never have embraced her, Everett thought, *it isn't fair on her.* The contrast between the warmth and comfort of holding her in his arms and the regret that she was promised to another, was evident.

Peter looked at him. "You look miles away, are you thinking about Isabella?"

"How did you guess? Did you sense it last night?"

"It's obvious you care for her. I know you admire her."

Everett let out a sigh. "And she's betrothed to Lawrence."

"Who has shown himself to have behaved fairly despicably in his quest to gain her fortune," observed Peter.

"It may seem despicable to us, Peter, but how many of the young men and women are out there searching for a way of securing financial stability through a match. In every recital ballroom I'd estimate that up to half of the guests are looking for an advantageous marriage."

"That may be true but he has not been truthful, or given her any indication of the extent of his debts."

Everett pushed the map to one side, standing and stretching his long lithe back, feeling a familiar knot of tension in the muscles.

"Maybe you should tell her how you feel," suggested Peter. "Why not be honest with her?"

"I have," Everett said simply. "I know she feels something for me, but nothing can change while Lawrence is missing."

Peter could only sympathize. "It's so awkward."

A figure appeared at the door leading out to the terrace. Peter opened it to let Clarissa in. "I needed some fresh air," she explained. "It's all so grim."

She turned to Everett. "I saw you with Isabella last night, out on the terrace."

"You shouldn't spy on people Clarissa," Everett admonished his sister.

"I wasn't," Clarissa pushed back against his accusation. "I was taking the air, and I came across the spectacle of Isabella and you embracing. Have you told her how you feel? Does she feel the same way?"

"We were just discussing that," said Peter. "It seems your brother is a stickler for the proprieties, and we all have to wait for Lawrence to return."

"It's the decent thing," insisted Everett.

"I'm not sure I agree," disagreed Clarissa, a thoughtful expression crossing her face. "I don't have experience of *ton* society. But I have to believe honesty is important in any relationship. Isabella has discovered her betrothed has been hiding the truth. You may have to tell Isabella how you feel regardless of circumstances."

"It's all a mess," Everett confessed. "I should have kept my feelings to myself. Now Isabella is wracked with guilt."

"I believe another way of putting that is that she's discovered she loves you," suggested Clarissa wisely. "You can have a double wedding," she smiled at Peter.

Peter was shocked. "What? You know about Penelope?"

Clarissa laughed at him. "Dear Peter, it wasn't difficult to realise that. Has she accepted you?"

He nodded. "We're keeping it quiet," then smiled at the irony of his next words, "till Lawrence returns!"

"It seems things will actually get more interesting once Lawrence is free. I feel better for spending time outside, just clearing my head. And I also notice that Isabella's gone for a ride. I suggest, Everett, you take your sketchbook and go for a walk."

"I might do that," he agreed.

"We're in a state of uncertainty, and you have to hold firm to the hope that Isabella will make her choices once Lawrence returns.

Everett smiled at his sister. "I know. There are just so many uncertainties. One of which is when the next letter with the location of the next rendezvous will arrive."

***

The afternoon shadows had lengthened across the garden at Drayton Park when the expected ransom note arrived. Mr. Fletcher had placed it on the silver salver and taken it through to Lord Drayton in the drawing room where they took afternoon tea.

Lord Drayton took the letter in his hands and broke the wax seal with visible frustration. How long could this go on? He looked up, scanning the faces in the room. "They want fifteen hundred pounds, and they state again it's the final payment.

"When do they want it?" asked Penelope.

"This evening, which is a surprise, at the castle ruins to the north of Drayton Park."

"Let's hope this is the end of it," said Miss Dymchurch. "It's exhausting, and I'm not the one making the exchange. I'm assuming they're asking for Isabella again?" she added with a note of anger in her voice.

Lord Drayton nodded. "There is a difference this time though, as they promise Lawrence's immediate return as soon as they receive the purse of money. They state this is the last opportunity to secure his release."

Lady Moreton stood and looked around the room. "Isabella must deliver the payment exactly as they instruct."

"I know you feel that way Lillian, but this is my niece who is being placed in considerable danger. I don't like this one bit." He turned to Everett. "Should we involve all the constables? You've held back from fully involving them in the last two rendezvous."

Everett nodded. "It may be our last chance to catch them."

"I cannot believe you're prepared to put my son's life at risk. I won't accept this," Lady Moreton cried. "This is cowardly and ungentlemanly behaviour. You should all be ashamed of yourselves."

"Lady Moreton, calm yourself," cautioned Everett. "As local magistrate I must act in the way I see fit. There is no way that Miss Drayton will go into a deserted castle on a dark, stormy night with no protection."

"I insist that the priority is the return of Lawrence. Nothing else matters," she insisted.

"And Isabella's life?" challenged Everett.

"The priority has to be the return of my son. I repeat, nothing else matters."

Lord Drayton looked at her aghast. "I believe it would be best if you retired to your bed chamber. You're clearly overwrought. We can send for Mr. Noakes."

"I expected more support from you, Henry! Lady Moreton turned on her heel and left the room, with Miss Dymchurch following closely behind.

Lord Drayton turned to Isabella. "I'm sorry, Isabella, her behaviour is shocking, and even if it is due to extreme anxiety, the way she expects you to keep putting yourself into danger is unacceptable."

"It's alright. I understand her anguish. She isn't thinking about the impact of her words.'

"That's generous of you, Isabella," Lord Drayton replied.

Everett could see that Isabella wanted to be alone as she excused herself. "And now I must go and speak to Cook. I'm sadly neglecting my duties as a hostess. Cook is more than capable, but I should show some interest in the menus."

The room felt empty to Everett after she'd left. He turned his focus to the map showing the ruined castle and its grounds.

"We must quickly develop a coordinated approach which balances Isabella's safety with the kidnappers demands. If we plan it, then there's no need for them to know there are any watchers present."

"At least we know the castle's layout, and potential observation points. We all played there as children," said Peter.

"Yes," replied Everett, "I only need to close my eyes, and I see the great hall and the stone staircase leading up to the higher level."

"I remember we were convinced we'd seen a ghost there once," added Peter.

"It was our place, our hide out as children. I doubt he realises he's chosen a location we know so well. Hopefully that will work in our favour."

"Will Isabella go alone this time?"

"Not if I can help it," Everett was determined. "I need to talk with her about it."

"Penelope will accompany her disguised as a maid again. That's something." It was as much a question from Peter as a statement.

Everett wasn't sure. "I'd be happier if there was something more robust, if one of us could accompany her."

"She won't be long with Cook I'm sure," Lord Drayton told them. "And with Lillian's histrionics, I totally forgot, but Isabella gave me this. He took the linen handkerchief out of his pocket and placed it on the table next to the other documents. One of the grooms found it near the second drop off site. He thought it unusual and gave it to Isabella this morning."

"It looks like it could be a lady's handkerchief," suggested Peter. "There's no lace but it's very fine linen. It could be a clue, or just a red herring."

"I do need to speak to Isabella about the rendezvous," Everett made the point again. "Can you keep working on the castle's layout and potential observation points?"

Peter and Lord Drayton both nodded. "As soon as Penelope returns, she can assist us," replied Peter.

Everett left the drawing room and went to look for Isabella. He found her in the small morning room looking through correspondence.

"I'm glad I found you," he told Isabella, "there's something I need to discuss with you."

The memory of a shared embrace the previous evening stood between them, and to avoid any awkwardness Everett spoke a little more formally than usual.

"I'm listening," Isabella told him. He noticed momentary confusion in her eyes and wondered if it was due to the formality of his tone.

"It's about the rendezvous this evening. I don't believe you should go alone."

"I won't be alone, Penelope will be with me," Isabella's tone was a little cold.

"I'd like to go with you, hide myself somewhere in the castle. I know it well, and I could even hide up the chimney."

"Absolutely not," Isabella told him.

Everett was taken aback. "What do you mean?"

Isabella's reply was insistent. "I mean that I shall go alone and follow those instructions exactly. I'll take Penelope as my maid, but no one else."

"You can't possibly..."

"You heard Lady Moreton. If you accompany me, and they discern your presence then they might hurt Lawrence. I cannot have that guilt on my shoulders."

"Isabella, listen to me. This is dangerous. I don't want you to go alone," he pleaded, but with the chill of certainty that she would not listen to him.

"I don't think you have any say in the matter, Everett. If I choose to go alone, you can't stop me. If you try to follow me…"

He recognized the expression on her face and knew that he'd failed to convince her. The unspoken words frightened him.

"I'm the local magistrate," he protested, desperately searching for something else to say.

"Everett, this is my betrothed. The man I will marry in three weeks' time. His life may be in danger, and I have the chance to save him. I must do this."

"It's too great a risk," he persisted, feeling quite desperate.

What has gone wrong with our communication, last night they had been so close, he'd thought there could be a chance of a future together. Today it had all changed. The connection between them seemed weaker somehow.

"My mind is made-up. I'd never forgive myself if you accompanied me and that led to them hurting Lawrence, or you. You have to understand this."

"I blame Lady Moreton for this. She's clearly distraught not considering others," Everett was struggling to understand her.

"I don't disagree, but she did say it, and it has stayed in my head. I need to go alone. Penelope will be close to me at all times. Peter and you won't be far away, but not close enough to endanger Lawrence."

"I can't believe you're doing this. It makes no sense."

"We are going to have to disagree," Isabella told him, a note of absolute determination in her voice.

And with that she curtsied, walk towards the door and left the room.

He stared after her in disbelief.

Everett didn't know what to say or do. Everything came crashing down around him.

She's doing this to save Lawrence. She must still care for him. I thought there was something between us, but it's gone. I said the wrong thing; I didn't involve her as a partner in decision making, instead I tried to direct her and as a result of my clumsiness I've lost her.

***

Twilight cast long shadows across the ancient stone walls of the keep. Everett forced himself to stay back at a distance, watching as Isabella approached the castle ruins. Once again he could see the leather pouch containing the ransom money held in her gloved hands.

The temperature had risen, and a strange wind whistled through the forest and through the crumbling archways of the medieval fortress.

From their strategic position surrounding the ruins Everett, Peter, the sergeant and Lord Drayton kept watch, making sure they remained concealed behind broken walls and overgrown thicket, well away from Isabella.

I will not allow harm to reach her, Everett promised silently, still devastated by the barrier between them.

Isabella hadn't spoken to him since their conversation this morning. It's seemed as though he didn't exist anymore. He had been wrong to think there was a chance of a future for them. She seemed determined to marry Lawrence.

Everett distracted himself by considering the kidnapping. *There's something very wrong here. I've missed something. I know I have. There are definite similarities between the writing and the ransom notes and the way Lawrence forms certain letters.*

He had shared his concerns with Peter and Penelope. Penelope would be closest to Isabella, and he needed her to be aware that there were suspicions around Lawrence.

Everett hoped he was wrong, but this whole kidnapping scenario has been filled with inconsistencies, and these bizarre ransom exchanges. The sites had all been carefully chosen and suggesting coordination by someone with local knowledge, but no experience in kidnapping.

He tried to imagine the sort of criminals who might stage this type of crime and kept coming back to it being one of Lawrence's creditors, working with someone who had close knowledge of Drayton Park.

He wanted to be closer to Isabella, he could hardly breath with fear for her safety, even though it was clear she no longer wanted him, and her course was set for a life with Lawrence.

Chapter 26

Throughout the day, thoughts of Everett and that strained conversation haunted her.

He must surely understand, I can't forsake Lawrence at this point. I have to do everything I can to ensure his safe return to his mother.

Yet the memory of the look in his eyes, when she had told him that she wouldn't accept his protection during the handover at the castle, made her feel sick with sadness.

I wanted to say, 'yes come with me, never leave my side, I can't do this without you,' but I couldn't. Even though he's lied to me my first loyalty still has to be with Lawrence.

Penelope walked a few feet behind, once again wearing the dress and bonnet of a maid. The dark shape of the ruined castle rose up before her, and her feet faltered as they crossed the moat, filled with thorns and hawthorn bushes. The castle itself was covered with creeping ivy, and Isabella knew it had been abandoned ever since Drayton park had been built three hundred years before. Her ancestors had inhabited this ruined keep, and she knew it well from playing here as a child.

We were always searching for a secret passageway or a dungeon, Isabella remembered. Today it looked like a gothic castle out of one of a gothic writer's novels. In fact, she thought there was a handover of ransom and a heroine at the climax of one of Radcliffe's books. So much about her novels seem relevant to this situation. She did feel she was living in a gothic novel plot.

The storm hadn't broken, only the occasional drop of rain from a dark sky filled with thick gray storm clouds. Isabella heard scuttling sounds around her and shuddered, hoping what she could only think were rodents, would stay away from her. Penelope drew closer. "Did you hear that?" she whispered.

Isabella nodded and squeezed her friend's hand for re-assurance.

Their footsteps echoed loudly as they crossed the stone courtyard leading to the main entrance of the keep. "Take care," Isabella whispered, "there are lots of cracks in the stone and it's very uneven."

Isabella took a deep breath and crossed the threshold of the deserted castle. She must have startled a nest of crows, as they rose above, their cawing sounding like laughter in the darkness.

"It's all right," she told them. "I mean you no harm.'

This has to be the final payment. We're following the instructions exactly, and there must surely be an end to this.

Once she was in the great hall of the castle the instructions told her to move towards the central chamber. She gasped, noticing more fallen columns than when she'd visited last time, perhaps ten years ago. The alcoves were perfect for concealment, and she looked around wondering if the kidnapper would emerge from one of them.

For a moment Isabella saw the central chamber as it would have been in medieval days with sconces lighting the walls, and a large fire in the hearth.

She stood still, trying to muster confidence and dignity, wondering if she needed to progress any further, or if the kidnapper would find her here.

The sound of a barn owl crying, the rush of the river, and the scuttling of mice and rats in the corners of the castle were all around her. Yet it felt eerily silent.

It's the silence of waiting for something to happen, she thought to herself, shuddering with fear. *I hope I don't look as scared as I feel. I need to stay quietly confident,* she told herself.

Isabella felt a sudden change in the air flow in the ruined chamber. Something was different.

A shadowy figure emerged from a darkened corner, and she kept her gaze steadily on the figure walking towards her.

Could it be? It was. It had to be Lawrence. She gasped, and tried to call his name, but found she had no voice.

This was a different Lawrence, disheveled and dirty, his once immaculate clothing torn and an unshaven face. He seemed confused and unable to see in the darkness as he called her name. "Isabella?"

"I'm here Lawrence, over here," Isabella called, forcing calmness into her voice.

Even at a distance she could see his face showing relief at her arrival.

She walked towards him, wondering why she didn't run and fling herself into his arms. They've never had that sort of relationship, and she couldn't actually recall him touching her except in the formality of a dance.

Still they were betrothed, and he'd clearly been through an ordeal, so she kept moving quietly towards him.

"Are you hurt?" she mouthed.

He shook his head. "No, but I'll be glad of a hot bath," he told her.

She smiled knowing this ordeal was over.

"You haven't left the ransom purse", hissed Penelope. "You have to put it in the hearth."

Penelope was right she had forgotten to put the leather purse in their designated place.

She took a step backwards and turned to the huge stone chimney, built so many centuries before.

She faltered, almost stumbling, as a masked, cloaked figure appeared from behind a broken wall. The figure held a pistol, pointed directly towards Lawrence's back.

Isabella froze, feet rooted to the ground and in that moment, it seemed as though time had stood still.

What was happening here? It wasn't like the other rendezvous. She felt nervous, taking air from shallow breaths, determined not to show the fear she felt.

Even in the midst of danger her analytical mind kept processing the scene around her. Something seemed strange.

Lawrence's bonds appeared loose, hanging by his side, despite his being held in captivity. The masked figure holding the gun must surely be the kidnapper who'd kept him in captivity for several days. Why loosen his bonds but still need to point a pistol at his back?

It flashed into her mind that Lawrence's position suggested a stage arrangement rather than genuine imprisonment. She didn't like the direction her thoughts were taking her.

She had to believe in Lawrence. He had no idea a pistol was pointing at him, or did he.

She needed to do something quickly. She cried out and bent over, as if in pain. This distracted the figure with the pistol, as their body language showed sudden confusion.

In that instant Isabella lunged forward, pushing the shadowy figure off balance with unexpected force knocking the pistol out of his hand. Penelope ran forward and grabbed the gun, and stood holding it in the direction of the kidnapper.

The figure lay on the floor, struggling to get up. Isabella pushed the kidnapper backwards again, towards the rough stone floor and then reached forward to pull back the masked figure's hood.

She gasped in surprise. This was a woman. In one movement she tore off the mask and heard a cry of dismay as she revealed the face of Lady Lillian Whitby, Lady Moreton, writhing in agony on the floor.

"This isn't how it looks," Lady Moreton croaked.

"I'm glad to see you have recovered from the hysteria and illness you've been suffering during recent days," Isabella said coldly.

She heard a noise behind her, and turned sideways, so she could continue to watch Lady Moreton.

Lawrence stood there; his hands free of restraint. *How strange, he's looking at his mother with anger rather than surprise.*

"Lawrence run quickly," cried Lillian Whitby. "The game's up, our cover is ruined. Grab that scheming minx. We need to restrain her," Lady Moreton continued barking out orders to her son.

"You may as well let us go," Lady Moreton said, directing her attention towards Isabella. "You're ruined now, along with our family. No one will ever be sure whether you were involved in this scheme or not, and I'll make sure I damn you with my last breath."

Isabella ignored her. "Stay where you are, Lady Moreton. This castle is surrounded by my people. You won't get away this time."

"I shall also waste no time in telling certain people in high places about your obvious attraction to Viscount Kennington. You showed none of the grace and manners of a young lady of *the ton*, and I'll make sure you're ostracized, even if I have to do that from a prison cell. The scandal sheets will follow you for months, there will be no escape."

"I care not for my reputation, but I intend for Lawrence and you to answer charges relating to fraudulent deception and extortion."

Lawrence stepped towards her carrying the rope that he'd used for his own staged bonds.

He looks so different; the carefully cultivated charm has disappeared. This man is evil. How could I have not seen it?

"Come with us, Isabella. As Mama said, you're ruined now. Join us on the continent or in America. You'll still have access to your fortune, and we're prepared to live with you as a ruined young lady."

He really believes I might go with them. This is insanity.

"Why Lawrence, why?" Isabella asked. "Help me to understand." Isabella chose her words carefully so he might think she was considering his suggestion of joining them.

"Our plan was always simple, a false kidnapping, followed by a controlled marriage giving us access to your inheritance. You would live quietly at Moreton House. We would give you a few plants to keep you happy, and we'd occasionally let you out into society so no one would guess that you were fully under our control."

Isabella couldn't help it, the words just spilled out. "That's despicable. You not only put me through the trauma of the last few days, but you returned prepared to marry me, before making me a captive in your home. A lifetime of imprisonment as your wife."

"There are worse fates," Lawrence replied, shrugging.

Isabella left it a moment too late, as he reached for her wrists, ready to restrain her. "Come quietly, it will be easier for you," he hissed.

"Stand back, Moreton", came Everett's voice, speaking with quiet but unmistakable authority. "You are both under the grip of the law."

Lady Moreton began to laugh. "You have to let us leave, or we'll hurt Isabella."

The ruins were still and quiet. Isabella could see her uncle, Peter, and a constable blocking each exit.

Lady Moreton looked surprised at the men's arrival. "You didn't follow the instructions," she accused Isabella.

Isabella smiled at her. "Oh, I obeyed them to the letter, it's just that everybody else ignored them."

Lady Moreton turned backwards, retreating to the archway. "Move out of my way," she commanded as Penelope blocked her path.

"You need to surrender," Penelope spoke with quiet firmness, holding the pistol steadily. "You won't get past me."

When Lady Moreton stepped forward, Penelope pushed her, and the once formidable lady of the *ton* tumbled to the stone floor.

Two constables took hold of her arms and guided her forwards on her journey to prison.

Penelope came to take Isabella's arm. They stood huddled together watching Lawrence attempt to justify his actions.

"I was forced to this by my mother," he claimed. "She's quite insane, and I had to do exactly as she told me."

"That's the most ridiculous thing I've ever heard", responded Isabella, stepping forward, fury in her face. "Everything about this scheme was coordinated and planned. Surely, you've got the decency to admit failure, rather than desperately justifying your actions."

"No one's been hurt," Lawrence continued. "You have to understand that I had no choice. I needed money to pay off my gambling debts."

"And did you ever have any regard for me?" Isabella asked with curiosity.

"All I could think of were my creditors, and as soon as we married, I'd have access to your inheritance. You were a way that I could keep my estate and good name in society."

"I see. I could call you all sorts of names Lawrence, but you're not worth the breath."

The constables guiding Lady Moreton stopped when she began to shriek at her son.

"I was forced into this by my son. You all know how ill I've been. I had no choice but to follow his instructions."

How sad. They devised this scheme together, and now they're turning on each other to minimize their own role.

Isabella realized that there couldn't have been any love between them. Lady Moreton prepared to send her son to the gallows or transportation. At the same time, he insisted that his mother was the evil genius behind the scheme. What they did know is that they were both in it together. They were equally guilty.

Everett signaled for the constables to remove them, despite their continued protests and accusations which fell on deaf ears. Everyone in the building could see the deception and devious nature of their planning.

Lady Moreton is carrying on as if she's a grotesque character in a comic opera, thought Isabella. She shuddered, glad to be rid of them.

After they had been led away Isabella just stood there, rooted to the spot in stunned silence.

I could have married him. Once married, she realized with chilling clarity, she'd have been totally under their control. This was evil indeed.

She looked around for Everett, but he'd already left with the constables. He hadn't even spoken to her.

***

Drayton Park was a beacon of light. The household staff had placed lanterns on the terrace, and candles were lit in all the windows

Isabella took a seat in the drawing room, with Penelope and Clarissa, making their statements to the sergeant. A sorry tale of a false kidnapping and attempted extortion.

Uncle Henry stayed close beside her as she gave her story, describing each ransom drop and the inconsistencies which formed a clear pattern, revealing Lawrence and Lady Moreton's elaborate scheme.

Miss Dymchurch looked exhausted and in a state of shock. "I had no idea, please believe me I had no idea," she kept repeating. "I knew they had financial difficulties, but not the extent of them."

"It's all right, Althea," reassured Uncle Henry. "We're all sorry that you had to be a companion to such a dreadful woman for so many years"

Isabella's calm composure showed none of the emotional turmoil under the surface at discovering her betrothed's true character. She kept her dignity while giving her formal statement, glad that it would help prevent the evil pair from preying on others in the future.

Uncle Henry stood up and clapped his hands. "I know it's late, but we should keep our strength up, so I've asked cook to set out a collation in the dining room." He turned to his niece. "Words cannot express how thankful I am that you've escaped a disastrous marriage. I never really liked him."

Isabella gasped in surprise. "Uncle Henry I had no idea."

"Oh, Hermes never took to him. In my opinion a spaniel can determine someone's character more easily than we humans can. I should have cautioned against the match, but you've always been your own woman, and Lawrence seemed to be saying the right things about supporting your research."

He took her arm in his and patted it gently. "Next time anyone comes courting you, Isabella, they will have to get Hermes approval before you can proceed" he added laughing.

She looked across the room to see Hermes standing next to Everett, who patted the dog's back, while it looked up at him adoringly. She felt tightness and regret that things had broken down between them. He hadn't spoken to her since returning, and she had convinced herself that he'd turned away from her, when she'd rejected him again by refusing his protection.

"There's been so much sadness," said Penelope. "Let's partake of this sumptuous collation and retire to bed. However, tomorrow I propose that we have a musical recital here between ourselves. Poor Clarissa, it's been such a dismal start to her coming out into local society. We shall have a supper gathering, singing, and maybe, if uncle will allow it, a little dancing.

"I shall play the pianoforte," offered Miss Dymchurch.

"That would be lovely thank you," Penelope smiled at her.

"Not for every dance though," said Uncle Henry. "I expect you to dance at least three sets with me, Althea."

Well done, Penelope, Isabella thought. *You're bringing us back to normal life, with a little society and happiness.*

Everett excused himself from the cold collation, and said he had to go to the library to work on paperwork as the local magistrate. "I'll take a plate in the library if that's alright," he told Uncle Henry and disappeared.

I feel as if my heart has cracked and is shattering like tiny pieces of porcelain, but I know I'm exhausted. I could have been kinder to Everett, rather than objecting to his plan. I only have myself to blame for this barrier between us.

Isabella remembered the thicket growing in the moat of the deserted castle. That's how it felt between them now, an impenetrable thicket with no way through.

Chapter 27

Everett remembered the sight of Isabella lunging towards Lady Moreton as she waved a pistol in the air.

She'd incapacitated the baroness, but she could have been killed in the process.

He didn't know what to say to her and also tell her how sorry he felt that Lawrence had used her so abominably.

He felt strange after their sharp words earlier that day, and he knew he needed to protect himself from further rejection.

Everett pushed the last piece of paper onto a pile, ready to send to the assizes in Hertford. His only concern was that he felt Lady Moreton was mentally deranged. She must have lost her mind to behave the way she did, and risk everything by spinning a web of false kidnapping and extortion. He hoped she would be placed in an asylum, rather than a women's prison, although neither prospect was appealing.

As for Lawrence, he didn't care what happened to the disgraced Baron, but, putting aside his personal feelings, he still hoped Lord Lawrence Whitby would face transportation.

The person who had suffered most from their scheme had been Isabella. Her betrothed had disappeared, and she had been subject to several traumatic handovers of ransom money. He felt angry that the evil pair had always stipulated that Isabella had to deliver the leather purse to the chosen site. He could see no reason for that and could never excuse that behavior.

Everett's thoughts drifted to Isabella. She'd stood with dignity while her betrothal and future collapsed around her. He remembered her fierce words of loyalty for Lawrence, and how she wouldn't abandon him while held in captivity by his kidnappers.

His breath caught as he remembered holding her close in an embrace the previous night. He would treasure that memory always. He would leave for his own estate tomorrow and give her time to adjust to changed circumstances. There would be much tittle tattle in *ton* society, but she had nothing to fear as she had been blameless and an innocent victim of two scheming criminals.

Everett felt a light tap on the door and, as it opened, he saw Clarissa's face smiling at him.

"Have you finished your administration," Clarissa asked, coming to join him at the table.

"It's all done," he told her. "We can forget about them until their trial."

"Poor Isabella, and Miss Dymchurch," exclaimed Clarissa. "They both have to come to terms with trusting people who had no concern for their welfare."

"I still can't quite believe that Lillian Whitby, Lady Moreton, was a master criminal, but I saw the evidence with my own eyes."

"So, brother, it looks as though Peter and Penelope will announce their betrothal within days, and if I'm not mistaken, I sense there may be wedding bells in the future for Lord Drayton and Miss Dymchurch."

Everett smiled. "All deserve a happy ever after. I'm glad for them. You really think Lord Drayton and Miss Dymchurch will marry?"

"It's been lovely watching the romance between them evolve. I predict a wedding within a year."

Everett sat back in his chair and closed his eyes feeling incredibly tired.

"And what of you Everett?"

Everett looked at her and smiled. "I plan to take a spaniel from Lord Drayton's litter. That's all the company I need."

"Incorrigible brother! I meant will you make Isabella an offer?"

He looked at her, his expression serious. "She doesn't want me, Clarissa. I offered her protection this morning and we had sharp words. I didn't feel she should enter that ruined castle alone and she disagreed with me."

"Oh Everett, of course she did. She's a young lady of grace and favour. She's betrothed to a man who's been kidnapped. His mother is insisting that she follows the directives of the kidnappers absolutely. None of us were to know that the mother was, in fact, a kidnapper. Isabella would have felt disloyal if she'd gone against Lady Moreton's wishes."

Everett looked at his sister, such wisdom in one so young. "Well, when you put it like that, I can see how torn Isabella must have been."

"She loves you. It's obvious with every glance. Do you love her?"

"I've always loved her, ever since I was about nineteen years old. I asked her to marry me then and she said no."

"Oh Everett this is hopeless. I'm almost the same age as Isabella was then. How would you feel if I told you I was to marry next month?"

"I would tell you I wouldn't allow it, and that you needed at least one season in town first."

"So what's different? I certainly haven't worked out how I feel about life, marriage, or any of those things. I'm enjoying being out in society here, although that's proving a little more dangerous than I expected; and I'm looking forward to my season in town in the spring."

"Oh Clarissa, I've been a fool, haven't I?"

"No, just a little hurt pride when your plan to protect Isabella was turned down earlier today. I'm sure you can overcome hurt pride, brother."

Everett smiled at her. "If I can overcome being wounded in the war, I can overcome a little piqued pride."

"Talk to her soon, don't leave it too long."

"I'll think about it," he said quietly.

"I don't know if I want you to have a double wedding with Peter and Penelope. It would be lovely, but I'd only have one bridesmaid gown," Clarissa said giving him an impish grin.

"You're way ahead of yourself, sister. At the moment Isabella and I are hardly on speaking terms. You've more chance of a wedding between Miss Dymchurch and Lord Drayton."

"I'm a romantic, I believe in happy endings. I know that as soon as you talk with Isabella everything shall be well," Clarissa told him as she went out through the door

"I wish I had your confidence," he said as she left the room.

***

Everett tossed and turned all night, Clarissa's words echoing in his mind.

Was it possible he could have a second chance with Isabella? It was all he wanted. He'd thought he should leave and return to his estate, and carry on with life without her. He knew though that it would be an empty life.

He got up and dressed early, going down to the stable to ride in the early morning mist. He wasn't surprised when he found himself at the lake. The rowing boat was on the pebble beach, and he remembered that rather idyllic moment in the forest clearing.

They could get back to that, surely? He loved Isabella, and he knew there was a strong connection between them.

Everett tethered his horse to a tree, and walked to the edge of the lake. He chose a stone with a flat surface, held it in his hand, and then released it to skim across the lake. It bounced across the water, causing ripples as it moved towards the center out of sight, before dropping below the surface.

Suddenly, he heard the sound of a horse's hooves approaching. Could that be Peter looking for him?

He walked back to greet the rider, surprised at the sight of Isabella on her bay horse. She looked equally surprised to see him.

Would she ride on or stay and talk? He hardly knew, as he watched her approach.

Isabella slowed her horse to a walk and then stopped beside him. He moved forward to offer her assistance in dismounting, and she smiled down at him. His heart felt warm, and his pulse began to race, as he helped her ease down to the ground. He took Melody's bridle and tethered the bay mare to a tree as well.

Isabella stood there, in her midnight blue riding habit, and hat with a jaunty feather. He knew in that instant that he needed her in his life.

I need to repair my clumsy words and frustration of yesterday.

"Everett, I'm so sorry I had no idea I'd find you here. I often ride by the lake in the morning. I find it clears my head, and this morning I really needed fresh air. I like to look at the water. The mist is clearing, but it often has an ethereal look on days like today."

Everett offered her his arm, and they walked together to the pebble beach where the stones crunched beneath their feet.

"There's something about being close to water. I find it incredibly relaxing," continued Isabella. Everett had yet to say a word, unsure how to behave.

"You would love the coastline and sea in Portugal," was the first thing that came to his mind.

"At your estate there?"

"Yes, it's close to the sea, you can smell the salt in the air." He wanted to take her there and walk along the beach in the warmth of the Portuguese sun.

Everett took a deep breath, hoping that his words weren't too clumsy. "I don't think I've made things any easier for you," he began. "I should have understood more about why you wanted to follow the kidnappers' directions and go into that castle without me."

Isabella began to walk towards the lake's edge, looking out towards the hills in the distance.

Everett continued. "I am sorry, Isabella. I should have listened to you and let you follow the path you needed to take."

"You usually do that, Everett. I know it was out of love and concern for my safety that you couldn't accept that I needed to go into that castle without you."

He felt hope rising. *She understands. For once I've managed to explain how I feel.*

"I still can't believe Lawrence deceived me that way. When they talked about how they would treat me after marriage I felt numb inside. I thought we at least had respect and affection between us. I misread the situation. I was totally wrong about his character."

"They set out to entrap you. Lawrence knew how important your research and field studies are to you. By saying he would support your work he made himself stand out from other men. He caught your attention."

"You're right. I knew we didn't love each other, but I thought that enough of love might follow, or at least companionship to make for a contented life."

"I'm sorry. They treated you despicably."

"Yet I didn't marry him. I'm free, and I've had a lucky escape." Isabella paused, gazing out at the lake shimmering pearl-like in the morning sunshine. "The mist has cleared and it's going to be a beautiful day," she murmured.

"I feel free this morning, as if a weight has been lifted from my shoulders. I don't think I have felt this light spirited since I lost my father and brother. I believe I may find some peace today, a sort of calm after the storm."

"You deserve it, although Penelope and Peter's plans for a musical recital mean we will no doubt have a late night."

"I'm looking forward to it. Everything has been so dismal and dull while we waited to see if Lawrence would return safely. Shall you sing a duet with me?" Everett asked.

"Of course," she said smiling up into his eyes. His pulse raced, and he felt a tingling charge of anticipation and excitement coursing through his veins. "Uncle was right." Isabella added.

"How so? Did he dislike Lawrence?"

"I don't think he had strong feelings. He didn't discourage me from entering into the betrothal. What he says about Hermes not liking Lawrence is true, but he never mentioned that till last night. It's one of his jests."

"But his view changed?"

"Yes, he saw how unhappy I'd become, and he sensed a closeness between you and me. He told me I needed to consider my choices when Lawrence returned. I believe the extent of the gambling debts shocked my uncle."

"I wonder if he would approve of me," mused Everett.

"Oh absolutely, Hermes adores you." Isabella laughed.

Everett joined in with her laughter. "I agree with your uncle, spaniels are an excellent judge of character."

"It's such an idyllic day after the rain and cold of yesterday. It's as though we've stepped into summer again."

Everett looked at Isabella. "I want to say something, but I have a fear if you do not like what I have to say I risk our friendship. I'm going to be brave and say what I need to."

"Then I shall listen carefully to your words," Isabella said quietly.

"You know that you've had a place in my heart ever since that summer when I asked you to marry me. Even then, it just felt as though we were right together. I don't think I had even realised what love was then. But I should never have asked you. I could easily have waited until you'd had that season in town, danced a few waltzes with handsome young men."

"I was rather looking forward to the season," admitted Isabella. "You did rather take me by surprise that day."

Everett continued, hoping he was doing the right thing. "I don't know when my feelings for you changed, Isabella. We were friends who had adventures, got into scrapes together, then one day I looked at you and it felt different, I had this strange sensation that I never wanted us to be apart.

"Oh, Everett I know that feeling. I would never want to smother you with affection, but I'm happiest when I'm with you."

Everett smiled hearing her words. "Something has developed between us, a deep connection which I believe is still there."

Isabella nodded, holding his hand a little tighter.

"When I met you again on the eve of that ball, I suppressed my feelings as you were betrothed to Lawrence," admitted Everett.

"How strange that we should meet again at my betrothal ball."

"As we spent time together this week, I knew I still loved you. The pain of you being promised to Lawrence was almost unbearable."

"I never loved him; it really was an arrangement of convenience."

"I have this certainty that we should be together. We're not the same in our approach to life or our thinking but, I believe we complement each other very well indeed."

A light breeze ruffled the surface of the water, and the leaves whispered around them.

Isabella moved closer, the physical distance between them diminishing, and Everett sensed the emotional barrier between them disintegrate completely.

Isabella smiled up at him reassuringly. "I knew that I loved you the moment I saw you arrive for the ball. I never hoped to see you again, when you walked into the great hall, I promise you that my heart leaped. I can't describe it otherwise."

"You hid it very well," Everett grinned as he told her.

"I had to, I suppressed it and pushed it away because I was pledged to Lawrence. Then he disappeared, and as each day passed you gave me the support I needed. I saw a man who reminded me of the boy I'd loved all those years ago but was now so much more." Isabella paused, looking up at some geese flying across the lake.

"You made me feel valued, Everett. Lawrence never did. He listened to what I had to say, but he never acted as though we were partners with equal influence over which direction to take. I believe that's why I was upset yesterday, because in your anxiety you were telling me what to do, and that isn't how it usually is between us."

"I misjudged that badly," admitted Everett. "I thought I'd lost you again. I have to say this, I'd rather spend my life alone than with someone who isn't you."

She's listening, she hasn't turned me down yet. I hardly dare hope.

"Oh Everett, I feel the same. When you held me in your arms after the failed ransom exchange, I had this strong sensation of coming home. Your embrace offered sanctuary, and I wanted to stay sheltered there forever."

He took both her hands in his, and she responded until their fingers intertwined with a natural ease, both feeling that strong magnetic pull of the connection between them. Everett freed one hand and gently traced a line down her cheek.

"I wish I could give you flowers," he said impulsively. "If it were the summer, I could pick you a scented rose and hand it to you. You would smile at me, and all would be well with the world."

"I love all flowers you know, so no need to restrict yourself to roses," Isabella jested with him. "I'm happy to wait for the summer for roses, but there is lots of beauty in the countryside in winter. You can pick me a Christmas rose. We have them growing in the forest here."

"I can do better than that," Everett said suddenly. "Close your eyes, Isabella."

She looked at him in surprise.

"Humour me. Close your eyes."

"Very well," she murmured, a little nervously.

He knew exactly what he looked for and found it within yards, at the edge of the beach. He bent to pick the blooms and returned to her with his wild posy.

"Here you are. Flowers found during a day in early November. There is no flower more resilient, flowering during most of the months of the year than this tiny, silvery plant."

She opened her eyes and looked at the posy in delight. "Of course, daisies. I overlook them as they are with us so much of the year and grow wild in so many places. Garstang, our gardener, always wants to pull them up, but I stop him whenever I catch him doing that."

"They remind me of you, the strength beneath fragility." He took a deep breath and knelt before her. "I love you, Isabella. I know this is unseemly, and we should wait, as your betrothal to Lawrence only ended a few hours ago, but will you marry me? I hardly dare hope."

He'd asked her to marry him before, all those years ago, and she'd been unable to accept his proposal. This time Isabella smiled with delight. "I wish you'd asked me again, all those years ago. I tossed and turned all that night and knew I should have accepted. I loved you then."

Isabella looked at Everett, tears glistening in her eyes. "You never asked me again, and I thought I'd missed my chance of happiness."

She pulled him to his feet. "Yes, yes and yes again. If I've learned anything it is to value love and seize it when it appears in life."

He raised her hand to his lips and gently kissed each finger.

"I love you Viscount Kennington," she gasped, as he pulled her into his embrace.

"And I love you Miss Drayton, soon to be Viscountess Kennington."

"There will be talk," she warned him. "I'll understand if you wish to reconsider."

Everett laughed. "Hush, I can't believe you've accepted me. I'm the happiest of men. I care nothing for *ton* gossip."

She smiled up into his eyes. "And we will be happy," she told him with certainty.

"I'd thought to live in Portugal once Clarissa is married and settled. I can change my plans, so you can keep compiling that encyclopedia."

"Oh, the research is done. I just need to write up my notes." Isabella smiled. "I believe having an artist for a husband might even enhance my book."

"So that's why you accepted me," he said laughing.

"Well, I took it into consideration," she told him with mock seriousness.

As the last strands of mist cleared from the lake, and the wintery sun rose in the sky he lowered his head to hers. She closed her eyes and met his kiss, sighing as his lips closed over hers, and the connection which joined them became stronger with every second that passed.

Chapter 28

They rode back to Drayton Park together, leaving their horses in the stables. Isabella looked at Everett. "I really need to tell Uncle Henry about this."

Everett smiled back. "I believe I too need to speak with your uncle. We should do things in the proper way."

"I'm not sure there is anything proper about ending a betrothal and then entering into another one in less than twenty-four hours," laughed Isabella.

"I can hold back and court you for several months if you prefer?" Everett said playfully.

"You know that such a course shall not suffice for us."

"And I'm not sure I have the strength for that," he laughed again, before kissing her gently, with the promise of more kisses very soon.

They both startled as Maisie's face appeared in the doorway.

"Oh Miss, I'm so sorry," she said quietly. "I needed to speak with you about something and thought I might catch you returning from the stables."

"It's all right Maisie," Isabella reassured her. "You can't say anything yet, as Uncle Henry doesn't know, but Lord Kennington has asked me to marry him."

"I can tell you've accepted him." Maisie's excitement covered her face. "I knew you belonged together. I told Mrs. Finchley it wouldn't be long before we had news."

"Maisie, really. You've all been gossiping about me?" Isabella's pretended to be shocked.

"Of course, Miss. We all want you to be happy. No one liked Lord Moreton. He was, in my opinion, a short tempered, arrogant man, and as for his mother …"

Isabella collapsed into peals of laughter. "I didn't know it was possible to feel this happy," she told Everett. "Speak to my uncle soon, or everyone will know from my face that something is different."

"There is something I needed to tell you about," said Maisie. "We'd all forgotten her, and it's very unfortunate."

"Who Maisie? Who have we forgotten?"

"Madame Annette, Lady Moreton's lady's maid. She was upstairs waiting for her ladyship last night. It seems her ladyship had taken to retiring to bed and insisting she couldn't be disturbed. Madame had taken to sitting, waiting for her mistress to open the door, and last night she fell asleep outside her mistress' door."

"And we all forgot about her!" Isabella felt so sorry for the poor maid.

"She's in a terrible state Miss. Mrs. Finchley is with her. She has no money, and her family are in France. She's always kept herself to herself when they stayed here, but she's never been any bother."

"Very well, I'll speak with her. She can stay here as long as she chooses, but I don't need a lady's maid as I've got you."

"Oh Miss, really? I'm not like Madame. I just make do and have had no training."

"You do very well Maisie. It may be Penelope, or possibly Clarissa is in need of a maid. Has Clarissa got a maid?" she asked Everett.

"I hardly know," he replied with a dreamy expression in his eyes.

"Everett, you're miles away."

"I was remembering a walk by the lake. Now what is it you need to know?"

"Does Clarissa have a maid to help her dress and do her hair? She'll need one when she goes to town for the season."

"No, no one like Maisie," admitted Everett.

"Then that's a problem solved. She can stay here for now." Isabella looked at Maisie. "You don't believe she knew anything about Lady Moreton's scheming?"

"No, Miss, she's having the vapors in Mrs. Finchley's parlor. We all feel sorry for the poor lady."

"Very well, I shall go and speak with her."

And so life continued. She left Everett to go and speak with her Uncle Henry and went to calm down a distraught French lady's maid.

***

There was so much to think about. In a few short hours she'd gone from being betrothed to Lawrence, to discovering the truth about his scheme to embezzle her inheritance. Now there was the joy of that unexpected conversation with Everett.

He loves me, he always loved me. There's no point waiting several months for proprieties' sake. We both want to marry as soon as it can be arranged.

She spent most of the morning with Penelope and Clarissa preparing the evenings recital. They were so preoccupied with excitement that they didn't notice the glow of happiness around her.

She'd missed having conversations about which gown Penelope would wear, or what soup Cook should serve for supper. All that had stopped whilst the ordeal of Lawrence's kidnapping had been happening.

It's good to be back to normal, even if that means discussing what gown to wear, or what flowers to dress the table with at supper time.

After a quiet luncheon with Penelope and Clarissa she went to her chamber seeking a few minutes peace.

She lay on the bed, closing her eyes, as exhaustion overcame her, and she fell into a deep sleep. Maisie awoke her when she came to lay out her gown for the recital.

"What time is it?" Isabella asked in confusion.

"Six o'clock miss, and supper is a little earlier this evening to give more time for the recital."

"I've been asleep for hours." Isabella looked out of the window. "It's almost dark."

"You must have needed the sleep, Miss. Now, let's get you ready for this evening."

As Isabella walked down the main staircase Uncle Henry appeared in the great hall. He waited for her, smiling openly. "I'm glad to say, you look more like yourself again."

"I fell asleep uncle. If Maisie hadn't come to help me get ready for supper, then I believe I would have slept for hours".

"I've spoken with Everett," Uncle Henry told her quietly. "It's what you want my dear?"

"More than anything. It feels right."

"Very well. I've given him my permission. He seems to want to marry in the next few weeks. Are you sure you wouldn't rather wait?"

"I know it's a little unseemly, but after all that's happened it feels important to move on with life as soon as possible. There's just one problem," Isabella added smiling.

"Tell me. After all you've been through, I'm sure we can solve it."

"It's whether Everett has the approval of Hermes. You did say that was essential before you give your permission for me to marry anyone else."

"Oh, no worries on that front, my Dear. They are together now; they've walked down to the stables together."

Isabella laughed. "Then there are no obstacles in our way. We can share our news with family and close friends, but I'd prefer not to make an announcement for a couple of weeks until the fallout from this business with Lawrence and his mother has faded a little."

Uncle Henry offered her his arm. "Let's go to the drawing room and wait for the others. I need to decide which song I'm singing later."

Isabella had an idea. "How about a duet with, Miss Dymchurch?"

"I hope to sing many duets with that fine lady," admitted Uncle Henry. "You guessed?"

She nodded. "It was Penelope who noticed it first. We like Althea very much."

"I don't want to cause any more gossip around the family. At least one of us needs to consider the proprieties. I thought we could ask Miss Dymchurch to stay as your companion, and act as chaperone for Penelope and you. It will only need to be for a few weeks."

"That sounds an excellent idea. I'm very glad uncle. I can see Althea makes you happy."

"It seems a day for happy endings, my Dear. I almost had a queue of young men outside my study door asking for permission to marry."

"Peter and Penelope?"

"Indeed, and as Hermes approved, how could I say no?"

***

The music room looked magnificent in the evening. Candelabras lit every corner, and a log fire burned brightly in the hearth.

Clarissa and Penelope had organized every aspect of the evening, and they gathered in the music room after a sumptuous feast prepared by cook.

The surprise first act was Uncle Henry and Miss Dymchurch singing a duet regarding a misunderstanding between sweethearts. Fiery comedy filled the room, and Isabella realized she'd never seen her uncle look so animated.

Clarissa played and sang a song beautifully, and as she listened, Isabella realized that she would soon be her sister-in-law, and she might be the one to bring her out into society in the spring. *There is so much that has changed in the last twenty-four hours. I hope for a few calm days without incident.*

When Penelope took to the harp and began to play a beautiful lament, tears began to form in Isabella's eyes. As she played her friend's eyes drifted to Peter who gazed back entranced. When Clarissa finished the piece Peter walked across the room to join her, and as she stood, he took her hand.

"Some of you know, and I doubt this will be a surprise, but Miss Penelope Drayton has agreed to become my wife. Immediately everyone broke into a round of applause and cheering.

They look so happy, and how dreadful that Lawrence's scheming meant they had to wait to share their news with family. We needed a day with happiness, and there are no dark shadows in this room today.

Everett joined Isabella. "It's time for our duet."

"We haven't practiced," she protested.

"Everyone will sing along," Everett assured her. "Come on Isabella."

As they walked to the piano Uncle Henry intercepted them and turned to the assembled group. "I don't want this news to go beyond family and close friends until a week or two has passed but there is another betrothal to announce. My beloved niece Isabella has found happiness with Everett, Viscount Kennington. I don't know if there will be a double wedding, but it won't be long before the bells ring out over Drayton Church."

Applause again rang out and Isabella looked at Everett and knew she could lose herself in his eyes. "Happy?" he mouthed.

"Very much," she whispered back.

As Isabella played the introduction to their song she knew that loving Everett was all she needed in life. She trembled as he brushed against her to turn the page of the music. Tiny flames ignited within her as she played the familiar tune. She had found love and realized that she had almost settled for an empty marriage, and then how diminished her life would have been.

Everett leaned forward to turn the next page. "You look beautiful tonight, my love," he whispered in a voice only she could hear.

Penelope and Clarissa organized the taking up of the rug and dancing, and Miss Dymchurch began to play a reel.

"Come, let's get some cool air," Everett suggested, as he took Isabella's arm to guide her to the door.

Everett looked at her. "I need to apologise, Isabella."

Isabella looked back at him with momentary concern in her eyes.

Everett laughed as he told her. "I'm afraid I couldn't wait any longer to kiss you again. It's all I've thought about during the day."

She laughed as well as he traced a finger down the side of her cheek. The tiny flickers which had been building throughout the evening transformed into a strong flame. She could hardly breathe as he gently pulled her closer into his arms. Isabella gasped as his lips brushed hers gently. "I'm going to need to kiss you every day, every morning, afternoon, and evening. I plan to start and end every day with a kiss."

She smiled up at him, feeling that flow of happiness through her body. "I shall look forward to your kisses in winter, spring and summer."

"I think I prefer autumn kisses most of all," he whispered as his lips met hers and deepened the kiss.

"Shall we marry next month?" he asked, his voice full of emotion.

She rested her head against his shoulder. "I don't think we should wait. I don't believe I need a betrothal ball, but I admit I'd like a midwinter ball on the day of our wedding."

"As long as I dance with you."

"Every dance is yours," she promised.

I love you Isabella,"

"And I love you, Everett."

The music of a country reel, combined with the laughter of their family and friends, sounded in the background. Isabella and Everett stood in harmonious silence, holding hands while gazing at a sky bright with autumn stars.

Epilogue

Six weeks later ...

"Come along," said Althea Dymchurch. "We should leave for the church in Drayton in half an hour.

"I can't believe I'm getting married today," said Penelope dreamily.

"Can I help you with your bonnet and veil?" asked Clarissa. "I'm ready, and so is Althea. The household staff are leaving in a few minutes to walk to the church."

Penelope shook her head. "Madame won't let anyone else do anything. She's gone to find a different curling iron. She isn't happy with my hair."

"Well, she needs to hurry," said Clarissa.

"Oh, I don't think anything can make Madame hurry," laughed Penelope.

Miss Dymchurch looked around. "Maisie, where's your mistress?"

"She's gone to fetch the flowers. She's prepared fragrant posies for us to all carry. She says it's an ancient tradition which should be revived."

Miss Dymchurch sighed in frustration. "She needs to hurry as well. Can you go and find her?"

Maisie dashed out of the room and almost careered into Uncle Henry who stood waiting outside the door.

"I'm so sorry, my Lord," Maisie said, her voice more flustered than usual.

"Make haste and if you're looking for Isabella then she's in the conservatory. I believe I'll return to my study. It doesn't look as if you young ladies are anywhere close to being ready yet."

The two veils lay ready for the brides. Isabella had decorated the silk covered bonnets with yellow roses for Penelope and white roses on her own. Penelope picked up her bonnet and held it up to the mirror.

"Non, non, non," came a shriek from the doorway. You must not touch those until the last minute. I will, myself, pin your bonnet.

"Of course, Madame. I didn't think." Penelope quickly put the veil back down.

"It is quite usual for a bride to be unable to think in the hour before her wedding. I shall forgive you," said the petite French maid who had already found a place in their hearts.

Isabella arrived back, closely followed by Maisie. "The flowers are ready downstairs. We should be leaving soon."

"We shall leave in ten minutes," Madame informed them. "As soon as I have dealt with Miss Penelope's unruly hair."

Isabella looked around at the scene of chaotic happiness. *This is all that I want. I'm marrying Everett, and my family and friends all look so happy. Life has been very good to me.*

The shadow of Lawrence, Baron Moreton, had receded into the background. He'd been sentenced to transportation and may even have already left the country. Everett had intervened for Lady Moreton, and she would spend the rest of her days in an asylum for those who had lost their reason. He'd been to see her once and come back shocked at the change in her. She hadn't known who he was and just kept asking for her baby son. She had lost her mind, and perhaps that made her fate easier to bear.

"I felt rather sorry for her," he had told Isabella. "She wouldn't cope with prison or transportation. She'll be well cared for in the asylum in Bedford."

Miss Dymchurch hurried them along. "We really need to leave for the church."

Madame placed Penelope's bonnet on her head, and then Isabella's own bonnet.

"You both look beautiful," Madame told them, standing back and taking a long look to ensure everything was perfect.

Uncle Henry offered them his arms as they walked to the waiting carriage. Going through the main door, Isabella looked up into the sky. Snowflakes fell all around them.

"How romantic," cried Clarissa. "Whenever it snows you will both remember your wedding day."

They climbed into the carriage for the short drive to the village. Isabella felt tears forming in her eyes at the sight of the whole village waiting to greet them.

Each bride and bridesmaid held a posy of winter foliage, with rosemary, lavender, trailing ivy, and hot house roses. At the last-minute Isabella had tucked several daisies into her own posy, remembering the day when Everett had proposed.

As they entered the Church the violinist, who had impressed Penelope so much at the ball, began to play.

"I'm so happy I could burst with joy," whispered Penelope.

"So am I. We're both going to start the new year as married ladies."

Isabella looked ahead and saw Everett, who turned smiling, waiting for her to join him at the altar.

Her heart melted, and she walked forward to become Viscountess Kennington.

***

After the wedding feast the orchestra began to play gently. "I'm not sure I've got the energy to dance," confided Isabella to her husband.

"There is no escape my love, you promised to dance at least three waltzes with me."

"I have no idea how I could have been foolish enough to promise that," she laughed.

"First, come to the library, I have a gift for you," Everett told her.

As the heavy oak door closed behind them, he drew her into his arms, his lips finding hers, in eager anticipation of their wedding night. A leather-bound book lay on the table, and she reached for it, opening the pages before gasping at the contents.

'You've sketched our life so far," she said in wonder, tears forming in her eyes as she turned the pages. "Oh Everett, it's so special. Thank you."

The book contained sketches of their journey from childhood friendship to marriage. Each sketch captured moments they had shared. The day she discovered her first orchid, to the day he had proposed and given her daisies.

"It's our path to how we found each other. As she reached the end he pointed to a blank page.

These are the pages where I promise to illustrate our future life together as we create it day by day.

Isabella couldn't stop the tears racing down her cheeks.

"You can't cry, our guests will think you are sad and regretting our match," Everett chided her.

"I know, and I couldn't be happier."

"Let's show them how to waltz then."

With those words he raised her hands to his lips and offered his arm to return to the ballroom.

***

Kennington Manor
Eight months later...

It felt good to be home for the summer after a late spring break at Everett's estate in Portugal. Penelope had stepped in to chaperone Clarissa at the late season events, and they had set sail to visit the vineyards where Everett felt most at home.

When it had been time to leave Isabella hadn't wanted to make the voyage home. They would return in the Autumn and might stay all next winter at the Portuguese estate.

Now, re-united with family, they were happy to be back.

Today Kennington Manor welcomed guests for a very special celebration. The drawing room and the music room had been transformed into an art gallery showcasing Everett's first public exhibition. It also happened to be their eight-month wedding anniversary, and they were so glad to have found each other after all those years apart that they made a point of celebrating their anniversary every month of the year.

Golden afternoon light filtered through the oak tree branches as Isabella stood proudly beside Everett, close to the herb garden that had been recreated on Everett's estate to match the one at Drayton Park.

In the distance the lake glistened, and Clarissa had her wish there was now not only one rowing boat but two as every day since they returned Everett had rowed Isabella out to an island in the middle of the lake.

When they had set sail for Porto, work had already started on building an expanded conservatory at Kennington Manor. Isabella's botanical collection had found a new home in this expanded glass house. Her carefully catalogued specimens were displayed alongside Everett's botanical illustrations, as part of the art exhibition, and in combining her knowledge of plants with Everett's skills as an artist they had created a true fusion of science and art. She felt that warm glow as she listened to the admiration of their guests for her artist husband.

The rare orchid that they both remembered from their childhood days, and which had started Isabella on path to being a botanical expert, now bloomed in pride of place, a symbol of that long nurtured affection that was finally allowed to flourish between them.

Uncle Henry moved among the guests with ease, his future wife Miss Althea Dymchurch on his arm. The couple had found love and companionship which augmented their lives, and the wedding ceremony was set for two weeks' time.

Uncle Henry's pride in both Isabella's accomplishments and Everett's artistic success was evident as he guided visitors through the exhibition.

"I'm hoping he'll sketch me in my wedding dress," Miss Dymchurch told Isabella.

"That would be wonderful," echoed Uncle Henry.

Isabella smiled. "Please say if you need help with anything else for the wedding. I enjoy planning the floral decorations and posy for the bride."

"Althea liked those posies so much at your wedding that she's determined to have her own," smiled Uncle Henry.

"I'll make sure it's a beautiful posy. We all want you both to have a perfect day."

Clarissa, home from her London season, drifted between groups of guests pointing out her favorite details in her brother's watercolors. "Who is that over there?" she whispered to Isabella.

"I believe it's Sir George Middleton, he's a baronet, and he was at Cambridge with Everett," Isabella told her in a hushed voice. "Would you like to be introduced?"

"I would indeed!"

After all the guests were settled, and Clarissa was happy spending time with the rather handsome baronet, Isabella and Everett themselves went round to look at the paintings, feeling proud of what had been accomplished in this exhibition.

One of the guests approached them as the exhibition drew to a close. "I'm Sir Percival Newstead, President of the Royal Society of Botanical Science. I wonder if you would consider doing a joint exhibition for us at our headquarters in London. The combination of Lady Kennington's scientific notes, and the beauty of Lord Kennington's sketches and watercolors is quite astounding."

They agreed immediately with great excitement. This was what Isabella had dreamed of, this recognition for her work in botanical science. Everett had gained prestige as a botanical artist, and he no longer felt the need to hide his art.

As dusk fell, Isabella and Everett slipped away from the gathering. He took her hand and led her through the rear entrance of Kennington Manor to the walled garden.

"Where are you taking me?" Isabella asked, intrigued by the determined set to his face.

"I've wanted to show you this since we returned, but we've been so busy preparing for the exhibition. Close your eyes, my love."

She obeyed, as he took her arm and guided her a few more steps. She heard him opening a door, and wondered why they were visiting this old, deserted building at the far end of the garden.

"Where are we? Can I open my eyes yet?" she laughed.

"A couple more seconds. Let me just light this candle. Stay just where you are."

Isabella stood still, rooted to the spot, waiting for his instruction to open her eyes again.

"Now, open your eyes," he called.

She stared at the most wonderful sight. "You've made me a laboratory. I can't believe you've done that for me." She moved around the ground floor of the renovated cottage, examining everything.

"If there's anything I've missed then let me know. I think Peter covered most things."

"I must thank him. I can't find words to express how I feel. This is a dream come true."

"There's more," he said, as he led her upstairs to a comfortable study with a writing desk looking down towards the lake, and a chaise longue to rest on.

"Everett, you made me a place of my own. You knew it was my dream to have a place where I could work without being disturbed. Thank you, my love."

He took her in his arms and kissed her, as she responded with love and joy.

"You've put your paintings on the walls too. I love that. I can sit here and think of Drayton Woods, and the house in Portugal. There is so much that is good in life."

"I remembered you telling me about how you longed for your own place to work, and it gave me the idea to transform this place."

"I didn't want to leave Portugal, and now I don't think I'll ever want to leave Kennington Manor."

"I'm glad you like it," he said simply. "Today you've been asked to exhibit at the Royal society, and I suspect you might be the first woman to have that honour. You should feel very proud of yourself, Isabella."

"I wouldn't have achieved it without you. They want us both to exhibit. Your art brought my work alive."

As soon as Uncle Henry's wedding is over we can start preparations for the exhibition. "He looks so happy, and so does Althea."

"Did you know they are going to the house in Portugal for their honeymoon?"

"I didn't, but I can think of nowhere more perfect for a honeymoon."

Extended Epilogue

One for sorrow, two for joy.

Five years later ...

Late spring sunshine warmed the gardens at Kennington Manor. Isabella walked through the walled herb garden with her tiny four-year-old daughter dancing along beside her.

Juno, their spaniel raced ahead, before returning to check they were still there.

"Can we go to the lake, Mama?" cried Marguerite, named after the tiny resilient daisy.

"Not today, my love. Papa will take you tomorrow. Uncle Peter and Aunt Penelope are visiting with baby Nathaniel to celebrate Papa's birthday. You can visit the island if you want."

"When I'm older I'm going to build a den there. I'll be able to row myself out."

"When you're much older than four years old that sounds a fun thing to do." Little Marguerite was always looking for adventures and getting herself into trouble. Isabella delighted that the little girl had confidence and enjoyed exploring everything in life.

"We're going to plant some wildflower seeds in each corner of this walled garden. The birds will visit, and in midsummer we should have lots of butterflies. You can help me plant the seeds. I gathered them last Autumn, and all we need to do is sprinkle them where the gardener has already raked the soil ready for us." Isabella got the small packets of carefully labelled seeds and showed them to Marguerite.

"Can Juno help?"

"She can watch. Dogs have a habit of digging up seeds, rather than planting them," Isabella laughed, as she threw a stick for the spaniel to chase.

After they had sewn the first corner with seeds, Marguerite insisted that she knew exactly what to do and didn't need any help. Her eyes, so like her mother's, shone brightly in the sunshine, as she concentrated on shaking the seeds across the soil ready for a display of wildflowers in summer.

"Look Mama," she said excitedly. "That Jenny wren is building her nest in the garden again."

"We must look out for the robin that fed from your fingers last year. I think Uncle Henry and Aunt Althea would be interested in meeting Master Robin Redbreast."

"Can I go and find them? They will finish breakfast soon." Isabella could see her daughter planning what she needed to do that day. "I must bring Nanny and show her where we've planted the seeds. She told me a story about a robin and a giant last week."

"That sounds very interesting."

"The robin became the giant's best friend," Marguerite continued. "They lived in a castle a little like the ruined one at Drayton Park."

Isabella shuddered as she remembered the evening when she had delivered the ransom money to that castle. Yet Everett was right, they had so many happy childhood memories in that castle that they could not let that one evening ruin it.

Isabella had taken on Maisie's sister Katherine as nursery maid, and then made her officially Nanny, and it had proved a great success. Maisie had married one of the tenant farmers at Drayton Park but often rode over in her gig to see Isabella and Marguerite.

"Oh, look Mama, there's Papa in the far corner of the meadow. Can I run to him?"

"Yes, of course. I'll finish sewing these last seeds and come to find you. You can take Juno with you if you like.

"Can I? Juno, come with me," Marguerite called racing off towards Everett, who was sketching a group of willow trees in the far corner of the meadow.

She liked how he'd transformed this field into a Medieval meadow filled with ox eye daisies and then poppies later in the season. Marguerite liked the corncockle and bluebonnets best and knew all the names of the wildflowers.

As Isabella wandered through the aromatic garden, she wondered about planting a special tisane bed. They took tea with fresh chamomile leaves, but it would be good to have dried leaves in the winter.

At that moment Uncle Henry and Aunt Althea appeared at the garden gate. Althea who usually looked bright in the mornings looked upset about something. She moved quickly towards them to see what had happened.

"Oh, my dear, it's nothing to worry about. It's my own foolish thoughts. Just being anxious about being away for so long."

Althea looked around her. "You've made a lovely job of recreating this ancient meadow. We must do the same at Drayton Park. I love to see the flowers. I can't wait to see the different ones in Portugal."

"I'm glad you're staying at the vineyard," Isabella told them. "It's a very special place. If you walk along the stream, you'll come to a waterfall with a hidden pool which you can swim in. It's summer, so it will be warm enough to swim."

"I can't wait," Althea, couldn't hide her excitement and worry at the same time. "Three months in Portugal."

Uncle Henry was equally enthusiastic for the journey. "Althea, remind me to thank him again for his generosity to allow us to stay there for so long."

"Uncle Henry, Aunt Althea," called out Marguerite, running up to meet them. "Papa was sketching the Willow trees, but now he's sketching me."

"Let's go and see what he's doing," suggested Althea.

"Come along," Marguerite tugged at Althea's arm.

They all gathered around Everett, looking at his sketch of Marguerite.

"Does it look like me?" She cried. "If it does then I look like a princess," Marguerite added proudly.

"Marguerite, you are a princess," said her father in mock seriousness, "and we must all bow before you."

"Let me see your sketch of Marguerite," Isabella peered at his sketchbook. "You've captured her personality in a few strokes of charcoal. I love it."

"Uncle Henry says I can ride a pony when we go to Drayton Park for the wedding. Can I? Please say yes," Marguerite was jumping up and down with excitement.

Isabella smiled at her. "Of course, you can.

"When will aunt Penelope, Uncle Peter, and Aunt Clarissa arrive?" asked Marguerite. "I wish baby Nathaniel was old enough to play with. He just wants to run around, and he never knows the rules of the games."

"He's growing older, and he likes you chasing him," Isabella assured her.

"Are we having a picnic Mama?"

"We are indeed, down by the lake."

As they walked back towards the house, Marguerite skipped alongside Uncle Henry and Althea.

Everett spoke quietly to Isabella. "There's something I wanted to tell you. It's not pleasant news."

"Oh really, that doesn't sound good."

"I went to visit Lady Moreton last week. You know I go every six months or so to check they're treating her well. I don't know why but I somehow feel responsible for her welfare."

"It's because you know her, and you're the magistrate."

"Something like that, certainly. She isn't doing well. The last couple of times I've visited she's thought I'm either her father or Lawrence. They don't think she'll make it through the next winter. She's very frail and retreated into her own world soon after the trial."

"I still see her as that rather loud, often rude lady who thought of herself before others. Except where Lawrence was concerned, and she would do anything to make sure he was happy," Isabella said quietly, reaching for her husband's hand. "I don't think I'd have got along very well with her son if I'd married Lawrence. We would have clashed continually. I have the greatest admiration for Althea, living as her companion for several years. I cannot imagine it."

"I'll go and see her again in the Autumn," Everett told her. "But I think that will be the last time."

Isabella sighed. "It's such a sorry business, we'll never know what compelled Lawrence to keep taking wagers and lose his home."

Everett looked up. "I think I hear a carriage arriving. It must be Peter and Penelope."

"Well, that will cheer us up," Isabella smiled. "Marguerite's hoping that Nathaniel will be old enough to play with her."

'He should be old enough to chase after her now," laughed Everett. "We can get out the sandbox for them to play in, and they'll both enjoy splashing on the pebble beach."

Penelope alighted from the carriage, turning to help down the heavily pregnant Clarissa. Peter and Clarissa's husband, Sir George Middleton, had ridden over and were dismounting. The nursery maid followed Clarissa with little Nathaniel, who insisted on walking and not being carried.

"He's growing up so quickly," Isabella looked at him in surprise.

"He knows your name now," Penelope told Isabella. "He calls Marguerite, Mageet. It's rather endearing."

"Come inside and rest," Isabella urged Clarissa.

"I will for a short time," agreed Clarissa. "But Marguerite assures me we're going on a picnic. It does me good to walk."

Later, as they walked slowly towards the lake, Penelope started to teach Marguerite a song about a magpie. The handsome bird with some blue feathers who liked to collect shiny objects.

"I swear that Penelope has a song for every occasion," Isabella told Clarissa.

"When is Everetts's next exhibition? George is keen to go. As you know we met at your art exhibition. You could say we fell in love over art."

Isabella smiled, remembering that day. "It will be in Bath over the winter months."

"We could all go to Bath together," Clarissa suggested.

"I'd like that very much."

"Oh look, Uncle Henry is giving the children more of those carved animals. That will keep them occupied for a good long time."

"Once we're at the lake Peter will make sure the children enjoy splashing about. It's a perfect day for a picnic. How are you doing? she asked Clarissa.

"I'm fine. I've another two months to go, and they are sending a gig to take me back to the house. I enjoy walking, but it can be tiring."

"You look well. Married life must suit you?" Isabella told her.

"We're very happy. How strange that I always thought that I'd meet my true love at a ball or recital, and it happened at Everett's art exhibition."

"There's the lake," said Isabella. "We're almost there, and I know Cook has sent down lemonade and ice. I love our picnics."

"Peter and George suggested that they take both rowing boats over to the island."

Marguerite had overheard them and showed her excitement, almost jumping up and down with glee.

Everett and Peter pushed out the boats and Peter climbed in the first one, ready to row it over to the island. 'We might find treasure," called Marguerite.

Isabella remembered how excited Marguerite had been at the prospect of pirates when they were talking.

Her imagination is quite remarkable, we just live in a world of fairies, giants and elves.

Little Nathaniel was more interested in pointing at the ducks, and she heard Penelope singing a sea song to her son as they sailed towards the island.

"It looks like it's just us," said Everett. "That's quite a surprise."

"You're right it doesn't happen very often," she laughed.

"I sketched you and Marguerite earlier, and I think it's one of my better attempts. I'll say it myself, but I think I've caught the essence of both of you in the drawing."

"You must show me. Is it in your sketchbook?"

He nodded. "I have quite a collection now."

"Well, you're not putting on an exhibition of me, Everett," Isabella exclaimed.

"That's a shame, Isabella, as I think that could be the most successful exhibition I've done so far."

"It's definitely not happening," she persisted. "An occasional portrait, but not a whole exhibition."

"Very well my love I shall live with the disappointment."

"Clarissa looks well. She suggested we join them in Bath for your exhibition."

"What an excellent idea. I look forward to that. I do miss seeing my sister every day."

"There's something else to look forward to," she told him, her voice quiet.

"At the moment I'm rather enjoying some quiet space and time with my wife. It doesn't happen often enough these days."

"We need to do something about that before the baby arrives," she told him in a matter-of-fact voice.

Everett looked at Isabella in awe. "A baby ... oh my love that's delightful news."

"I thought this morning of that old rhyme."

"One for sorrow, two for joy, three for a girl, and four for a boy."

"I have seen four magpies today, so I suspect we might have a boy this time."

"It doesn't matter; I'd be happy with another little girl."

"It looks like they're returning. Yes, there are the boats setting off from the island."

"Let's make the most of these quiet few minutes," he suggested, a playful grin on his face.

He drew Isabella close in a gentle embrace, his hands cradling her face as he lifted it to share a light kiss. "I still can't believe I have you in my life. Yet every morning I wake up and there you are with your face on the pillow next to me.

"And you're there in my dreams, as well as in my waking hours. I feel excited about this new chapter of our life. Everything feels good, and I savour every moment we spend together."

His lips found hers, and he heard her sigh, and their kiss deepened as her lips responded to his and they celebrated their love and the strong, enduring connection between them.

The End

Printed in Dunstable, United Kingdom